Thank you for your help.
Fran Edelstein

Set to Music
And Other Stories

Fran Edelstein

iUniverse, Inc.
New York   Bloomington

Copyright © 2009 by Frances G. Edelstein

All rights reserved. No part of this book may be used or reproduced by any means, graphic, electronic, or mechanical, including photocopying, recording, taping or by any information storage retrieval system without the written permission of the publisher except in the case of brief quotations embodied in critical articles and reviews.

This is a work of fiction. All of the characters, names, incidents, organizations, and dialogue in this novel are either the products of the author's imagination or are used fictitiously.

iUniverse books may be ordered through booksellers or by contacting:

iUniverse
1663 Liberty Drive
Bloomington, IN 47403
www.iuniverse.com
1-800-Authors (1-800-288-4677)

Because of the dynamic nature of the Internet, any Web addresses or links contained in this book may have changed since publication and may no longer be valid. The views expressed in this work are solely those of the author and do not necessarily reflect the views of the publisher, and the publisher hereby disclaims any responsibility for them.

ISBN: 978-0-595-49686-0 (sc)
ISBN: 978-0-595-51993-4 (dj)
ISBN: 978-0-595-61209-3 (ebook)

Printed in the United States of America

iUniverse rev. date: 02/24/09

Dedicated to my husband Bill, my wonderful children and grandchildren, for their loving inspiration and assistance in the writing of this book.

In memory of Mom and Dad, and my sister Estelle.

With thanks to my teacher for advice ever valued, and to my rabbi for his wisdom: "Birth, the beginning; Death, the destination; Life, the journey."

Contents

Set to Music

ANNE CAUGHT HIS ATTENTION when she struck a wrong key on the piano. Maestro's arms froze high above his head along with her sour note, and a catlike glare scooped up the discord and shipped it right back to her in a stinging look of scorn.

What would he like me to say— "Ladies and gentlemen, dinner is served"? "Please excuse me, Maestro," she managed in a low voice, her head bent with chagrin toward the keyboard of the polished grand. But the conductor's pose remained unchanged. Suspended above his cool gaze, both arms resembled stalactites in her personal cave of mortification. Anne searched for something to blame for her error, but came up empty. Though this was a rehearsal, it was as important as their first London performance only two days away.

"Do not save that one for opening night!" the man bellowed. Just as suddenly, he flashed a dazzling grin. "It happens." Directing his famous fingers back to the orchestra, he seemed to forget her. Alexandre Raynor never used a baton. He conducted solely with his hands.

In the spring of 1972, opportunity was knocking for Anne David, chosen by the Moscow Philharmonic to be guest artist at this year's Command Performance in London. She had heard about Raynor's perfectionism, how abrupt he could be, how hard he worked his musicians.

The following morning presented a different challenge. "How long will it be?" she asked the specialist.

"A year, two, or three... or more. It can be slow. We hope so," Ted Naftoly responded with a glance through the window of his Grey's Inn office, as though a more promising diagnosis might be found in the English garden below. He turned back to her. "That bad tumble, the shadows crossing your vision... What you are experiencing has been caused by severe traumatic injury, resulting in complex retinal detachment and vision loss affecting both eyes. Someday—soon, we hope—there will be a tried and true procedure to correct this, but there isn't one yet. I am sorry, my dear."

Anne sat unmoving as the renowned Theodore Naftoly confirmed the diagnosis back home. "I refuse to fret, Doctor. Even in darkness,

3

I shall always have my music." Ugh. Pollyanna! In truth, she felt as rebellious as one of her horses.

"Loss of sight could occur gradually or suddenly," he added as she rose to leave.

Or not at all, she decided.

———

London in April was months ahead of Canada with its botanical booty: in lush green lawns, gardens bursting with bloom, barrels of flowers lining the Haymarket. Anticipating a spring rain, Anne was surprised by the bright sun that greeted her as she left the medical building.

On the corner, a girl was selling jewelry at an outdoor table. What struck Anne most was her auburn hair as it cascaded out of a flowerpot shape hat in a torrent of curls halfway down her back. Color. Light. Beauty. Anne would not relinquish her ability to see them. The walls of her world must not close in on her that way!

She declined the box that came with a novelty ring she fancied: a gilded band sporting two dangling batons, which she immediately placed on the third finger of her right hand. "Thank you, Mum," said the vendor. Bathed in the girl's beatific smile, Anne responded with one of her own… into sightless eyes as green as a Caribbean ocean. Stung by what struck her as a cruel preview of what might lie ahead, she swiftly turned away.

"Where to, Miss?" Rolled all the way down, the window of a black cab exposed the face of its cabbie as he called to her from at least a dozen feet away.

His voice was merry. Her spirits rose. "Royal Festival Hall, please," she called out, hopping in as he coasted to a stop.

The driver tore through traffic, periodically twisting himself a full ninety degrees to provide his fare with running commentary. She wondered at the flat cap, sure to fly off, that sat like a tweed pizza crowning his large egg-shaped head and jolly, florid face. "Where ya from, love?" he asked.

"Canada."

"Ah, we like Canadjyans over here! They're easy to talk to and not as difficult to please. Most others, if ya don't talk about women, business or taxes, they think you're crazy!" From the seat beside him he lifted a musical instrument. "I don't talk much. I just serenade 'em, and they come back and say, 'I want that driver!' "

Anne was hardly eager to be serenaded by some blithe spirit tearing through the fast-merging lanes of London's mid-day traffic. Instead of a request, as he likely hoped for, she admired the object of his pride. "A fine clarinet, beautifully kept."

"Eight pounds!" he beamed. "That's what they asked. But I got it for five and a half! Five. And. A. Half," he repeated slowly to impress upon this 'Canadjyan' the brilliant bargaining that produced such a deal. "And it's almost ebony!" Encouraged by the girl's interest, he continued on, "I been taking lessons for four years... mostly classical. Kinda shakes ya up—though I do like Woody 'erman."

"So do I," Anne responded, wondering what 'almost ebony' was. "May I have one of your cards, too?" she asked when they reached their destination. *Reward him. He works hard to amuse, after all, and he is interesting.*

Like one blessed, the cabbie-musician replied with an ear-to-ear grin. With his left hand he produced a card. He pivoted in his seat and opened her door with his right. She paid him through the window.

"Holy Gawd, it's Christmas!" Shaking his head and spinning his hat, he plunked a wad of change back into her hand, and exclaimed, "No, young lady, you've overdone it!" At the same time, fortified by the girl's generosity, he decided to share yet another tidbit. "It's all love n' gush," he blushed, offering a copy of a poem he had written. "But if the papers likes it, it must be good." Off he drove, with his pizza cap whirling in its place.

Anne stuffed the poem into her handbag and unzipped her wallet to pocket her change. Holy Gawd, she echoed. He'd taken no tip at all!

———

When Anne resumed her place at the piano, Conductor Raynor gave her an oblique look. It was ten minutes before rehearsal, and the orchestra was still short of members. She wasn't late. What was bothering him?

Raynor was elated, but he hid that under a scowl. *Others be damned; she's here.* He raised his arms, directed his fingers at the first violinist, and commanded, "We will take it from se top."

When was the last time she'd heard that expression? Not since high school. She thought about how easily newcomers to a language fall prey to the lure of phrases and clichés, and hid a smile.

Thoughts quickly sobered as the remaining musicians, nervously consulting their watches, scrambled to take their places. The scrapings of chairs and rustlings of sheet music lent havoc to the opening strains of Dvořák's *New World* Symphony. All disregarded by the conductor.

He has an Ozawa complex, thought Anne, watching his entire body enter into the performance. *His T-shirt raises and lowers as though launched on a bungee string! And his silvery mop whips 'round, like one pitching for a shampoo commercial!*

A pair of Russian eyes flashed inarguable directives. Raynor's stance brought to mind that of the god Mercury, alternating from sprint to backstep, leaping forward to jab at the orchestra with ten separate finger puppets, each delivering their personal message. Suddenly he halted.

He was only thirty-eight. Despite such displays of energy, he appeared much older than his years. In a clouded countenance, sat eyes bathed in a veil of creases and an expression like one breathing fire. *He works too hard,* the girl ascertained. *Or perhaps he is not strong.*

Accustomed to moments that warned of swift anger, and sudden switches to reverence and personal passion, the musicians gave their full attention. Raynor began his daily lecture. "Miracles only happen in se Bible! You have to work at it, cajole it, make love to it—perhaps INSAWLT IT in order to get what se composer GAVE HIS GAWTS FOR!! You have to LIVE it!"

He pivoted to face Anne. "'I LOVE YOU!' or 'I HATE YOUR GAWTS!' Se music must say somesing to conwince its audience to indulge in its spell and embrace its message, to journey along and celebrate its TRIUMPH!" He lifted his arms to the orchestra. "Again please."

After rehearsal, "Uh, Miss David, kindly sit back at se piano," Maestro beckoned. "I must have words wis you."

Anne removed her jacket. *Uh-oh. I knew it. Something's wrong.*

But one surprise was to follow another. "Yew are an excellent pianist; yew perform brilliantly," Raynor stated. "I need to tell you sat. But you seem to lack se confidence yew should have."

"Is that what comes through, Maestro? Please forgive me, especially for that very bad error during yesterday's rehearsal. For some reason, I was nervous."

"One must be nerwous in order to perform well!" Raynor snapped. Alarmed by his own tone, he continued softly, "I am not going to be easy on yew. I hope yew don't mind. Yew have an exceptional talent straining to be recognized. And yew must be se best sat yew can be."

Anne squinted at the man through the glare of stage lights being tested behind him. "I am grateful for your interest, sir," she breathed, not quite sure of the direction of her leader's critique, feeling privileged yet wary of some possible conflict.

Raynor didn't intend to keep the girl guessing. He fastened his sloe eyes upon her, "Now sat we are alone in sis room… "

Anne remained calm but alert to a possible suggestion hanging in the air. *No. This man is too dedicated to music and is too renowned for his talents as a conductor. He's wrestling with our language— there's a culture gap here.*

"Come here," Raynor gestured toward the podium. "On second thought, I will come sere." He joined her at the piano, maintaining a respectable distance between teacher and student; but his fingers shook as he pointed to the opening bars. "Not soft, you see. But *crescendo!* *Crescendo! CRESCENDO! IMMEDIATELY!* Do not fiddle timidly wis what yew want to say; enter wis it *DIRECTLY! YEW* are se passion at sis time. *YEW ALONE* must lead se entire orchestra *wis YEWER passion!* "

Startled by the magnitude of her role, Anne lifted a worried head to the conductor. "How?" she began.

"How?" Raynor's dark brows furrowed. Again, possible fury. He paused to allow it to dispel, then began again, "Sink of your room as a child." Noticing a faint smile, he forged on. "Sen, as yew grew older, how yew changed it, added to it, put away se toys." He could tell that she didn't have the slightest idea what he referred to. He lifted the music and waved it in the air. "Sis is not just paper to read from, or to play 'following-se-leader'! *It is singularly yewrs!* A giant priwilege meant for all musicians who inwest their entire selves for as long as it takes to play a piece! *Play! Like you own it. Like it is your last song! Like yew are deweloping wings and reaching for heawen!*"

Silence.

Breaking the silence after some minutes with a fortifying smile, followed by a deep search into Anne's face with eyes that rejoiced as they challenged, he spoke again. "I believe sat is what Dvořák wants."

Anne sat enchanted. *He speaks of the composer in the present tense, as though he still lives. But of course he does; his music is immortal—which is why maestro's reputation has become legendary.* Anne deemed the moment sacred. To her, the man would forever stand on hallowed ground. She would learn from him, develop her talent under his brilliant tutoring for the duration of their tour. She smiled into the windows of coal-black eyes, their centers shining with diamonds.

"We have four weeks tour. We will work on sis together," he stated in a low voice. "Let us, as yew Americans say, 'grab a coffee,' while yew tell me about yewerself."

Not a request, nor an invitation. An order. Not to be disputed or hesitated about. Anne picked up her jacket and followed her leader out the stage door and into the London night.

Raynor consulted his Rolex. "Almost sewen." He turned to her. "Perhaps we should have dinner?" Sensing her hesitation, he swiftly added, "May I have se pleasure of yewer company?"

Anne smiled up at him. "I'd like that." But she wasn't exactly sure. She was ill at ease about spending social time with such an icon.

He wasn't much taller than she was. Her eyes met his chin. His mop of hair gave added height. His face was classically sculptured with a narrow nose and high cheekbones. Wrong for a Russian face, she thought. But so dramatic.

He knew London. And he knew his wines. He took her to Swallow Street, where they were seated in a seafood restaurant at a table centered with candlelight. Anne watched the wine steward fill her glass with a golden elixir.

"Mind if I smoke?" Raynor inquired, prepared to place his cigarette back into its case if Miss David objected.

Anne waved away the notion and admired a single rose draped across her dinner plate. "One rose. There is so much beauty in just one. Look," she beckoned, drawing his attention to the flower's delicate form, "How can one count the number of songs dedicated to this beautiful thing?"

Raynor's eyes shifted unnoticed to her heart-shaped face, framed by the opalescent sheen of ash blond hair swept back into a thick braid. "Beautiful," he repeated.

Anne analyzed the low rasp in Raynor's voice. He smoked too much, she determined. And from the lull that followed his last comment, she also concluded that the man felt quite comfortable choosing the length of his quiet moments.

"Tell me about yew," he resumed. "Not your credentials; I know sem. Rather, how yew spend se other part of yewer life."

"It's a long story," she answered, then emphasized, "Really, it is!" to the lifting of brows that questioned the long history of one so young. "My father owns a ranch in King City, just north of the city of Toronto. My mother was a piano teacher. She died a year ago" Anne quickly waved away any sympathetic response by lifting a hand against it. "I have good memories.

"We train two-year-olds, my dad and I, along with a fellow named Carney."

She was sure his latest cigarette would burn his fingers. He held it to the end between thumb and forefinger and trained his gaze on the slight girl before him. "Yew? A horse trainer?"

"Contrary to what many people think, it's not just a man's job. And not at all like you see in the movies!" protested Anne. "We simply hold them, put the bit and saddle on them, close the fence and let them run. After about ten minutes they're subdued enough to mount. My dad gave me a horse for my sixteenth birthday which we groomed to race."

As the waiter placed before them platters of seafood with various sauces, Raynor grew more intrigued. "I wonder, how do you manage to train se horse to obey more san one rider?"

"In that case, we didn't have to. I rode him. In the very first race my jockey was scratched because he weighed in two pounds heavy, so I rode him myself, and continued to. But to answer your question: a racehorse needs to get used to a few people other than his jockey, such as the owner, the veterinarian, the hot walker, and sometimes different exercisers in the mornings."

"A chockey... you," murmured Raynor, studying the girl's face for a telltale stretching of truth. Again, his brow reacted. "Was it not wery dangerous, sis racing round and round, faster and faster to beat out all se others? I would sink it would be wery dangerous, yes?"

"Yes, it can be," Anne smiled, amused by his description of a race. "One must train for racing. I fell off a few times in the training, but I could always sense it coming."

"So what do yew do?"

"Hang on with all my might!"

"Were you ever hurt?" Alex persisted.

Anne lowered her gaze to the scampi on her dinner plate. The tumble against the rail fence burned in her memory with its pain, headaches, gray patches... No fault of the horse: she hadn't tightened the saddle properly.

She reached into her handbag and pulled out a small folder. "This is a photo of that first race, when I was up," she indicated proudly. Raynor's eyes focused on the sexless figure in pink and black silks. Enjoying the effect she was creating, Anne pointed out, "That's the win picture."

Alex barely found his voice: "You won it? Incredible."

Because I am a woman? "It was only seven furlongs on a slow track." Had she come upon a chauvinist here, burdened with moth-eaten concepts of male and female roles?

"It says you did it in one minute and twenty-seven seconds."

"That was 'Last Spring'. He was the One Horse all the way."

"Yewr life... it seems full of trust and sonshine," Raynor commented with a wry smile.

Was that a smile or an admonishment? "I like to think so," Anne responded openly, satisfied that she had indeed experienced a happy childhood, secure in the fact that she needn't apologize for it.

Alex would not waver. "Are you one of se women liberationists?"

"Oh no, Maestro. I was liberated long before I was a woman!"

For a moment, his lashes swept down over his eyes. They were full and long and very black. Lifted, they exposed deep curiosity. He would learn more about this unusual girl.

As she would learn more about him.

He was a sensitive man, but not about himself. Likeable at some moments, he was equally bear-like at others. This time it was she who raised a brow. *If there ever was a chance to head him off at the pass, this is it.* "It took a seventeen-year-old redheaded boy with a face full of freckles, who faced an agonizing handicap, to teach me to be true to myself, to accept and like myself. His coping skills helped me to detour around the growing pains that come with adolescence. I love him."

Alex signed the tab, lit his fifth cigarette of the evening, and leaned toward Anne with interest disguising a sense of encroachment. "Se boy next door?"

"Yes. For a while. Until he moved into the big house, he lived in the bunkhouse with the hired hands. I was just nine years old when Carney showed up, tired of mucking stalls in a circus. He loved horses, and they responded well to his manner. I followed him around like a puppy, always asking questions, watching the loving way he tended the animals. I felt secure with him and happily carried out the small, manageable tasks he assigned to me at my dad's request. Carney never said a cross word. I learned a lot from him."

Did she mean to chastise him? He said nothing.

She continued. "Carney had a speech problem. Some consonants took so painfully long for him to pronounce, people lost interest and walked away." Tears jetted into Anne's eyes at the memory of the boy who had displayed the same intense look of consternation in his deep amber peepers that her beloved horses had in theirs.

"When he knew that Carney was with us to stay, my dad took him under his wing and made sure that he received speech therapy. Anytime I showed signs of teenage agony or dreadful shyness, Carney shared with me some of the social tools that helped him make it through. 'As long as you mean well,' he said, 'don't be afraid to express yourself. If others misunderstand, they're the losers, not you.' I grew up believing that, and I still do," Anne concluded, lifting her wineglass to the light.

Raynor was struck by her spirit. *Ser is magic in sat gesture,* he thrilled. *Se light above enhances ewery perfect feature, but is superfluous to se light she projects.* Aloud, he said, "Yew were lucky to learn sat at such a young age. Is Carney still there, on yewr ranch?"

"Carney—Dr. Charles Carnaghan—is now a veterinarian," Anne announced with happiness showing.

"Why did you decide to put music first, ahead of the ranch, which you seem to love?" asked Alex, reverting to a subject more familiar.

"As I said, my mother was a piano teacher, and would have gone on to be a concert pianist had her health allowed it. No, I am not fulfilling her dream," Anne quickly interjected at the repeat of an eyebrow lift. "I remember as a toddler falling asleep to the soft sounds of her playing. I could make out her image at the piano, multiplied nine times in the beveled glass panes of the French doors that separated us; and I would count them, like some count sheep. I loved falling asleep that way. Very often, there would be a student; and Für Elise became one of my favorites!" she laughed.

"I was at the piano before I was three. Later on, the Royal Conservatory back home recognized some potential, and I was groomed by them and my mother for a musical education… but with an eventual choice of career. Both my parents allowed me to make that choice, without pressure. By the time I received my degree in piano performance, I couldn't help but be excited about the prospect of further study in Paris."

"Where you earned your Master of Music degree."

"As you know, Maestro." Anne left out the amazing reviews she'd received at the Paris Concert Hall prior to graduation.

Though Alexandre Raynor was aware of them, he questioned, "Ever regret yewr decision?"

"I love music. No matter what happens in life, I shall continue to pursue it. I also haven't lost my love of horses. Unless Fate announces otherwise, I believe that I can enjoy both."

"Let us start by yew calling me Alex, which is my name," he said, rising from his chair to help Anne into her coat. "Shall we walk for a while? It promised earlier to be a lovely evening."

"I would like to compose a symphony called 'Puffins on Oxford Street'!" Anne joked, as they joined the parade of people, looking neither left nor right in their purposeful walk. "There's hardly room here to swing arms or take full steps!"

"Puffins have no arms!" laughed Alex, in an attempt to be as playful.

"They have wings and they keep them flat at their sides, I know. They are the image of hustle and bustle and they have funny little feet! I can picture them with brollys in their beaks, sporting black derbys on their little heads, can't you? Stiffly erect, using slow foot movements, just like the Palace Guards, and that calls for a symphony, don't you think?"

"Not a wery quiet bird. I heard sem in Norway. Seir calls sound like chainsaws. What kind of music would come out, do yew suppose?"

"Heavy metal!" she laughed. "Up and coming!"

Raynor scratched the side of his head in contemplation. "Have yew ever written music?"

Anne consulted the countless stars overhead. "I've hummed some, but never got the notes down on paper," she answered absently.

"Would yew like to?" Raynor's expression was sincere, however charming and disarming.

Such a question brought Anne back to earth with a leap. "Oh my, yes!" she exclaimed. *Am I dreaming?* Relaxed by now with maestro's lack of affectation, she dismissed the comparison to Ozawa. Other than in his high cheekbones and the bounce of his blunt-cut bob, the parallel ended. He was like no one else.

It rained on their side of the street. They took refuge in the lobby of their hotel.

Anne wore gray to match her eyes. Raynor paced nervously backstage. A hum filled the hall. One could smell the furs, dampened by a cool spring rain, paraded for such occasions despite the season. A heavy rustle of programs helped to announce that the house was full.

Her skin looked like blush china. Her hair, combed to the waist, lay in shimmering waves over bare shoulders. Anne trembled with excitement.

Raynor, who never dressed for rehearsal in anything but a black track suit, was majestic in a white dinner jacket. He took to the stage; with feet together, arms loose at his sides, he inclined his head to the Royals. Black lashes, that appeared to blanket half his cheekbones, did not flicker as he pivoted to acknowledge the mounting ovation. With an arm extended toward his guest artist, the conductor of The Moscow Philharmonic welcomed piano virtuoso, Anne Quincy David.

In a tight taffeta gown, its skirt caught up in a train, Anne looked sleek and feline as she swept onto the stage. With nervous fingers, she pressed imaginary wrinkles at her hips, then drew her hands together as if in prayer. How in the world was she going to curtsy in such a tight dress? How had they missed considering this!

Maestro had thought of everything else while lighting and sound were tested during the morning's final rehearsal. "We will run through it all again." Anne hated that elusive state called perfection, so sought after, yet so fraught with bug-a-boo, a superstition dictating that once attained, it could never be repeated.

"Se more experienced you are, se more perfection se world expects," Raynor had coached.. "For years and years we are working and working to be somesing. And now we are sair. Ah! Is sat it?" he challenged over the clatter of cables and litter being cleared from the wings. "No, my friends, it is chust se beginning!" Above the scraping and scratching of chairs slung into groups, Alex forged on. "You should have se necessary jitters; yewr excitement must be mixed wis torment at sis moment. Will se music and se audience marry? Se musical aristocracy—will sey recognize our ability to transform our audience into ardent spirits? It is important also to inspire a good review. To do sat, you have got to be better and better, better san se night before."

All Anne wanted to do was play the piano. But she listened intently in order to digest maestro's message. She loved him for what he was teaching her; she needed him to teach her more. She hoped, though, that her need would not lead to dependency. Not only must she learn, but she must also be able to make her way by herself.

In answer to her initial dilemma, Alex reached for Anne's fingers and lightly entwined them in his, their slight movement guiding her into a very gentle curve from the waist, followed by robust applause. Had the audience been holding its sympathetic breath?

The pianist acknowledged her conductor, warmed by the mixture of excitement and pride that shone from his countenance. But his words, grumbled behind the ovation, were not in keeping. "See sat guy hanging over se balcony up sair?" Raynor's gaze was pinned to the left of the Royal pair. "I'd like to take him by se seat of his pants and throw him over!"

Did I hear that correctly? Anne wondered. Despite what he said, his smile didn't waver. *What in the world brought that on? And what a time for a wisecrack! Yet, at such a formal event, it has to be funny!* Would it be his way to individualize the people before him, when she, in her nervousness, simply saw a floating sea of faces? Anne followed his gaze, and barely made out the figure of a young man with red hair who had just turned his back while taking his seat.

Our leader has European elegance: so graceful, so attractive, so smooth, Anne determined, turning back to the conductor. *Gaining popularity way beyond the Continent, he's being labeled "the musical de Mille of his time'" by some critics; by others "an unbearable curmudgeon," most likely because of the growling or the glaring that accompany his eternal quest for perfection!*

He's deserving of a knighthood, she decided in an appraisal that presented its own cautious message to one wise enough to know that awkwardness comes with worship. To chase it away, she mustered her discipline and awaited direction.

Like the first shimmers of daylight, flickers ignited themselves in maestro's dark eyes. Out of the air, his fingers carved their own New World as he wooed what he desired from a musical group with extraordinary genius for translating his gestures.

He beckoned to the woodwinds, stepped back toward the strings. His hands cupped their plea to the brass. He played them fast, whisking his audience into anticipation. Before the drama tumbled forth, the piece teased" Adagio... stillness. This maestro's je ne sais quoi. Reckless, many would say, but an extraordinary interpretation of the intention of Dvořák.

Her cue. All at attention, Anne inclined her head to the keyboard. Stage lights dimmed to allow a single spot to focus on the girl's shimmering hair and pearl lashes extending their effect to Raynor's sensibilities.

The acoustic kaleidoscope made Anne shiver. Following her leader's gestures, she played like one on enchanted territory. Alex enticed her with all the sorcery at his command: Anne partnered him as one would a lover. *Crescendo! Crescendo! CRESCENDO!*— to diminuendo, with joyous submission awaiting her next cue.

Such playful engagement, in cadence or at odds with the composer's intentions, extended brilliantly to a hushed and spellbound house.

Raynor's curious pantomimes transported his musicians on a course that seemed to contain no gravity. As the music rose, and the piano re-entered, syncopation produced a levity that had the audience soaring. Free to fly and conquer, maestro's imperious fingers triggered from his orchestra the heat and passions he lived to impart.

Anne thrilled to the symphonic layers washing over her, and maestro's ability to stun an entire audience of musical souls. People seemed pinned to their seats. There wasn't a rustle. On this night, the pianist learned how the silence of hundreds could be more audible than the roar of a crowd.

Approaching the finale, Anne marveled at how it had all come about. *Had there been some kind of electricity?* She had played as the conductor demanded, and she had experienced his rapture. *How can one define how a company of players, united by one goal, is able to enchant an audience and each other so totally? How can it be explained that every performance can be new under one man's unparalleled leadership?*

Like a leap of the god Mercury, it was over—to seven thundering ovations, sure to be heard all the way up the Thames!

Conductor Alexandre Raynor grinned a slow, satisfied grin.

———

The performers greeted the Queen backstage. "Thank you, your Majesty," said Anne, with two bright spots on her cheeks. "I am very happy that you enjoyed the performance." In response, Anne felt an unexpected little squeeze of her hand, preventing her from having to take another bow.

"Let us, as yew say, 'duck out'?" Alex proposed, as the guests departed.

"I must get out of my gown," answered Anne.

"No, no! Come as yew are. It is beautiful!"

What is? My gown, or something out there in the night? Anne did as she was bid, praying that it had better not rain because water spots can damage silk.

Raynor moved aside to allow Anne to precede him to the stage door. He was aware of her perfume, her grace, the serene sway of her hips. He was alarmed with the beat of his heart.

With their chins resting on their mops, two night cleaners flanked the exit like palace sentries in a Disney animation. The futility of their jobs and the loneliness of the night filled eyes heavy with dreams gone by. Lowering them with respect to maestro and his companion, they stamped an image, unimportant to her at the moment, but one that would remain forever in Anne's memory.

———

Charles Carnaghan waited for the Queen and her entourage to exit the theatre. Anne always loved surprises. Eagerly, he inquired his way to her dressing room. He knocked once, again a little louder. Slowly, he tried the doorknob, and faced an empty room.

———

A heavy drizzle had ceased. In the dissipating fog, the riverbanks beneath them seemed strung with ribbons of dewy lights. Anne and Alex crossed the bridge toward The Strand in a city freshly showered and welcoming a few stars. They walked in silence, steeped in the first quiet moments necessary to embrace their success, to search out and preserve, in each of their minds, the various contributions to it. They spoke at once.

She: "You certainly present Dvořák differently!"

He: "I don't know what you've got, but I like it!"

"You first," they chanted together.

"Maybe we shouldn't analyze things too much. I like your last comment, just the way you phrased it." Anne stretched her arms toward a starry sky. "This evening was just… amazing!"

"No past tense, please. We have another four days of performance, sen weeks of recording."

"And we're supposed to make each performance unique?" Anne locked his gaze with hers. "I hate to be a nuisance, but can you give me another little hint how?"

"Do I detect disbelief?"

"Absolutely!" laughed Anne. "But would that make a difference? Would it?"

Her candor astounded him. And her innocence. Challenged by the vast difference in their cultures, he chose to be just as plain-spoken. "We make each performance unique by trying somesing new each time. But sometimes when you don't try," he fixed her with his eyes, "It happens... anyway."

They reached the Savoy, across the street from their hotel. Alex took Anne's arm and steered her into the bar. "Somesing new," he explained with a grin, inspired by his budding talent for manipulating the English language.

"In celebration," he proposed, toasting the evening with Anne's choice of vodka on ice. "Does everyone call you Anne, or do some call you Ann-yee?" he wanted to know.

Tipsy with adrenalin and alcohol, Anne assumed a splendid smile. "Ann-ee," she imparted, dallying with the name reserved for those who knew her well. Annie was intrigued with the man, most assuredly with his pronunciation of her pet name, "Ann-yee,"... like a woolly lamb.

Raynor lifted his glass once more. "Then here's to you, Ann-yee. Do you sink we can write some music in se time left to us... ah, your puffins on Oxford Street, perhaps? Or maybe you would prefer your racehorse, Last Spring?"

"Oh Maestro—Alex—how thoughtful of you!" Anne exclaimed. "It would make me very happy to compose with you... especially a piece about Last Spring!" She pondered for a moment, laced her fingers under her chin, and looked up wide-eyed. "Do you first pick the topic, then set it to music? Is that the way it works?"

"Yew pick a passion," He answered gruffly. "Se music follows."

"You make it sound so simple," Anne contemplated, stirring her drink. "To me, it seems beyond reach, as it might be into waves that wash up on a beach... to catch bubbles that drift and break and disappear."

Alex studied the girl before him. "Yew have a way wis words. Even yewer mistakes are delightful! Bubbles break, but still they are preserved. When you throw yourself into those waves... reach out wis determination, infinite tenacity, constant originality, and boundless enthusiasm. It's a constant pursuit, because bubbles are, as you said, not possible to possess. Yet, as you must observe, it is not se bubbles we lust after; it is sair essence, se impressions sey leave after se waves recede."

He wrapped both of her hands with his and looked seriously into her eyes. "Achievement worthy of recognition requires such essence, such bubbles, as yew say. And se essence thrives in those endless moments of ecstasy enjoyed by our audience, and by ourselves as artists. We must make sure se bubbles do not break too soon. We multiply sem wis variation, innowation… somesing original and more reflective each time we play a piece, though we may have played it hundreds of times before."

Alex patted Anne's hands and let them rest on the table. "Call it hard work. I prefer to call it adwenture… with constant application and devotion, of course. Sair is no full artistic life wissout such ongoing application." Alex lifted his hands, palms outward, in a gesture that suggested a choice. "Sat is, if we are to be a team."

Anne felt her heart smile. "May we trade biographies? Would you tell me about your life in Russia? That is, if you don't mind my asking," she quickly added, wondering if this famous man had a wife or family to care about him. This time, the hard look that she was becoming accustomed to failed to intimidate her, even though a troubled edge to his rejoinder made her rethink her boldness.

"I had scarlet fever as a child. It is explained sat is why my hair is all gray." Anne tried to picture Alex as a boy, but the gray got in the way. "Sere was no time set aside for childhood as you know it. No horses, no playsings…. My father, a surgeon, was born and raised in Germany. He expected perfection in all family endeavors. He was not what yew would call a companion: I must say he was there, but I never really knew him. My mother was se granddaughter of a Russian count; her family had many riches before se Rewolution, I'm told. My family maintained a modest home just outside Moscow, wery ample, even by old standards. We maintained a country home in se Black Forest where my mother loved to give parties. My last memories of her bring to mind how she looked in a white ermine cape, wis diamonds in her ears… also in her beautiful eyes.

"She died when I was fifteen, and my father married his mistress, a school teacher from a family of teachers formerly employed by Czar

Nicholas to instruct se young people of se palace. She was not a bad person, but I couldn't live wis se rules she set, so I got on my bicycle and rode like hell to se city, where my aunt Tasha took me to her bosom—er," Alex hesitated, "okay to say?"

Anne blinked her eyes in affirmation, and pleaded silently for self discipline to hide the ripples of amusement fighting to effervesce.

"To reward Auntie's faith in me, I worked hard at my studies and lessons wis cello." Alex surprised Anne with a chuckle, "Not like life in se fast lane, eh?"

Her smile was polite.

For a moment neither spoke. Then Alex continued, "I was married once. Not for long." Anne's eyes searched his and he answered them. "No kids. I'm not much for kids." He paused, lifted his glass to the waiter for a refill, and switched course. "May se road rise up to meet you. May se wind always be at yewr back… an Irish toast, I believe."

Cliches and proverbs. But the toast was sweet and Anne accepted it with grace, despite a tongue that felt locked as it searched for the right words for what she wished to know.

Alex proceeded. "In our life, we learn as we go, not just go wis what we have learned. Sat, too, must be an old saying."

"How do you remember so many of them?" Anne queried, hoping her exasperation didn't show.

"Se way I learn English. Sey teach me more san mere words: sey teach me yewer values, yewer sympathies… no, sat is not se right word.… "

"Sentiments?" she offered, ashamed of her previous impatience.

"Esactly. Sentiments. Yew are a good partner. You will be a good music collaborator. Do I get to keep yew?"

Anne blushed and lowered her gaze. Shimmers of excitement skipped through her like little spikes.

"I do what I do to keep my audience where I want sem," Raynor quickly continued, in an attempt to rescue her from his possible lack of tact. His voice was soft but firm. "We must exercise our constant right to change, or we put public to sleep."

Anne laughed at the image.

Alex brightened. "Mine are an incredible group of musicians, Annyee; always open to change. Sey speak to me through sair instruments. I listen; sey listen. We laugh, we cry." Alex pointed to his temple, his features dancing with merriment. "We are having an experience up here when most people sink all we are doing is playing music! We celebrate each night of performance! How many can be so fortunate? We share one of se strongest passions known to humankind: Music. Se euphoria of sound. People walk out of se hall glad to be alive. And se applause never ends as long as sey keep standing in line to buy tickets."

Though Raynor was open-minded and logical about life, he was not unguarded about his privacy. He loved the arts, but experienced no need to see and be seen, rarely taking time to attend most functions, or even to enjoy a good book. He was married to his work.

As he told his story, weariness crept into his eyes. *It all filters down to the demands upon him*, Anne decided, *and how uncompromising he chooses to be. Fame makes its demands, no question. How faithfully he is saluted for his genius!* Curious about his relationship with the orchestra members, whom she referred to by the instruments they played, Anne asked, "Do you socialize together, or, like the captain of a ship, are you revered and isolated up there on the bridge?"

His answer was immediate. "Do we know each other as indiwiduals? One day, if you like, I will tell you about each of sem. Do sey regard me as father figure? I am sere if sey need me. Not by choice am I elewated somewhat, but it is necessary I suppose to maintain leadership. We socialize together a little, but not excessively." He thought about his cellist, Sergei Malankoff, a former brother-in-law, and a problem.

Sergei drank too much, skipped rehearsals with a sense of entitlement based by him alone on their former relationship, and was, to Alex's chagrin, a compulsive liar. Alex had helped him through a few financial squeezes, but by the man's increasingly shiftless periods of irresponsibility, felt betrayed by him. He didn't like him. He didn't trust him. But that had to remain a private matter. Alex swung the conversation back to Anne. "Wis reference to composing music about your horse, what is se first image coming to mind?"

"Carney... training Last Spring."

Alex's expression tightened. "So sis is to be about yewer stable boy? Tell me why you will sink of him first when we write about Last Spring?"

"Because the piece must resound with heart," Anne promptly replied, her cheeks burning in opposition to Alex's description. "Carney's loving heart helped to train my horse. It also led him to form a riding school on our ranch for handicapped children—twice weekly during the school year, three times in summer. With my eager participation, and with my dad's, of course. But it was Carney's heart that did it. I guess he wanted to give back to other children some of what he considered his good fortune, though he worked hard for every success he achieved. He was hardly a stable boy! His huge heart brought joy to many young faces. Teaching handicapped children to ride—some severely handicapped, I must add—was an exceptional feat. A real waltz, I called it.

"I love children," she added softly. "And I am very fond of Carney, the boy who taught me how to train Last Spring, and so much more about heart than what I already knew in a family brimming with heart."

Raynor's smile was steely. "All sose children. Children can be brats."

"You were a child once," she challenged.

"True. But I was my parents' brat, not mine. It just wouldn't be my choice." Raynor lifted one of her hands in his, and produced a wistful smile. "However, I wisit some schools to acquaint children wis instruments, challenge sem wis sounds, rhythm, for music appreciation— "

"Heavens! How does that work when you dislike them so?"

"It is for se music. Sey must learn when sey are young, no? If sey are ever to become great musicians."

Anne rested her chin on her hands and contemplated this paradox of a man with the belief that one day, when the time was right, Alex Raynor would love his children as every father surely must. Retreating to familiar ground, she stated firmly, "I very much loved Last Spring. He was my friend. We bonded. I felt safe with him."

"Is he still living?"

There was a moment's hesitation. "He went... blind," Anne murmured. "We kept him in pasture for the first while, but it was agony to watch him flounder around in there. He wanted to run, you see. And he couldn't. So... he had to be destroyed."

With an attempt to comfort, Alex squeezed her hand gently. "Sey shoot horses, don't sey? People wis insurmountable afflictions are not so lucky."

Right. Anne took a heavy breath and plowed on. "I seem to continually rely on someone to point my way. First my mother, then my dad, and of course my teachers. Along came Carney, and now, composer-director, possibly music-collaborator, Alex Raynor. I am grateful for his leadership. I need to learn from him. Am I destined to go on this way, depending on others for direction for the rest of my life?"

Chatter at the bar increased. Raynor regarded the girl so seriously in search of herself. He indicated a quieter table. "One isn't born knowing," he said, pulling out a chair for her. Seating himself, he searched carefully for what he wanted to say. "Though one may be priwileged with talents and intelligence, sese sings require direction, inspiration—at first, anyway." He leaned forward with one hand under his chin and eyes riveting her with their sparkle. "Yew are young. Wis experience yew are deweloping strength. Sense of worth comes from inside, too.... Deweloping is like a pendulum. It goes like sis: deweloping, deweloped, deweloping, deweloped. From each 'deweloping,' a new 'deweloped.' See?" He smiled and the corners of his eyes crinkled. "Sat is art. Musical or other kinds. One never stops discowering, seeking stimulation. Deweloping. Yew can make any wish come true if yew pursue it: no one else can set your goals." Maestro's grin was sudden. "Long-winded, eh?"

Singular... and fiery too. But he listens, and one can tell that he regards every word as important as his own. "Thank you for your faith in me." The ring of Anne's laughter was melodious. "I return the toast: to you, Maestro... my teacher, possibly my partner in music—and probably my psychologist!"

It was after midnight. Most people had left the bar. The few who lingered were guests of the hotel whose recognition of the man and the girl caused the room to fall silent with speculation: Were they romantically linked? Expectant faces sobered however, as Alex, maintaining his public smile, took Anne's arm and guided her out the door.

The entire sky was bursting with stars. *I am reaching for them,* Anne ventured to herself. *Or are the stars reaching for me?*

"Tonight, stars is shining for yew," Alex declared.

Anne was startled. *He is reading my thoughts! I am not drawing on his attention, but I am certainly receiving it!*

They crossed The Strand as a light sprinkle began. Moments ago Anne wanted to bathe in the stars; now she worried about rain spots on her gown. There had been no flashes of lightning, no rumbles of thunder to announce an approaching rain. And a few twinklers still peeked between drifting clouds.

Though Alex had placed his jacket around her shoulders, she arrived wet. She shook the rain off, returned it, and turned to the door of her room with key in hand. "Allow me to do sat for yew," he offered. Shoulders touched as he maneuvered the key in the lock. The door swung open but he didn't step back. "Yew are tired?" he whispered.

"Somewhat. But not for a foot-up and a hot drink if you'd like," she said, with no warning lights flashing. They entered the suite. She moved toward the coffee machine with its packets of fixings. He stepped up behind her and watched her put it together.

"You are a beautiful woman," he announced suddenly. "I sink I would like to kiss you."

Anne caught her breath and felt foolish when all she could think to say was. "Why?"

"Because I have wanted to ever since I first saw yew."

Anne felt her pulse beat. The man frightened as much as fascinated her. She shivered and her answer surprised them both. "Why don't you then?"

A hint of a smile touched his lips. He pulled her to him. She didn't pull away. Eyes of glass and opals fixed themselves into his. "Madness?" she said softly, "or 'something new'?"

"Perhaps both," groaned Alex, taking her into his arms and burying his face in her cloud of hair. She smelled of roses and limes. "But yew left out one sing."

"And what is that?" she whispered, limp with the warmth of him.

"Adoration."

"Symphonic. And… somewhat religious," she trembled.

"Yes."

Time stopped.

Raynor ran his hands along Anne's shoulders and down her back. She felt his breath on her forehead. "We will write music tomorrow," he soothed, removing the coffee cup from her hand and setting it down.

Oh no, thought Anne, *we are writing it now....*

He unfastened her gown, lifted it away, and let it fall to the floor. *Rainspots on silk might not be uninteresting,* she told herself as he carried her the rest of the way.

Adagio. Slowly, tenderly, as though she might fade from his sonata, he trailed his kisses to her throat. She closed her eyes, shocked at her own deft removal of his clothes. Without them, they no longer seemed separate.

His body was richly tanned. "Rio de Janeiro," he explained, following her gaze. "January tour." He was more muscular than she had imagined. His waist was slim, his arms and shoulders graceful, and he swept his magic hands over her as lightly as silk.

"Mallorca," Anne formed the word languidly and with anticipation, as she ran her fingers the length of her lover's back. Slowly, she moved into the curve of him, and felt him respond. "They say it's... *exquisite!* I've never... been."

Fraught with desire, Raynor's body seared and his breath shook. "At sis time of year, *yes!* my dear, it is... *blazing hot!* Ahh, *yes!...* but, indeed, *exquisite!*" His kisses began to peak her sensibilities. "To... keep cool," he murmured with difficulty, "I... ahh ...swim as much as possible... in se sea...."

"*Yes, yes,* among the waves," Anne joined in.

"Ah, *yes!*" he echoed, fathoms deep in harmonious waves. In concert, his legendary hands summoned the tides of passion to claim her final response. And they rose to meet their own crescendo, rich and holy, to capture and possess them both. Floating back, Raynor whispered, "Now you must please be mine."

Anne sighed. They slept in each other's arms.

In the black of night Anne opened her eyes, aware that something was different. She studied the face on the pillow next to her. It hadn't been a dream. A breeze blew in from the open window. She slipped out of Alex's embrace and went to close it when she was caught by an event playing itself out below.

Another rain shower had cleared, and the street was wet. The effect was surreal with its cluster of performers in some nocturnal pantomime, doubling themselves in the puddled setting like puppets on a mirror. In their midst, a young bobby maintained a good-natured but watchful eye on a parade of hookers, drunks, and garbage pickers sifting through their findings with nimble fingers and assumed dignity. He touched his helmet to the homeless; with mild admonishment he wagged a finger at the inebriated who gingerly walked the night, drowning themselves in the "last one" that would never find its bottom.

I love the night, thought Anne, hugging herself. *I love these people with their strange drama floating their way into my quiet contentment right now... lending urgency and dimension to a city that seems to be sleeping.* All of this, capping an extraordinary night of love.

Two arms encircled her. Once more the man and the girl cocooned themselves. Just as those below were unaware of what was happening above, their audience of two was unmindful of anything but their hunger for each other.

"Yew are shaking my fences!"

"No, no!...You're 'rattling my cage'!"

And so Anne and Alex began their own symphony, loving as intensely as they played. Changing direction, challenging, teasing, and rehearsing each other's moods and versatilities, slowly and deliberately, so that each time would be brand new.

———

Together they read the morning reviews:

The *London Times*: "Compact in stature, gargantuan at the podium, Alexandre Raynor conducts the Moscow Philharmonic with a combination of wild authority, amazing skill, and floppy hair... on this circuit, providing the first European tour for Canada's pianist, Anne Quincy David.

"Ms. David has mastered her art brilliantly. With the introduction of Raynor's own piano arrangement for Dvořák's *New World* Symphony, she brings new life, new adventure. Together, they bring the audience to its feet..."

The *Daily Guardian*: "Conductor Alexandre Raynor merits a throne seat for his riveting control of the Moscow Philharmonic's New

World Symphony... penetrating in the hands of Canada's beautiful Anne Quincy David, interpreting maestro's piano adaptation on the keys. Together, they richly honor Dvořák with their passion and sense of freedom, timed to perfection through racing fingers and supreme partnering...."

The *Morning Sun*: "Alexandre Raynor can always be counted upon for surprises. Not unlike some cat burglar in a white dinner jacket, he steals into Dvořák's *New World* Symphony with nimble-fingered cool. Sufficiently teased to anticipate the familiar, we are disarmed by Raynor's own flourishing passages for piano in partnership with the sensual sparks of virtuoso Anne Quincy David.... Symphonic incandescence, unmatched ..."

Night Out London: "He is here. And there is no one else like him.... Akin to a buccaneer at his inaugural, Alexandre Raynor leads his Moscow Philharmonic with swashbuckling brilliance. In perfect accord with the conductor's famous hand magic, guest pianist Anne Quincy David scales musical heights with an extraordinary sense of teamwork, electric to the crowd's last roar."

Stagemag UK: "Like some dam breaking loose, its magic bubbles percolated by a Russian sorcerer and his amazing Canadian apprentice."

"Looks like yew might beat me at se game of popularity!" Alex exclaimed, with no attempt to hide his jubilation. He planted a kiss on Anne's cheek, then kissed her ring finger sporting the two batons. "Se critics are correct. Yew are compelling... and wery, wery beautiful."

The London engagement of the Moscow Philharmonic would be remembered for a long time. Four days stretched into two weeks. The three weeks of recording were moved ahead. After hours, Alexandre Raynor and his collaborator hummed and scribbled a symphonic tribute to the "One Horse." Anne's fingers needed no prompting to simulate the flight that appeared to multiply their numbers on the keys. Last Spring was sure to be immortalized.

"It is easy to associate music wis spring," declared Alex one morning, propped by a ring of cushions on the floor, where the two did most of their writing.

"When everything comes alive," Anne agreed. "However, many great pieces were written and composed in or about winter, too… especially in your Russia! I'm also thinking of' "Un Hiver a Majorque," written by George Sands about her affair with Chopin, which certainly confirms that winter brings its heat!" she chuckled.

"Winter is not winter in Mallorca, you funny lady!" Alex laughed.

Removing the pen clenched between her teeth, Anne said, "Personally Alex, I love snow. I'm a snowbird after all… and really, so are you!"

"I hate snow," Alex retaliated. "It gets dirty. I want to wipe it away!"

Anne snuggled close and stroked his fingers. "Not the first snow. Besides, winter is when the blood thickens, to keep you cozy—like this."

"Winter, summer, who cares?" Alex argued, pulling her to him. "Now. There is only now, which is when se blood quickens. When it gets cold out, instead of wandering through tulips and forsysia, we will make beautiful love by se fireside, my snowbird and me. Yes?"

"I look forward to that," sighed Anne. "But for now, let's practice."

The days went by swiftly, like rippling pages of a book. The connecting doors to both suites remained unlocked for the duration of the Moscow Philharmonic's London engagement. They were joyful days and loving nights.

Anne learned to appreciate and respect the dedication of the symphony members, and to admire their deportment in a country that was welcoming yet politically cool. Through music, the world could indeed become one people, she pipe-dreamed.

They, in turn, were quick to predict Anne's growing popularity as a renowned artist, and ready to do their utmost to compliment her extraordinary talent. In deference to her relationship with Maestro, the women kept their distance in a formal, respectful way, which meant that there were no favorites among them.

She did not appear to miss one. Ms. David remained exciting because she was excited. About her music, her travels, her lover, along with a growing awareness of her own emerging potential: "Deweloping-deweloped." For Anne, music presented a very personal area of development. Not only did it involve her, but it also involved, in some degree, Alex' perception of her and the mutuality they shared. Both derived a great deal of pleasure from working and living together, and responded as one… caressed and possessed.

Not only was Anne a natural beauty, she was also an attractive woman: jauntily dressed with attention to fit, quality and style, even in jeans. Her hair, worn in a thick braid that fell fully down her back, could have been judged medium brown if not for the silvery gold streaks running the length of it. Lithe and gamine-like, Anne was physically strong. She loved to run, breathing in the morning air at the break of dawn. In all things, she was female.

Raised in an era when women burned their bras, Anne had remained pretty secure with who she was, but with enough open-mindedness not to oppose those who were not. She was bright, gentle, but determined to live life as fully as the late Sixties would allow a teenager with some healthy rebellion in her soul.

She had never believed that her role was secondary to that of men. To credit her wise and devoted parents, once she'd learned her tasks well, all ranch duties had been equally shared. Regarding the piano, "With application and your God-given talent, you are bound to succeed," her mother had predicted.

For the first time in her young life, the girl was facing a wall, with no idea how to surmount it or pull it down. Conscious of its slow and insidious inroads, as little by little long periods of clarity submitted to brief periods of haziness, Anne feared that blindness might loom suddenly like a thief in the night. While denial was still possible, her fears about the future seemed set free for a time in the arms of the man she was beginning to know so well. With Alex, she was no longer afraid. She would tell him… soon.

Right now she was happy that the man she loved wanted to love her. Tenderly, blissfully, over and over. In his arms she discovered a quiet calm. If they were parted for an hour, she was eager for his return. Still a tough taskmaster at the podium, Maestro had mellowed noticeably, was becoming more affable, and at times displayed a sense of humor. Less and less was he communicating his dark, inner places.

Anne examined her own behavior in terms of the decade's roles of men and women, soon to be fractured, rearranged or reversed. She and Alex decided that each would pursue their careers, though they might be parted for months at a time. She felt secure with that. She would not marry Alex: a career-minded woman, in her estimation, would not be self-sacrificing enough for the wife of a genius. He desired no children. This was a perfect coupling. Anne felt sure that Alex would agree to keep it this way.

They talked about where they would meet after her final appearance with the symphony in Mallorca, scheduled for the latter part of June. Anne would accompany Alex to Madrid, where the Philharmonic was to fulfill a week's engagement in August. Not featured for that, she nevertheless looked forward to their being together a little longer before she returned to Canada for two appearances with the Toronto Symphony Orchestra. All of July, they would languish in Palma.

"Other than se piano," Alex asked, during their last week in London, "what are yewer wishes and goals for se future?" He was looking at the one woman who gave meaning to his life. Convinced of his commitment, he had to be sure she felt the same way.

Anne hesitated. *Now might be the time... no... maybe not. The threat might still go away.... No, it won't go away.* She would lead up to it, half-tell him: "I would like to open a music school... for blind children," she began.

"A school? You, Anne? Sat is for people who, for one reason or another, cannot perform. *Sey* teach. But you... wis such a brilliant career before you? And why se blind?—Ah yes, Last Spring."

"I assumed you meant the far future," Anne lied, satisfied for now with the reason he'd just provided. "Most important, Alex," she began on a serious note, "I want to be me. Really me, with all that can be worthwhile in me. There are heights I want to scale beyond personal recognition. If I continue to make it in the area of music, I want to share what I've learned, and sharing can be boundless." With those words, thoughts of Carney occupied her mind. If one could use horses to mend lives, why couldn't she do it with music?

Alex kissed her frown and ran his lips down her neck to her shoulder until she grasped his face in both her hands and focused on his deep and probing eyes so exquisitely pinpointed with diamonds.

Wrapped tightly in each other's warmth, their bodies slowly circled, igniting the sparks of arousal. He ran his hand to unbutton her blouse, then teased her with his tongue until she began to moan her little sounds. His breath caught with the ecstasy of her touch, their mounting mutual ascent and waves of bliss. Anne gasped, "Oh Alex—now!" Two spirits, caught in the magic of night and the torches of desire, slipped over the precipice saved for lovers... and into the divine.

"Hello to you," Alex whispered.

"Hi," Anne murmured, content in the crook of his arm.

Seconds later Alex jumped from the bed like an eager child. He opened a dresser drawer and removed a brown paper package tied with string. "I have gift for yew," he offered with an expectant grin.

Like a kid in a sandbox, Anne dug into the wrappings and caught her breath. "It's Last Spring! It is! How did you do this?"

Jubilant with her reaction, Alex confessed to enlarging the photo she had shown him on their first evening together. His smile was shy and guilty. "I snuck it—but I put it right back," he quickly amended. "Sair are many good sculptors here in London; I had one make a sketch, sen a mold of se animal. Se result yew see before yew. Yew like it?"

"Like it? Oh my!" Anne ran her hands over the statue to feel each feature so accurately reproduced.

"No problem sen?"

"Problem?" Her throat caught, and her eyes spoke their love. "You could never be a problem to me!"

Cast in bronze, which emphasized the true color of his coat, the animal looked as graceful as he had been in life. Regarding the inscription on its base, which read *FAREWELL TO LAST SPRING*, Anne cried, "It's too much!" She hugged the man for his gift. For him most of all.

Life was good. "For yew, my darling," said Alex, "nossing will ever be too much."

———

The lobby of the Hotel Nixe Palace on the Paseo Maritimo was cool in marble, brass and glass. Across its width, a wall of windows glazed and framed the scenic Bay of Palma, an arm of the Mediterranean

Sea as blue as its reputation. On surrendering their passports at the reception desk, Anne and Alex were presented with keys to their suites, hooked to heavy brass knobs to prevent pocketing. "Elevators are to your right," announced the concierge, beckoning a bellboy who chalked the suite numbers on their luggage, "to take you down to your floor."

"Down?" Anne questioned.

"Yes, Madame. The hotel is built into a cliff. You must go down to all suites. And they all face the sea." Promptly, the concierge turned to the next guest.

Anne's suite was the color of roses, its walls lined with pink silk damask. The thick white carpeting was deeply luxurious. Bleached furniture of Louis XVI design included a tall armoire fitted with doors and drawers, two delicate chairs upholstered in silk, and a pair of matching tables flanking a four poster plump with pink satin pillows. Beyond an archway was a sitting room with two side chairs and a lady's writing table. Electrified gas lamps flickered on the walls.

The adjoining quarters were the same, but tailored with striped wallpaper and mahogany furniture.

Like twin atriums ablaze with color, both terraces overlooked Playa de Palma, the beach below, and offered a magnificent view of an indigo stretch of sea. Anne tingled a bit to think that just beyond the horizon lay Tangier.

Tea was served in the bar, a walnut-paneled room off the main lobby. Here, they were able to relax for the first afternoon in weeks. Anne wrote a letter to her dad, describing the people around her as they appeared....

"Rubbish!" cries a portly Englishman. "All cars are rubbish, except for the Mercedes!"

"I shall have six children, then tie my tubes!" declares a six-year-old, here to assist her grandmother.

"My Gerald sleeps all day and all night," complains a raven-haired beauty to the bachelor sitting next to her....

"I'm here to find a girl I met during the war. Haven't seen her in thirty years," twinkles a doctor from "Winneepeg."

And no less amazing, two men named Sydney, friends for forty years, announce that they never share a table in the dining room because they're both too picky!

Each character found their way into Anne's letter. But not Alex. Not yet.

During their weeks in Mallorca, Anne and Alex were romanced nightly on the dance floor to strains of some of the world's most beautiful music_Chopin's *Polonaise*, themes from *Love Story*, *The Godfather, Romeo and Juliet*— by a five-piece orchestra, largely inspired by the couple's obvious chemistry. It hardly mattered that the musicians were not highly professional. The aura created by that chemistry, the syncopation in tune with it, stretched each evening well into night.

The couple took time to tour Polenca Formentor, home of the Gypsies, high in the hills where windmills still pumped irrigation from the sea. They drank cerveza at Son Amar, an ancient walled village surrounded by trees so laden with oranges, their branches swept the ground. They danced at Tito's, a spacious discotheque featuring Spanish dancers and endless champagne. They climbed the surrounding cliffs and perched on their ledges like a pair of love-struck gulls. They exhausted themselves. And they were happier than either of them ever dreamed they could be.

Auditorio de Palma hosted eight successful concerts. The program listed Chopin's *Minute Waltz*, Rachmaninov's *Piano Concerto Number 2 in C Minor*, and concluded with excerpts from *New World* Symphony. Reviews in many languages resulted in a sellout of seats by the second night and ovations resounded across the Bay. When the engagement ended, most members of the Moscow Philharmonic departed for home, except for the few who preferred to remain on the island so close to their next stop, Madrid.

Each Sunday morning Alex played tennis with his percussionist. Anne would hunker down under a blanket to indulge herself in a little more sleep. During the weeks of performance, rehearsals had been grueling. At last they had come to an end and there was time to rest, play, or leisurely work on "Last Spring."

Anne would have a late breakfast, a midmorning swim, then practice for an hour on the baby grand in the solarium. By that time, Alex would be back. But on this last Sunday prior to their departure,

Anne decided to make a brief exploration of the old city of Palma, to
see some of what she and Alex had missed.

She ambled through streets so narrow, they would have been called
alleyways at home. Each residence loomed tall and formal, their doors
and windows heavily adorned with ironwork. Though cloistered by
trees, gardens were lush enough to belie the obstruction of sunlight.

On one of their walks, she and Alex had observed the tall spires
and artistic appointments of King Philip's sixteenth century palace,
which later served as a residence for Generalissimo Franco when he
chose to visit Mallorca. Today Anne passed through its wide arches
into a cold gray interior formidable with ponderous furnishings. She
found the atmosphere burdened and concluded that ancient castles
were not to her liking. She remained just long enough to study some
wall tapestries by Goya.

With quick gestures that only they could interpret, groups of elderly
men occupying the benches in Palma's main square, wagged or nodded
their appraisals of new tourists as they appeared. Artists concentrated
on the surroundings, and heavily-robed priests strode with alacrity
in and out of a lavishly adorned edifice reputed to be Palma's oldest
cathedral. All part of a time-honored scene in an era altered by the
zoom of minibikes pumping their tin around its venerable core.

With the ascending sun, the square filled with Palma's citizens.
Out walking their owners, a whippet proceeded his Englishman, a
pincer pranced with a German, and a poodle proudly showed off her
Frenchwoman. *People do resemble their dogs; not the other way around!*
Anne observed, laughing to herself.

There were warships on the Bay of Palma. Their crews, part of the
U.S. Sixth Fleet, were well-informed of when young ladies of various
nationalities visited the island. This day, swaggering in crisp whites,
they evaluated a flock of new arrivals from Sweden. Anne from Canada
chose to pass on all winks and whistles, though she did enjoy being the
object of them!

The market area with its bakeries and sweet shops, lured her with
their intoxicating aromas into the first piazza that beckoned. "That's
why she's so skinny!" a mother lectured her daughter, as Anne passed by
with a muffin, a bunch of grapes and a cup of coffee on her tray. "You
think she's pretty? Think again! It is not pretty to be skin and bones!

You need to have meat on them… here! Here! And here!" she huffed, pinching her daughter's plump rump, upper arm, and indicating with a gentler poke her already budding chest.

Anne's mother, of Spanish descent, had made sure that Anne learned the language. She cast a sympathetic look at the tubby ten-year-old, then chose a table behind a row of tropical plants, open to the sea and its breezes.

She was spotted by Sergei Malenkoff, seated with a young woman in the nook next to her, pretty well hidden by greenery. Though she didn't know the man well, it was easy to tell that he was hung-over. "Our wedding breakfast," purred his companion, stroking his fingers. Anne peeked through an opening to capture the couple's happiness. But the man's expression seemed one of dawning regret, like one with a foot out the door. Anne wished she were somewhere else.

Malenkoff worked hard to focus on the woman facing him. She wasn't someone he'd just picked up. He'd met her in a bar the last time he was in Palma. But how had she managed to manipulate him into this? He'd been drinking, but he'd been loaded many times before, and had never ended up looking for a priest! He would rid himself of her somehow, get an annulment, whatever was required in this place. Meanwhile, he patted the lady's arm to keep her quiet, lifted a demonic eyebrow toward the green hedge, and with a leer to match, cunningly planned how he would take advantage of such an extraordinary opportunity.

With a lift of his voice, Sergei trumpeted, "I belief sat our maestro is living it up again here in Palma wis his latest squeeze. I dunno. He's not esseptionally good-lookink. I always wonder what ser is about him sat gets all se gorchuss girls! Like se one he marry."

Anne was further jarred by the scraping of a chair, pulled to form a huddle. "Who is she?" the woman wanted to know.

Relishing his words, Sergei shook his head, placed a noble finger to his lips and loudly whispered, "She's guest artist, like always. He gets around, eh? Wizzout hafing to move wery far!" There was loud laughter: His. "Ewery year a different one… pianist sis time… wery pretty… fell for our Alex, like, how you say… a load of blocks?"

The woman surveyed her new husband, and took a moment to answer. "A ton of bricks." She was uncomfortable with Sergei's vicious account of Raynor. "I attended a concert, remember? Miss David is beautiful and talented. And your conductor makes exciting music. I like how he uses his hands."

"So do lots of women!" roared Malenkoff with more laughter. "He passes them over ewery new dame sat comes along!"

"How many years have you actually been with him?" the lady enquired, alarmed with the menace in her husband's voice.

Devoid of conscience and on a roll, Sergei could not be discouraged from his mission. "As long as Raynor has been leader of Moscow Philharmonic—about sewen years," he calculated. "You can belief it, I know him well. Married my sister Tatyana. But for him, career come first, like she is inwisible. He's okay guy, but a wery bad husband."

The exposé sounded like a soap opera, dramatic and demonic. Anne flushed with the heat of it and lifted her eyes from her untouched muffin to the botanical embankment. Had they seen her come in? She preferred to believe that Malenkoff was unaware of her presence and that to find her here would be an embarrassment. Not that she cared.

Anne did not know that Raynor had always been kind to the brother-in-law whose coarse nature led him to confuse kindness with weakness. Sergei resented Raynor's success, and it showed in his mean lack of appreciation. He was fully aware that if Maestro were to re-select his orchestra members, he would no longer be one of them.

Now, gratified by the deep quiet on the other side of the greenery, Sergei forged on with his maniacal tirade. "Sey haf no children; he neffer wants sem. Work is his baby, along wis se babes he manages to pick up—all he wants!" This opportunity would serve, Malenkoff concluded, his need to get even for what seemed to him the abandonment by Alex Raynor of himself and his sister. The man was especially gleeful to spot Anne's grip on her coffee cup tremble in midair.

There were no tears. One could say that Anne was too stunned to indulge in them. Unaware of the man's rancor, she did not suspect a motive. She left by a seaside exit.

Anger came next, though Anne knew it was unjustified. She really had no claim on Alex Raynor. They'd been lovers, but had made no commitment. She'd been content with that. It hadn't occurred to Anne to research the man's reputation… so what right did she have to feel so betrayed? *Of course he's had affairs; he's almost forty, for God's sake!*

Thoughts of other women wouldn't normally bother her. But the way his alleged tendency for wooing them had been recapped and bandied about—as if she were simply another piece of flotsam, part of a collection open to scrutiny, as that scathing disclosure seemed to imply—was too hard to absorb. *Oh no.*

Oh no, Alex. Their relationship must not be as perfect as she had imagined. It had been too quick; not like her at all, really. Which probably meant that her child side had been leaning on him far too much. Now she felt... unwholesome.

Alexandre Raynor. Promiscuous? Indiscreet? A predator? Or all three? The more she considered this, the worse he seemed. Heck, she didn't really know him, did she? As her state of shock widened into a mass of distress, Anne's anger changed to resolve. Love is a trickster, she concluded. Not unlike a fake painting. Fully in its grasp, a woman can be fooled into creating, in her mind, a glorious image of the person she thinks she loves. She chooses to trust, and that trust can lead to fuzzy judgment... a duel between decency and... wantonness.

Would she have felt the same attraction had Alexandre Raynor not been up there on a pedestal? Her conductor, her teacher, her leader... she was always looking up. In her heart and mind, that's where she had kept him, where he'd had to be.

Protective of her self respect, she flogged her gullibility. How could she have been so reckless? Something had indeed been wrong with her judgment! In her agitated state, Anne began to argue with herself, then to mourn the death of what she had believed was her singular significance in her lover's eyes.

And just look what she might have had in store for him! The doctors were right. There were bad times ahead. Her loss of vision would certainly have divided them.

Thoughts of romance between Chopin and Sands on this island left her young heart empty. She had to take stock of her situation. If there could be no more engagements, if she were unable to progress, there would be nothing to hold the two of them together anyway. She would merely be a pianist out of work.

She walked slowly past a row of homes, each protected by a brick wall embedded with shards of... what, exactly? Moving closer, she attempted to focus on a crust of colored fragments sparkling in the sun, when the sight in her left eye danced like a wonky picture show. Anne grasped the edge of the wall and remained where she was.

A small hand slipped into hers. Her broken vision strained to focus on a small child of maybe seven or eight who studied her with wide-eyed intensity. "Gracias," she responded weakly, as he led her to a vacant spot on a bench. He was steady. She was not.

When Anne was seated, the boy stepped back, hesitated, and observed that the woman still needed guidance, so he remained there. A grin split his face for the coins she took out of her pocket, but he didn't plan to leave until she demonstrated, by rising and walking around the bench, that she was no longer impaired. As magically as he had appeared, the child left.

Anne felt alive. *I want one of those*, she told her heart. *A sweet child to fill my aching arms.* It would take more than dreams; it would take a miracle. She could no longer wrap her future with denial. With loss of vision progressing, first and foremost she needed to strengthen her independence.

But a hand to hold... There is so much beauty in that. Such a little tyke, yet so like a shepherd in a storm. Maybe he was an angel lending her the strength to change her life... beginning now. With vision clearing, Anne searched the direction taken by the child, past an apothecary shop on her left, a wine store, a shoemaker. There was no sign of him.

Adjusting to the light, Anne squinted at an azure sky uninterrupted by clouds, then at the indigo sea in full view. *Look hard,* she demanded. *File this in your storehouse. Your sight is going; you'd better believe it.*

———

It was after six when she arrived back at the villa. The sun was making its last sojourn of the day across a jewel-like bay and surrounding cliffs. There was no movement in the branches of the twin olive trees on the patio. All was hushed.

Alex was still in his tennis whites, stretched out on a chaise, a glass of vodka nestled in his hand. Hiding his concern for her lateness, he waved cheerfully through the screen door. "Yewer martini is in se fridge!" Behind him, from the shore to the horizon, the blue of the Bay of Palma had deepened to cobalt, and was strafed with gold from the sun.

Anne offered a perfunctory greeting and turned away. As she changed into a caftan, she despaired at how one person's few vicious words managed to tip the balance of her perfect world.

"Would yew like to go to se docks later to see se boats?" Alex innocently suggested. One day, time permitting, he was determined to own one.

"A fat lot of use you'd get out of a boat in your Russian winter!" Anne sniffled under her breath. "I don't feel like it tonight!" she barked, feeling under the bed to make sure of her suitcase. She made her way to the patio.

Against the inky effect of approaching twilight, all cloud shapes blushed pink. The last fragment of the departing sun, as it clung to the horizon, invaded Anne's vision. She moved her chair under the olive trees for shade, and took a deep, nervous breath. "We need to talk," she said, not unkindly.

"So serious yew are," Alex teased. "Why not save serious business for tomorrow, when we leave here, maybe? It's a beautiful evening. Tonight is still… tonight."

By now Anne had it all thought out. "There will be no Madrid, Alex. I am not coming with you."

Alex's chest constricted. He felt a sudden chill. His impulse was to reach out for her, but she repelled him with her distance. "What is se matter? Why aren't you coming?" he asked with a sense of foreboding.

Anne jammed her hands into the pockets of her caftan, catching its surplus yardage around her body like a protective shield. Preferring not to answer directly, she began, "You've built your empire the way you want it to be—" She bit her lip in hesitation, finding it difficult to go on.

After several moments, "Sat's wery philosophical," Alex stated carefully.

Half-crazed by what she had to say, Anne searched for her voice. She had no desire to wound this man in the process. "No pressure, Alex. You stepped into my world. But I let you in. You turned my life upside down, but I helped you to do it. We wrote some nice beginnings together—your lines were especially professional—but right now I merely feel like a paragraph in the chronicles of your life. Now please give me the space I need in order to redeem the meaning of mine."

"I fail to understand where all sis is coming from."

"To defend your title is where your reputation rests. Be careful, Alex, not to trivialize the rest of it," she added testily.

As darkness swallowed up the branches of the olive trees, Anne seemed more and more a stranger to the man. He almost wanted to salute her. By now the patio was lined with lights. The moon slipped out of a cloud and was full, lending its shimmer to the man and woman who looked to be enjoying their nightly view of the bay as they stepped off the patio onto the beach. Tiny waves lapped meekly at their feet.

"Impossible to keep," Anne sobbed. "No more bubbles."

Alex moved toward her, but she quickly moved away. Stars appeared like old friends, and she seemed more resolved with their presence. "We were all filled up with a destination, you and I... for ourselves and for music. It was a commitment, sort of... but for you, it would mean imprisonment." While her eyes commanded Alex to say no more, Anne longed for his embrace, though she wouldn't accept it now. Imprinted in her mind were Alex and his women, with one affair following another, she among them, possibly inserting herself into an existing marriage, for all she knew... where she had no right to be.

Alex remained motionless with his arms at his sides, waiting for Anne to quit her craziness, or to explain it. She'd claimed she loved him... often. What was getting in the way of it? "Are we talking about yew, or are we talking about me?" he enquired.

"We are talking about you... and me... and a dream." To Anne, he was once more Conductor Raynor; no more Alex. Theirs was a relationship she no longer wished to be in. She glared past him into the night. To him she was more beautiful, more passionate and inviting than ever, despite her anger and his confusion. He awaited the rest of her statement. "That's all it was, Maestro—a dream."

"Annyee! Please stop sis. Yew must tell me what is se matter here! What happened to make yew like sis?" He couldn't fathom the ice in the girl's eyes.

"Nothing that I care to add," she assured him, as images of liaisons with women streamed through her imagination like bonbons on a conveyor belt. "Nothing happened."

"Very well," he answered, as though he'd been physically slapped. He regarded the stranger before him in an attempt to digest her words and the abrupt end of their relationship. "I will collect my belongings in se morning."

Anne steadied herself, took a heavy breath, and said it like a woman who had very much made up her mind. "Goodbye Alex."

They would have dined by candlelight on this last evening in Mallorca. But the bundles of fresh mussels, scallops, sea bass and colossal shrimp meant for Alex's favorite boullabaise, would remain uncooked.

Dream over. Anne suddenly recalled the night cleaners flanking the London stage door, and pictured them blinking themselves awake, removing their frilly caps, to glare slyly at her with the malicious features of Malenkoff.

She shuddered and dug into her handbag for the airline tickets that would need to be re-scheduled. Beside them was a folded piece of paper.

'I was once a wealthy man, but now I drive a cab.
When I take stock of what I am, this is what I have:
Jewels.
The kind that can't be bought.
Mine are songs that fill the air,
From tales of wonder caught
When listening to you back there.
A wealth of knowledge held in trust
To me, from you, my friend.
And this is why, until I'm dust,
My jewels will never end.
P.S.: If something does not feel right,
Walk away....
To feel what's right another day.
That's what I did! And I never looked back.'
.... P.F.N.

"Right, P.F.N. Your poem is right on," Anne agreed with a heavy heart. Then a memory streaked through it. "P.F.N'? Puffins! On Oxford. Street! Guess what, Alex, someone else got there first!" Was she laughing or crying?

Hidden in Anne's suitcase was a slender package tied with silver ribbon, purchased in London as a keepsake for maestro: a humorous, meaningful symbol of their happiest days. She couldn't do anything about the inscription: *Your Anne*, which scoffed at her naiveté. At least he'd remember what year, in the chronological order of things, she'd joined the lineup! Convinced that it would never be used, she placed the baton atop his suitcase, packed her bag, and returned by taxi to the Nixe Palace Hotel.

During the time she and Alex were together, Anne had felt tenderly and honestly loved. She could brave the wrench. She knew that she could part from Alex, but very much doubted that she would ever succeed in extinguishing his imprint on her life.

In the morning, she took an elevator up two floors to the main desk to arrange a flight to Canada.

Alex spent the night wondering what happened. Obviously something had. Did she know something he didn't? He'd been proud of her achievements, had considered her his equal, even when applause at times seemed louder and stronger for her. Ego had not entered into their relationship, nor had either of them felt the necessity to test the other's love. He had shown her respect, and had given her all the attention he possessed. Why had she broken away so suddenly, with no explanation?

Conductor Raynor was left with a baton and memories of a sylph in a watered silk gown. To him, she had no equal. He had been stupid enough to believe she had felt the same about him.

———

The following day, Anne's flight set down at Toronto International Airport. She was met by her father, Hamilton (Hap) David, and driven to their King City ranch in his brand new station wagon. "It's so good to be home!" Anne exclaimed, stretching her arms toward the open sky in an attempt to toss off the strains of the last thirty-six hours, and to once again become the carefree girl who left King's Meadow just three months before. She admired the new vehicle. "I thought you were determined never to get rid of the jalopy you were so fond of," she teased.

Lifting her suitcase into the hatch, Hap observed the shadows under his daughter's eyes and her forced cheerfulness. "I didn't. It's an extra for toodlin' around with the animals. With care, it'll last forever," he lectured. "However, on an occasion like this, to meet a princess at the airport—well, I thought I'd update her chariot." He waited a moment, then declared, "Anyway, life's too short not to indulge in the odd luxury, eh?"

Stamped by shared characteristics—though Hap's were toughened with time— there was no question that they were father and daughter. Both were slim and graceful. Hap's hair, once dark gold, was now quite gray, but still thick and wavy. His wide smile and opal eyes shone with kindness. The comparison ended in his ruddy skin, as tanned and creased as vintage leather, but so in keeping with his firm muscles, youthful stride and closet full of blue denim.

King's Meadow. Home. Hap tore around the car to open Anne's door. Immediately she was caught by the scent of clover mixed with pine. Ahead were acres of fields dotted with bundles of grain to feed the animals. Alfalfa was going to seed, and bags of oats already lined one wall of the barn. It was coming up harvest time... with its highlight, pumpkin time. What a great place to be raised!

Driven by a yearning she could not resist, Anne ran into the house and up a flight of stairs to her bedroom. It smelled of roses. Aware of the girl's love of them, Pan, the houseman, had placed a large bouquet on the mantle above the fireplace.

Cabbage roses decorated two knee walls hugging a window seat with matching chintz cushions. Years ago, when Anne's allowance wouldn't cover the cost of an authentic *Gone with the Wind* lamp, she'd painted a discarded fish bowl with flowers, turned it upside down and balanced it on an old iron stand. It still occupied her night table, with its recollections of a runaway imagination and a madly undisciplined paintbrush slathering an iron bed white, a wicker rocker to match, and a wood cradle smothered with decals, to hold her music. From the time she was little, this room had been her private sanctuary. In it, Anne had always managed to think things out, set her goals, and... imagine 'something new'.

She placed the bronze horse next to the roses, and looked about to make sure all else was the same. Fronting the white brick fireplace, a pair of brass andirons shaped like hitching posts boasted their antique patina. On a dressing table skirted with white eyelet, her mother's smile shone from its silver frame. And her single attempt to braid a rag rug, its deep turquoise looking gorgeous against the mellow pine floor, still felt welcoming under her bare toes. Home was her favorite port of call, fortified always by the familiarity of her room. "As a child."

Her riding clothes were where she'd left them, hanging neatly in her closet. Blue jeans with extra patches on the inner thighs, long sleeve top, dark blue vest with many pockets. Anne put them on. The boots, in which she'd invested serious dollars, were highly polished, thanks to Pan. She felt good, she looked good. Now for a good gallop to help clear her mind… and hopefully her heart.

Out of the corral that penned the two year olds, Hap was leading a sleek and feisty albino.

"He's new. What's his name?" Anne asked.

"Winter."

Un hiver de… Symphony not over yet, Alex? Well then, let's begin a song about you, Winter. But first things first, laddie. "May I ride him, Dad?"

"You can do better than that, Honey. You can own him."

"You bought him just for me!" exclaimed Anne, her affection bursting for the man. "I am sure to be the luckiest girl on planet Earth!" She hugged Hap and ran to do the same around Winter's majestic neck. "He's magnificent, Dad. Exactly the horse I would have chosen for myself." She ran her hands lovingly along the animal's alabaster flanks and pondered a moment. "May I… change his name, though?"

"Mmm, guess he could tolerate that. If you must," Hap grinned.

"I would like to call him Chopin."

Anne mounted Chopin. To Hap, no queen upon a throne could rival the sight of his daughter on her white stallion. Still, his heart was heavy for her. "Mind if I come with you?"

For the next hour, Anne followed her father across a meadow, then through a wooded path to the foot of the rolling hills. They crossed a gully and meandered alongside a stream for almost a mile. The trail led back through a heavily-wooded valley between two ridges covered with wild flowers, then leveled on the grassy meadow where it joined a different path leading back to the paddock. As Anne grabbed the pommel of her saddle and dismounted, father's and daughter's eyes met.

Hap placed an arm about the girl's shoulder. "Mine is a funny age, Anne. Sometimes stuff just ducks out of my head. Often, things we said or did together only moments before challenge me to recall them. But I know my girl from way back, where many of my memories are securely stored." With a look full of meaning he declared, "I know all is not right. So if anything's on your mind that you want to share, I'm your buddy."

"You're flat-out right, Pop. I've just walked out on the love of my life, that's all."

"There's no such person, darlin', for one so young. You're entitled to a few loves before choosin' the one and only."

Anne thought hard. "Possibly. All I know is that I am Alex... and Alex is me. I can't get rid of him. When I was with him I was floating twenty-four hours a day. People noticed, and felt it, too... like some magnetic thing."

Hap stroked his chin with a memory of his own. "You fell that hard, eh?"

"You bet I did. I'm twenty-eight; old enough to know the difference between falling for love and being in love. But I suppose I 'm still naive about some things. There would likely have been mammoth problems ahead. Though I couldn't foresee any," she quickly added, not about to worry Hap about anything more. Until it happened—*if* it happened. "Alex Raynor wouldn't have enjoyed our bison steaks, Dad. Let's just say he would not have... fit."

"That's my girl," Hap soothed. "Wise enough to know that what's meant to be, will be."

"Well... this one won't be, my darling philosophical parent. It's over." That said, she smiled with a look that invited no comment.

Hap touched his hat with respect for her wishes, and was about to go on with his work when an added thought nagged to be expressed. "You'll not find another Last Spring, honey. But, as you see, that doesn't mean that there's no other to love." Before she could respond, he lifted a hand and gestured toward the barn. "One more stop," he said, making his way to a corner where a furry creature slept fitfully in a basket. "This little guy was delivered just before we rode out...

and I think he has your name on him." Anne took the pup into her arms. "Should help chase those blues away," her father winked. "Name him."

"He's a chaser alright!" said Anne, with an uncontrollable rush of moisture filling her eyes. She allowed it to dispel while hugging the puppy to her chest. "Name's Blue," she winked back.

———

Throughout the month of September, Anne was happy to be grooming and training both Chopin and Blue. She practically lived in the stables where the animals nuzzled against her as soon as she appeared, yelping or snorting their joy.

Anne reveled in sunrise, when the misty world was silent except for the muffled thumping of horses' hooves on the powdery track. As dawn etched its way through the trees, Anne kicked up dust with the thoroughbreds, though none were listed to race. Trotting past Old Snowy, who, she was sure had occupied his place on the fence at the same hour and on the same tilt for twenty-five years, Anne yearned to chat up the old owl, but recalled as a child being swooped upon and quickly rescued when she'd tried calling, "Whoo-whoo!"

Her parents had soothed away the tears. "He thought you were another owl, come to claim his territory; that's all, honey." Lesson learned: Old owls wanted to be left alone.

Late summer in Canada seemed plated with coppery light, when life's cycle depended upon hurried wings or scurrying feet, poking and butting and scavenging, to scoop up the season's bounty in order to survive winter: all creatures using the implements endowed by Nature, whatever was their way, in their race to gather. And to waltz to a job well-done in the early autumn air. It was Anne's favorite time of year.

After her ride each morning, she would stop at a mirror hanging in the entrance hall to touch the track dirt on her face as if it were powdered gold. There were roses in her cheeks, whipped up by wayward tresses that refused to stay anchored in her braid. She belonged to the earth as well as its music, and was content with the duel spell.

Now and then, her eyes played tricks. She began to see bits of things that weren't there, caused by shifting light creating odd images. Anne was learning that discernment was a derivative, in large part, of an interplay of light with darkness. Shapes, shading, texture, color, were all products of a co-dependency. If light was unable to penetrate, if something blocked or distorted its path, vision would become dim.

With the advent of Indian summer, tall grasses bleached and bent to wavering waves of heat. Winds blowing over the meadows and through the trees were heavy with humidity, but the nights were cool. An hour before sundown, Anne would saddle Chopin, and with Blue alongside, ride leisurely through the forest where she was sure to encounter Alex's image in the sprawling maples... from their vibrant palette of colors, boasting his triumph over her heart. Out of sight, out of mind? Should be... but he wasn't. She bit her lip. She was as edgy as Chopin prior to a run.

———

Nippy winds announced the arrival of late autumn. Carney and Anne arranged to meet at the stables for their annual "wild ride" beyond the vast acreage of the ranch. Leading the albino out of the paddock, Anne encountered him grabbing armfuls of firewood away from Hap, disallowing the older man the effort. With a grin to his daughter that verged on apology, Hap made an excuse, "The more I do, the behinder I git!"—which seemed out of character, but after all, her dad was no longer fifty, the age she would choose to keep him if she could.

When all logs for five fireplaces were stacked, Charles leaned against his pickup and regarded the girl attending to her mount. Washed in sunlight, moonlight, or stage lights, Anne had to be more beautiful each time he laid eyes on her.

Charles was a well-favored man, characterized by a kindness that illuminated a face bright-eyed and handsomely chiseled. He had a cleft in his chin and little creases that could be called dimples, bridged by a broad mouth and a wide smile that showed itself often. His coppery hair was streaked by the sun; his muscular body bronzed by a summer spent mostly out of doors with his animals.

Anne gave him a hug and exclaimed, "Carney, you would have loved Command Performance! If only you could have been there, I would have reserved a seat for you, right next to the Queen!"

"I did!" he laughed, hugging her back.

"Did?"

"I was there at Command Performance, Anne. Not far from Her Majesty, I might add! And yes, I did love it. Afterward, by the time I found your dressing-room, you'd gone off with that fellow, Raynor, I was told."

"Maestro Raynor." Anne stood unmoving and saved the next thought for herself : *You, Carney, have got to be the guy with the red hair—the one he wanted to throw off the balcony!* Aloud, she asked, "Why didn't you wave?" Taking a dim view of that suggestion, they both burst into laughter.

Charles offered a theory: "Sometimes when you stare at people, concentrate on them long enough, it works for their attention like a magnet. But it didn't work for me that night !" he laughed.

But it did work... on Alex. He stared you away, and you promptly turned and took your seat. "What were you doing in London?" Anne asked. "Why didn't you tell me you were coming? Why didn't you ask Dad where I was staying, so you could find me the next day? Why did you just disappear?"

"Whoa, girl!" Charles'grin rippled a face full of freckles. "I was on my way to France for a veterinarian's convention, and London happened to be in the way." To Anne's chagrin, he quickly added, "Don't you be upset, now. The surprise was my idea, and it certainly wasn't well thought-out. As for the next to last question, my flight left London at eight the following morning." Charles brushed some wood chips caught in the sleeve of his riding jacket. "Never mind, my lovely friend, I was very lucky to obtain a ticket at the hotel desk. I hadn't planned well for that, either. And honey, I was so proud of you. The performance was thrilling. You especially."

"Where did you stay?" Anne asked, pressing his hand affectionately, but still with a forlorn expression.

"Just across the river at the Strand."

How different life might be if this man had found her in her dressing-room, or entering the lobby of the hotel. With Carney in town, those hours with Alex would not have happened. The three of them bar-hopping? Alex would not have welcomed it—he was too courtly, too private then... and not yet mellowed out of his dark places.

Then again, their so-called chemistry would have pulled them together at some point. After all, when a womanizer has an objective …

Are you still determined to believe that of him?

Well, where there's smoke, there's fire, isn't that right? Anne dueled with herself. Now, with time and space between them, such impulsive thinking was beginning to ring hollow.

Anne mounted Chopin. Carney was up on Warrior, a lofty black stallion. Watching them depart, Hap did some hard thinking. These two were, had always been, a great pair. As long as Carney was around, he hadn't been gravely concerned about Anne's safety and good sense. He was content with that thought for the moment… but only for the moment, before he took to chiding himself for his inability to smooth a happier path for his child.

The sun was gilding the treetops, its golden scintillations streaking through the branches, to hover over a shaded trail wet with dew, where patches of bluebells wagged their heads to a brook gurgling over a tiny waterfall. Though Anne and Charles had left together, the girl swept far ahead with the spirit of the horse flowing in her veins. "Go, Chopin! Go!" Anne's laughter trilled over the hills and through the trees—her first since she left Mallorca.

Skilled in this chase, they ran with the wind, against clouds racing across the sky, and a hawk diving for prey. Carney gave Anne the lead. Their laughter rang with the sweep of their horses and the clopping of their hooves.

Charles loosened the reins and came alongside Anne. Neck-and-neck with him, she looked up into sparkling hazel eyes and a forehead teased with spikes of wind-tossed hair the color of Last Spring's mane. He swept past her, blending as one with the rolling, painted hills, as if to impart that, as a skilled and mannered sportsman, he truly belonged to this scene. And how unlike Alex he was.

She watched him on the next high ridge point to a lake on their left. Hart Lake, a familiar spot. Very small. With no waves.

Regarding a swiftly looming bank of clouds, but with voice full of delight, Anne called, "We're heading into a storm!"

Charles pushed his cap back, looked up and studied the whirling cloud formations. "Seems so, but it's veering away from us, toward the city!" he yelled over a sudden gust.

Unwilling to relinquish the prospect of a tempest, Anne argued, "Which isn't very far away!"

Charles nodded. A bolt of lightning, no matter how distant, could spook the horses. Dust sweeping up from the road was smothering. A flash of light from the west had no effect, but he heeded its warning. "Head toward the Inn!" he called. Too quickly, the sky darkened above. A fork of lightning shot through it. Warrior reared.

With beating pulse, Anne watched Charles maintain control while reassuring his mount, though man and beast were pivoting like toys. "Stay with him, Carney!" she applauded, her heart racing madly, her braid slashing the air like a whip. For a full minute the storm hit with huge drops, then swung to the east.

"That was close!" Charles joked, his white teeth flashing. Like Anne, he too was elated, though both were soaked through. A fickle sun teased its way through the overcast. Anne breathed in the aroma of wet grasses as one would a rare perfume. They followed the lake trail steamed by the warm earth, cantered up to a log structure built like a long house, and hitched their dripping horses.

"We made it, Carney!" the girl's heart pumped with pleasure. Birds began singing their heads off like a choir full of kids.

"With thanks to the Old Log Inn—because,..." Charles looked up warily, with echoes of the storm cutting back around, "I think that baby likes us!"

"Hi Doc!" waved a man behind the bar, as they ducked through a doorway in time to dodge the second downpour. "And hi there, Miss Anne! Nice to see you again!"

Before entering the main room, each gave their heads a canine shake. "Do you still come here often, Carney?" Anne asked, breathlessly patting her face and neck with a kerchief she'd pulled from her saddlebag, and waving to Barney Fellows, manager of the Inn since she was old enough to visit a bar. "It's hardly next door for you anymore."

"Once in a while, when I visit your dad. Sometimes we'll ride over together," he answered, gratefully accepting a hand towel from an assistant waiter. "Last time was a month or so ago," he added, against a streak of lightning and a loud rumble.

"How is Mr. David now?" Barney Fellows interrupted, raising his eyes to a too-close crack of thunder. "Had us worried for a while." The turbulence ceased. One could cut the silence.

Charles stilled Anne's alarm with the same steady calm he applied to all situations. "Your father's doctor simply wants him to rest more," he assured her. "He's in pretty good shape for a man of seventy-nine." He cast a warning glance at Fellows and said, "We'll have a couple of those toddies today, Barn. I've touted them to Anne for a whole year!"

When they were alone, the girl placed a firm hand on her companion's wrist. "What did Barney mean, Carnaghan?"

Taking both her hands in his, Charles faced Anne directly. "Your dad had a heart attack shortly after I returned from France." Anne started. Charles pressed her fingers. "The doctors said he would survive it, and he did. He warned me not to call you to come home, and I wasn't about to cause another by defying him. I was with him at King's Meadow, Anne, keeping a sharp eye until the day you returned. He's doing very well, and promised not to overdo if I kept the secret." Charles' remorse appealed to her understanding.

"You did keep the secret, Carney," Anne breathed, struggling with the shock. "It wasn't you who gave it away." She paused for several seconds, then rose to her good manners. "Thank you dear friend, for looking after Dad." It was difficult to absorb the strange news, just as it was to deal with her feelings of foreboding.

Charles kept her hands in his as his thoughts ran on. *I didn't give it away, but I was leading up to it, Anne, because I was going to tell you, despite the promise. His heart is not strong. You need to know. The prognosis isn't great; your dad's health is failing, and doctors feel that he isn't a candidate for surgery.* But Charles' lips, for the time being, remained sealed. She had to adjust to one piece of news at a time.

———

Hap was resting on the porch swing when a rambling thought intruded on his nap. *Over, she says. But the whole thing might just be sleeping. I only hope she gets that guy out of her system.* Once again he laid his head back, complaining to the skies. *Haven't got it in me anymore to make things right.*

When she arrived home, Anne regarded her dad asleep with a book on his lap. Her smile faded. He looked suddenly... old. "Just you watch," he had recently boasted, "I'm going to live to be a hundred!" It was hard to imagine Hap old or infirm. He had to go on forever with the same jocular manner and the same good sense that she was used to. If he should leave, there would be no one to banter with, bounce ideas against, get strength from... there would be no one for her to care about... or to care about her. She left him sleeping and, with a heavy heart, mounted the stairs to shower.

A few days later, Hap set out for his usual after dinner stroll to check on the animals. A dry cough had wracked his chest on and off all day. Otherwise he insisted that he felt fine. After an hour or so, Anne began to worry and Blue started to pace, scratching at the door and whimpering. She tossed a jacket over her shoulders and the two ventured out to meet him.

The night air was chilly. "Jessie, where are you?" Hap called. "I hear your voice, but I can't see you because the mist is rising and the path is going the wrong way. I can't reach you yet, but I'm workin' on it, baby." Hap's muscles strained with his errand. His breathing turned to dry heaves. He bent to pick a bluebell poking through the fence, and looked about to match it to his wife's eyes. "Here Jessie, I'm bringing a blossom for you," he coughed. Then another thought hit: "But before I leave, I gotta get one for Annie."

... Annie found Hap beside the paddock with a pair of bluebells crushed in his fist. She put her face to his lips. He was not breathing. She felt for a heartbeat, then for a pulse. "Daddy, no!" she cried, her words stricken by grief and eyes burning with hot tears. Spokes of anguish stabbed at her heart. He'd almost made it to the house. But he hadn't made it to a hundred.

———

Winter arrived in October. For Anne, who always felt sheltered by snow, it provided a needed refuge. Hap wouldn't expect his daughter to cave in, but she had to mourn, and preferred to do so at King's Meadow. "I'm not giving in," she explained, watching flames dance in the fireplace. "I'm just holing up for a while, Daddy." And this time it seemed to be Carney she was leaning on. When he'd offered to occupy his old room for a time so she wouldn't be alone, Anne hadn't refused, though it meant miles of commuting to his kennels through icy back roads each day.

Anne felt her stomach lurch for the fifth time in as many days. She lay on her bed and counted with her fingers. She was late, but she'd been late before. Was this a trick, or what? How long had it been—How many weeks, and days—and nights? Fright consumed her as Alex' words resounded, "Even yewer mistakes are delightful." *The time is not right... like the order of my life!* She made an appointment with her doctor, wishing that she didn't already know the answer.

The next day found Anne beside her mother's grave. "There are choices, Mom... I need you to help me with them." A soft wind rustled the red maple planted by Hap behind Jessie David's grave. Anne waited for a sign, but none came.

Slowly, she started Hap's station-wagon, switched on the radio and drove from the cemetery. "If Ever I Should Leave You" came over the airwaves. Anne's flesh prickled. Her mother's answer was here, in the music. "If ever I should leave you, it wouldn't be in summer, or springtime"—when the baby would be born—"or fall." It would be never. Jessie David would never abandon her child. Nor would she, though she had abandoned its father.

She must find an apartment in the city, not far from the concert hall. She had to sever her dependencies. She was going to have to learn to rebuild her life... to walk before she could run. Everything still hurt too much and she wondered how to reach some vital inner resources to help her to forget about the past, and face what lay ahead.

———

A full moon coated the meadow. Anne left her bed, opened the front door and walked out into the silvery light in her night clothes. Her friends, the stars, were faithfully in attendance. A tiny animal scurried at her feet. "Where are you now, Alex?" she asked aloud. "Are the same moon and stars shining for you? Are we looking at the same heavens, haunted by the same memories?

"The stars know that I'm going to have your baby, but they can keep it a secret." She got into the old jalopy and eased it quietly out of the driveway... to somewhere, anywhere. Something inside her was broken. She could see no future. She mustn't leave her child. But she could take her child with her....

Struggling with an overwhelming feeling of discouragement, Anne stood beside the bridge. At three in the morning, no one was around. It was a long way down, through the trees where she would surely meet him. But he wasn't smiling this time. He wasn't even there where he promised to be. *But then, he did break promises, right?* She lifted herself toward the top of the railing, and felt a hand clamp her upper arm like a vise.

"Tell me," a voice asked gently and carefully, "What's down there that's better than what's up here?"

The voice was jolting. Anne's numbness disappeared. "Carney! Why are you here? Where is this?"

Charles threw a car blanket around Anne's shoulders. "Blue woke me. He heard you leave the house."

Anne buried her face in his chest so he couldn't see her tears. He caught her when she fell, and kissed them away. "I can't see you very well, Carney," she whimpered, in what for her was the deepest of darkness.

Charles Winston Carnaghan and Anne Quincy David were married by a Justice of the Peace at King's Meadow, on October 31st, 1972, in the garden bordered by crimson maple trees. It was a frosty Halloween evening, illuminated by three dozen tiny pumpkins casting their blessings upon two people who felt at home with their arms about each other. The few who attended were close friends and neighbors used to a nip in the air, all good-naturedly bundled up around a roaring camp fire, toasting everlasting love for the happy pair, not conscious of how difficult their wishes might be to fulfill.

Doctor and Mrs. "Charles" lived at King's Meadow with the faithful Pan and several hired hands to tend to the animals.

A few years later, during a return engagement in Mallorca, Alex learned the truth about Anne's defection from an unlikely source. A woman entered his dressing-room, by appointment, after the second performance. Alex scrutinized her cupid face, permed hair and short round body, having seen her before, but unable to place her. "Yew have captured my curiosity," he said, offering her a chair. Boldly, he looked her up and down. "You say you have some mystery to impart?"

Calista giggled nervously with the conductor's description of her mission. "It won't be a mystery for long, Conductor Raynor," she assured him in a little girl voice. "What I have to say won't take a minute."

Alex lit a cigarette and peered at her coldly through wisps of smoke. "Let's have it sen," he stated warily.

It took more than a minute. When she was finished, Alex shook his head in disbelief. "You were hidden behind se embankment and saw her leave?"

The girl nodded, twisting her scarf in her hands.

"Are you sure she overheard Malenkoff?" grilled Alex.

"Oh yes sir! I wondered why he was looking at the plants, but talking to me. He pretended it was all a secret, you see, but he was shouting. After he said all those terrible things, I saw Miss David leave the table next to us. She would have had to be deaf not to hear him go on and on! I recognized her as the person Sergei was talking about— the girl who played the piano."

And Anne accepted his words as truth.

"Why are you telling me after all sis time?" questioned Alex, seeking a motive. His eyes bore into hers, and she momentarily turned away, but then turned back. She would finish what she had come to do.

"I knew he had done an evil thing. I didn't know the reason, but that didn't matter. I had to get my mind right, by thinking it out. It took time; I was struggling with what I didn't want to do and what I knew I should do. By that time you'd already left Mallorca." The woman paused in her narration. "I don't think he likes you." She shifted in her chair and patted her skirt in place. Alex judged from her manner that her mission was as she claimed.

"Sergei can be mean-spirited, Mister Raynor. For three years now, that day has bothered me. During this trip, when he gloated about Miss

David leaving before you were supposed to go to Madrid together, I right away knew that I had to set things right for my own conscience." Calista Malenkoff did not tell of the marriage which her father made sure was not annulled when she found herself pregnant. These days she remained in Mallorca with twin sons—a situation that suited them both.

"Thank you, Miss Calista," groaned Alex. "It was brave of you to come."

"I should have found a way to tell you before this, but it was your personal business and I didn't know if you'd believe me, or if you'd think I was nosy and had a nerve. A note maybe? A phone call? But I didn't do either. You didn't know me, you see. I didn't know how …"

"Not your fault, my dear. Not your fault," said Alex, with a heart full of lead.

———

Carney was a good man and a sensitive husband. Anne was appreciated and adored. "There's something sublime about the aroma of a chicken roasting in the oven," he said, kissing Anne's forehead on the occasion of their first home-cooked dinner.

Anne loved him; she always had. True, there wasn't the same chemistry, but when she caught herself looking to her husband for the traits she had loved in Alex, she was reminded more than once that she and Charles were exceptionally good friends, close partners, and planned to be fine parents. Certainly enough.

During his wife's pregnancy, Charles was undemanding and patient. With the passage of time she found great comfort in her husband's arms.

Anne's son was born in May, 1973, on a beautiful spring evening, exactly one year to the day that she and Alex had discovered their love for each other. "Even yewer mistakes are delightful," was now, to her, an amazing prophecy. She observed her son with loving eyes and heart. "Not a mistake, Alex. God's work," she assured him, with her habit of conferring. "He is beautiful! How would you not love him?" Anne named the child Nicholas, culturally Russian, so that, if father and son ever did connect, the meaning would be there.

Charles marveled at the infant's size and delicacy. He was careful to treat him as some kind of breakable. "He's a good deal more sturdy than he appears!" chuckled Anne. "You're a doctor! You deliver dozens of babies yearly! Human babies are just as tough... you'll see. In three months you'll want to toss him around like a football!"

Charles looked doubtful. "Such a little thing."

Three months proved right. The infant more than doubled his weight and Charles was tossing him high into the air and catching him in his arms, which resulted in squeals and chortles that could rival those in any animal hospital.

At age two, Nicholas expressed curiosity about the piano. Beside himself with glee, he played Chopsticks at three. But it wasn't just the keyboard that captured his interest. When he turned five, his rhythm proved remarkable on a set of traps given to him by his beloved stepdad, who joked, "Always wanted to have a go at those things, but I've got no talent for it!"

What Charles did have was a heart so big and a love so great that harmony in his home was ever present. He was a giant of a man, not in stature, but in generosity, scope, and dedication to what was important for his family, his patients, the world, and himself—in that order. Charles accomplished by thirty-five what might take a lifetime for others: A solid sense of priorities, that worked.

Doctor Charles Winston Carnaghan would reach great heights and become world-renowned for his accomplishments. Carney from the circus had always been a healer. Now he tended all animals with the same loving care once reserved for Hap's horses, to the benefit of those filling his teaching hospital, the first in the country to perform heart surgery on animals and birds: reported by the media to be "a giant contribution to veterinary medicine."

But it was family first, and from that Charles never wavered. Nicholas was a cheerful, active child, in large part because his stepfather spent much time with him. They rode together often, shared experiences, trusted each other, and talked... about everything and anything important in a young boy's life. Charles inspired respect, the kind that disciplines easily because it is based on fairness.

Determined to find help for Anne, whose sight had weakened rapidly by the sixth year of their marriage, Charles contacted universities and clinics all over the United States and Canada. With the advent of the computer and its far-reaching access, he located an eye surgeon in Ottawa who offered a glimmer of hope.

"It's not as far-fetched as you might think," declared Brendon Sommerfield M.D., F.A.C.S. "Doctors are considering eye transplantation in animals, and will be experimenting with it one of these days. Success with humans will take longer, of course, but it will come. And one day, mark my words, scientists will discover a way to repair one's own eyes with a simple injection. Right now, this is what we do: Because you are experiencing corneal topographic changes from an underlying cause, the term for it unimportant for you to memorize, we will start by replacing the corneas. You know, the first corneal transplant was done right here in Ottawa, back in 1958. Trust us; we've been at it a long time!" Sommerfield reached for Anne's hand and patted it. "Imagine! New windows for those beautiful peepers!"

"We perform successful corneal transplants using live human tissue." Sommerfield leaned forward with an elbow on his desk as he planned the next statement. "Soon, those windows will be manufactured. Right now, we're limited to what donors can provide. As the public becomes more informed, needs increase, but so does the shortage of donors. So hang in there a little longer. It will happen for you."

While waiting, Anne asked that Blue be trained as her guide dog. She was refused. According to the experts, such animals had to be trained from infancy. But Anne would not accept that, simply because Blue was already so attuned to her requests, and with full instinct seemed to be shadowing her every move. She hired a trainer, and together they honed all of the animal's senses for the protection of his mistress.

Anne had her music school in a winterized carriage house not far from the main house. Here, she devoted countless hours to blind toddlers, children and teens, and was known to give a concert for a single child. Through music, she dedicated herself to improving the well-being of children with various handicaps.

Anne could no longer read music. She couldn't make out the notes. But she was still fascinating audiences in Toronto, and recording her music for listeners worldwide.

"Not many European orchestras visit our city, and very few conductors receive as much attention at our Canadian box office as Alexandre Raynor, conductor of the Moscow Philharmonic, seems to be attracting. As testament to how he hones his players round the clock into perfection, Maestro Raynor promises to lead them once more into triumph through scores that thrill with unusual momentum and amazing attention to detail. Toronto will be privileged with a new symphony, name withheld until opening night ..."

Charles snapped a finger on the Globe and Mail so that Anne would expect his next words to address what he was reading. "Alexandre Raynor will be bringing the Moscow Philharmonic to Massey Hall in three weeks. Would you like to attend?"

A stab in the heart followed his wife's simple "Yes," from across the breakfast table. She had obviously known of the impending concert, but had kept it to herself. "But not on opening night," she added. Had she heard about his appearance via the media or had she been following the man's career? Rather than second-guess, Charles was going to see the matter through. It was time.

The next few weeks were fraught with mind-changing anguish invading Anne's mind almost to distraction. The rift with Alex had long ago faded, ousted by the obvious power he'd cemented in her soul. *It's dangerous to go. Or is it? Why is it? I am blind!* Why would she want him to see her now? *What's past is past.* She was happy with Charles. She had a secure and peaceful life.

In the seven years since they'd parted, Conductor Raynor had taken the Moscow Philharmonic around the world... to Rome, Prague, Paris, South America, Mallorca, and many times back to London. In Toronto for the first time, the orchestra would be playing selections by Sibelius, Rimsky Korsakoff, and Beethoven, as well as some new composition making its entrance.

By the second night, the entire engagement was sold out. Maestro Raynor crossed the stage punctually at eight. Anne made out the shadow of his figure, and fell once again into the pattern of analyzing his weary posture. *They are buying his name, his reputation, his dynamics, his passions, as well as his music. But the man is a man, who works himself to exhaustion. All that glamour costs him dearly.*

Anne couldn't tell if he still wore a white dinner jacket.

She wore slate gray, pure silk, fitted and fashioned by her dressmaker… with ash diamond earrings, a gift from Charles, to match her veiled eyes. Her thick braid was wound at the nape of her neck. She looked very chic. "They will stop music just for you, Missus!" Pan had exclaimed without his usual reserve.

"That wouldn't be very good!" she'd laughed, with a lump in her throat.

Pan placed a cane in her hand, a black and gold one chosen by Charles for formal occasions. Blue sniffed at her feet, hoping for an outing. "Not tonight, boy," she responded, with the caress in her voice saved for this buddy. "There's always tomorrow."

How did Alex look ? With vision so scarred, it was like peering through layers of webbing. *Was he grayer, had he aged?* She couldn't ask Charles. But he knew: "Raynor doesn't seem to have aged with the years, except for his white mop of hair. Seems to me it was more salt and pepper back there in London. In the energy department, it's just as you hear it: he's waving that baton like a trainer of tigers."

Baton? Oh my dear Alex. She looked the other way to hide the welling in her eyes. *Such a crazy mist of a man!*

The sounds that poured forth from the stage might have been arranged by angels. That they were unprecedented was not surprising. However, Anne could not have come close to predicting the finale, staggering with motion, desire, love… and anger. Raynor's announcement of "The One Horse," credited to its composer, "Anne Quincy Daywid."

"No." To Charles' chagrin, Anne didn't care to go backstage, proof to him that she was still wrestling with feelings—for the man, the music, or both. She just wanted to go home, to King's Meadow, she said… *to sort out my heart in my sheltered place,* which she didn't say.

"We need a piano tuner," Charles announced the next day. "When will ours be back from that sabbatical he's taken?"

"Not for another week," said Anne.

"I'll locate one to come tomorrow when you hold no classes, Anne. Would you stay in the main house please, just in case he can't find you in the school?" Charles had a busy agenda and it was Pan's day off.

His English was much improved, but she immediately recognized the voice of the piano tuner. How could Charles have expected to fool her? *I'm blind, not deaf!* She had always thought of her husband as omniscient: surely he knew that she would rebel against this type of manipulation. Or perhaps that's what he wanted.

Nicholas! Her face paled as a current of panic tore through her. The boy would be home any minute. Alex was going to meet his son! And her son was going to face this stranger. Did Alex know of him? How was she to handle this? Anne tried to swallow the knot in her throat, but it wouldn't go away. She began to tremble, but reminded herself of her husband's gentle wisdom. Sensitive to a wife who seemed unable to forget her former lover, though she never spoke of him, he'd made this decision. He was forcing her to face the present, with the possibility of losing her altogether.

The discipline she'd had to live with since losing her sight served her now. Anne remained calm. "Welcome, Alex. Please come in. I was just going to have a martini… would you like one?"

"Anne. I could never win a mystery game, could I?" he responded.

"Most certainly not," she agreed with a half smile. "This mystery wouldn't be your idea; I know it had to be my husband's." *Seven years. So much time… In view of how we parted, how will we interact?*

Alex moved to help her fix the drinks, but Anne stopped him with a hand up. "I'm well able … but thank you." *He knows about my loss of vision. Charles would not have invited the poor man without a briefing.* She reached up, removed a glass pitcher from a shelf, swirled in it some vodka and vermouth, then bent to a bar fridge for ice and lemons. Alex wondered at her skill with things she couldn't see, then remembered her fingers on the piano, triumphant with practice and retention.

Automatically, he lifted his glass to her, then felt foolish doing so. Both spoke at once: "Here's to yew, dear Anne," he began formally.

"Here's to continuing success, Maestro."

Remembering how often they'd cut in on each other with similar thoughts, their laughter loosened the tension. Both silently speculated that had they remained together, the strange phenomenon would likely have continued.

"If yew have ever given thought to... I want you to no longer wonder ..." Alex began, voicing the first thought that came to mind. "I know what happened, Anne." She remained still while he explained, "If what Sergei said seemed true, yew were justified in walking out of my life. However, Sergei Malenkoff is a bitter person continually looking for grudges. And sat one found me." Alex coughed and laughed at the same time.

"How much of a liar is he?"

"Pardon, Anne?" Was she about to sound him out after what he'd explained?

"Were you still married, Alex?"

"Hell no!" Anne could imagine his black eyes blazing. "I told yew—"

Anne rose from her chair and walked toward him to offer him her hand, which he took. "In all that, I discovered a thing about me that I didn't like. So sure that I was stepping liberally into the era of bra-burning and sexual freedom, I wouldn't have questioned you about other women. Your life, before we met, was none of my business, so it didn't occur to me to question... to my way of thinking that was an attitude compatible with trust. However, Sergei's report stung. Was I experiencing jealousy, possessiveness, a wish to control? Or thoughts of being used? I hate them all. Not what I wanted for us, Alex. I didn't wish you to be tied to me, as I didn't wish to be tied."

Raynor offered no response. "Oh Alex, I was losing my sight! Though Sergei's malevolence did send me through all the paces of shock, anger, and flight, my imminent loss of vision made the decision for me. Until that day, I had been living in denial, telling myself that the doctors were wrong, that it wasn't really happening. That I really was fine.

"The unsavory experience with Malenkoff jolted me into facing life as it would be for us, into facing the realization that, under such circumstances, there could be no bright future together, don't you see? Please accept the fact that I was the one who pulled up lame.... uh, a saying which means—"

"I know what it means." Raynor sensed her wish to wipe away whatever guilt he might be harboring, and for that he longed to take her into his arms. "What yew or I did before we met is of no consequence, yew are right. But I want yew to know sat yew are the only woman I have ever loved. Whatever problems may have come our way, I have se feeling sat we would have dealt with them. I shall always love yew, Annyee."

There was no need for Anne to see Raynor's sincerity; she heard it in his voice, along with his emotion. "Come with me," she said, leading him to a nearby building filled with dozens of instruments, including two grand pianos. With pride lighting her face she announced, "I have my music school, Alex... just as I said I would. Remember?"

Alex watched her move. Though her stride now coped with an impairment, the same slim body carried the same eager grace. This was a woman with unfading beauty, now courted by something that eluded him: Distance. Her world apart from his. Naturally What else could he expect? "I am happy sat yew have what yew want. It is marwellous," he said sincerely. "I understand sat things have come together for yewr husband also, sat he has his own hospital."

Had he kept advised about them, or learned this in conference with Charles? No matter. "It took a good few years for him to put the concept into action," she answered. "Nothing came together right away. But yes, it's up and running, as they say. They are working miracles there, Alex."

He found himself adding, "The kind that only happen in se Bible?"

Once again Anne's heart leapt and frayed. But she knew, given the choice, she would not have married this man. He was far too intense for a girl with her free spirit. Their short time together had been essential to their lives, and to the birth of their son, no longer an unexplainable happening.

"Thank you for finishing 'The One Horse,' Alex. It resounds with your understanding of my joy in him, and my distress in losing him. It thrills with all that I imparted... entirely absorbed by you, and so successfully translated.

"He canters, gallops, races, and whinnies as though you, Alex, are in command of him! The finished work is, to me, a rhapsody. I heard the trumpeting of his breath, the thundering of his hooves, while I relived the excitement of outrunning the wind in those amazing highs and lows figured into each bar. In the course of it, he and I—and you—share an experience that will always live." Her eyelids lowered, her lashes moist. "You, Alex, are the true composer and should be credited as such."

"Sis time you do not speak in past tense, Annyee. That music, it is yours… ours, if you like," Alex stated with difficulty, as a door slammed and shoes were being kicked off.

Nicholas bounded into the schoolroom, his face flushed from running. "Nicholas," Anne began, trying to hide the tremor in her voice, "come and say hello to our friend."

The discipline that Alex was so good at made her grateful now. "Hello, son," he said quietly. But the wonder in his voice did not go undetected by Anne. Thankful that she had reared Nicholas with knowledge of his father, though without expectation of meeting him so soon, she reasoned that the word "son" wouldn't startle him. Everyone used it, even Pan. She knew that Alex would tread cautiously. He had a wonderful sense of timing. He was maestro, after all.

As Nicholas looked at Alex, Blue burst through the open door of the schoolroom like a thunderbolt and plunked his affections on his young friend without a by-your-leave. Anne smiled inwardly. There had been no children for her and Charles. With diminishing sight, Anne was afraid of her ability to parent more than one, especially if it were a girl who would need a mother in increasing ways. Though Nicholas was an only child, he was not lonely. The schoolroom at King's Meadow provided constant opportunity for one as sociable as he to be with other children. And there was Blue, his best friend.

Blue placed his large paws on the boy's shoulders. Groomed with dual purpose, the dog knew that this form of endearment was confined to his young master, and he took full advantage of it. In a stream of grunts, squeals, and tail-twitching, the animal conveyed his adoration while reveling in his daily reward, the child's roughhousing attention.

Nicholas looked like Hap. He was strong and reedy. His skin tanned readily in the sun. His curls were dark brown, streaked in summer with shades of cornsilk. His eyes were jet… with diamonds in their centers.

He sat a horse with authority and was allowed daily time on the track. For his sixth birthday, Charles had presented him with his own mount, a yearling the color of gold. The boy named him Popcorn.

Nicholas regarded the man whose curiosity rivaled his own. He looked to his mother who stood close by with her hands tightly clasped.

"I brought you somesing. Here." Shyly, Alex thrust a giant package into the boy's arms. With an affirmative nod from Anne, the boy tore off the wrappings to discover a curiously shaped... what? He lifted his eyes to his mother and at the raising of her brow, began with the best of his manners, "A... an instrument!"

Alex beamed his amusement. "Right yew are, my friend. An instrument called a balalaika. In my country, Russia, wery popular—almost as popular as se guitar in sis country."

"Awesome!" The boy exclaimed. "Look Mom!" he added, not sure how to proceed.

"It's a wonderful instrument, Nicholas. Want to try it?" Anne was pleased with her son's curiosity. They all laughed at his attempts to pluck at strings which sounded very different from those of a guitar.

"Don't stop," said Alex. This was his beat. He liked the way the boy held the instrument... with assurance. He strummed a few chords with him. Nicholas followed. In no time he was coaxing a tune from the strangely shaped box with its double strings. "Sink yew can handle it from here?" the man challenged in a voice full of pride. Anne heard it, and envisioned the diamonds sparkling in the windows of both pair of eyes.

They played, joked, and ate cookies from a tin kept full in the music room. Nicholas sensed a strong measure of approval from his new friend, which made him feel very grown-up and comfortable about sharing with both adults the events of his day. "This girl, she follows me on her bike, asking me about homework. She's always following me around and asking me something," he confided, puffing and crumpling his lips with exasperation. In unison, his parents realized that too quickly a new stage was approaching. Alex had missed so much... for which Anne was sorry... very sorry.

A half hour passed. Anne grasped her son's hand and pressed his fingers lovingly. "Nicholas, I want you to know that this friend, who came to see you especially, is Alexandre Raynor."

The boy stood stock-still. The diamonds in his eyes pierced through two pools of jet, deepening with consternation. "No!" he protested, wildly abandoning his anticipation of such a moment. "My daddy is my father!" He hid his face in his mother's sweater with torment flooding his eyes.

"And he always will be," Anne said, gently coaxing the child out of her embrace. "Do you remember our talk about birth parents? How Carney is your dad, and Alexandre Raynor is your birth father?" *How confusing this must seem!*

The lad regarded Alex with hostility, but raised with a visually impaired mother, he knew that facial expressions didn't count as much as words. Hanging onto Anne's arm, he answered, "Yes… but…."

"Shake hands with your father. He wants to be your friend, Nicholas. Nothing is going to change, except that you will now know your father, and have another true friend in your life." Anne was determined that the child would not be alone with this, or threatened by it. To lighten his anxiety, she added, "He won't be staying, but he will visit with us when he comes to Canada—all three of us—you, me, and Carney, who will always be your dad. Come now darling."

It happened slowly. A reluctant handshake from the boy invited a strong but tender hand on his shoulder, placed by the man who looked like he had just been given the keys to a kingdom, and wished he knew how they worked. As Nicholas gathered together the bit of trust he was able to muster, eye contact with his father was followed by an effort to relinquish his scowl. The man's hand was firm, yet gentle. The boy felt something inside go quiet, and returned the beginnings of a smile.

As though born to be released from there, Raynor's passions had always centered in his hands. Both hands now found their way to the shoulders of the boy with two bright spots on his cheeks, pulling him into an unaccustomed but gentle embrace. Uncertainty struggled in the child's duty-bound response; hence, a contingent acceptance. With the genesis of their life-altering discovery, two pair of dark eyes told the story of a starting point for now. "We'll let Mother know it's okay, yes?" whispered Alex, his face radiant with this new miracle.

Throughout what others would call silence, Anne picked up the essence of those profound moments in the smallest of sounds. It was done. It hadn't been easy, but thanks to Carney, it was done, and in a short time the anguish would fade for the boy. Once more, her husband had chosen the right thing to do.

Nevertheless, he should have consulted her. When they were once more alone, she asked, "Why have you done this, Charles?" using his formal name as she was wont to do when addressing issues of importance. Anne needed to hear his reasons besides determining them herself.

Charles' manner was neither soothing nor apologetic. Anne had to be aware that this was her moment, a time for her own personal assessment of her life. There could be little reaction from him, he said, until she was sure of her feelings. He handed her a martini and summed it all up with one word, "Reality."

"That can be a harsh word," she conceded. "It can update a person."

He topped his drink and studied it. "That's okay. I'm a modern man."

"What you and I feel for each other has nothing to do with Alex Raynor," Anne stated, running a finger along the frosty rim of her glass. "Like one cannot compare it to my love for Nicholas... or what I felt for my parents. What Alex and I shared was an interlude. We took a detour together, that's all." Anne's eyes clouded with the simplification.

"Maybe it was love. For our son's sake, I must convince him of that. Maybe it was something next to love: you and I would do well to agree about that. What we did give each other is all in the past. I can't be sorry, Charles. I would not change it. Nicholas is the result of it. It was you who convinced me of that before he was born, for which I thank you from my very soul. Now we must put it all where it belongs."

Charles put down his glass and placed an arm around his wife's shoulder. "There's nothing we can't work out, you and I.... I can be by your side, Anne, you know that. But we also have to reach for our rainbow together, because the only time that's real is now. You seem to spend much of it very far away."

Anne recalled this same hand brushing back spikes of coppery hair spinning around hazel eyes, and tightening Warrior's reigns to control the speed of the run. She remembered a broad smile flashing at the return of a storm, and a new sun born from the clouds. Most memorable were the arms that sustained her when she was lost in confusion. Perennial images firmly rooted, despite the fogginess of her world.

She placed an affectionate hand over his.

———————

One week later, Pan opened the door to a burly man claiming to be a friend of "se lady who plays se piano." On checking with Anne, Pan ushered the stranger into the music room where she was indeed about to play the piano. "Thank you, Pan. You can leave us now. It's alright."

She made out his heavy silhouette standing in front of the window, turning the brim of his hat round and round with nervous fingers. "What do you want?" she archly demanded.

With a whine imitating concern, the visitor announced, "I hef come to tell yew sat Maestro is sudden wery ill. Sere is word of operation in Toronto hospital. All I know." He turned to leave.

Anne felt an anxious stab. But she couldn't be sure of the veracity of the man's statement. "In concert, just days ago, he seemed perfectly alright to me," she shrugged, disallowing him the pleasure of her alarm.

"He is sick wis his heart. I am sent to yew by orchestra peoples. Sey remember yew and Raynor being, uh… friends." *Namely Calista, who is promising to tell everybody what I done if I don't come here.* "Sey sink yew would want to go see him, yew know?" *Okay pest wife, don't phone me no more… I'm done what you said, now lemee alone.*

With Malenkoff's grim announcement, Anne's heart plunged. But her face remained expressionless. "Where is he?" she commanded stiffly, striving to conceal the abhorrence she felt for the man and the terror screaming within. *Nothing is over. Once it happens, it can never be over.*

———————

She held the glass to his lips so he could sip the water. "Ah, Annyee, how do you manage sat?" Alex marveled, as though she had fed him an elixir.

"With my fingers," Anne responded lightly, placing a hand on his arm. "Remember these?"

He remembered them "tripling themselves on the keys." His white head lay slanted on the pillow, to look fully at her, his jet eyes tender with submission. He caressed each finger. "I love them.... I love you." His breathing was troubled.

Anne clutched his hand with hers. "I will always love you, Alex. And I will always love *your* amazing fingers... though I'm told that some silly woman gave you a baton."

"Not silly. Foolish, in underestimating my love for her. It hurts me to concur sat se words of a mental midget could destroy such happiness."

"Then we must not give him another victory," Anne stated softly, daring her patient to let a blind girl come into his arms.

Alex pinched the ring finger of the hand in his. The ring was still there with its two dangling batons. "Your fingers will play again. Fed from se eyes, you will see."

"Now you are a dreamer!" she laughed.

With her head on his chest, Anne was able to say what was uppermost in her mind. "I am grateful that you welcomed the opportunity to meet our son, Alex, and that you forgive me for not informing you of his birth. I was never sure how your coming together would affect him... remember how you felt about children? So I did the unacceptable: nothing. But I knew the day would come. He needs to know you. Because he likes you, he has something extremely precious. Love. From a most important source."

Alex held Anne tightly to him and whispered, "One day we must meet again... at another time... in another place... another world. In sis one, if I'm granted more life, part of you will be by my side always." Anne kissed him on the forehead, on both sides of his face, on his mouth. The diamonds, inherited by her son, shone wearily in the windows of his father's sunken eyes.

"My turn to say please don't speak in past tense, Alex. I am the very proud mother of the child we made together... your most beautiful gift of all, in a bevy of them. Gifts that are forever. God grant that you will get to know your son in the years ahead...."

"It is said sat all gifts must come in srees," Alex's voice trailed as a nurse administered the last injection of the day, and sleep began to take over. "But I wish to... send... yew... somesing... like a mira..."

For a reason Anne couldn't explain, these words fell from her lips, "Wherever you go, don't forget us."

"Not... a chance," Alex gasped, holding onto her fingers. Drinking in her presence, he whispered, "After... all, I... am sis minute... still mortal."

Anne stayed with him until she had to consider the stablehand waiting to drive her back to King's Meadow. It was past midnight.

She remained awake throughout the night. In the morning she called Intensive Care.

"Are you family, Madam?"

She had no trouble answering, "Yes."

"I am sorry to inform you that Mister Raynor died during the night."

But I just saw him. He held my hand only a few hours ago. He was very tired... but to me he seemed... so alive!

As the minute hand of the clock crept around its face, Anne sat steeped in shock, with her palm still resting on the phone. No. Alex Raynor would never die.

Hap... Alex... Charles. Amazing men. Her men. Real men. One had given her life, another bliss. And her husband, endless devotion.

Anne needed to ride, but hadn't soloed for a while. Consumed with the tears she must shed, she wouldn't want Charles along. With emotions full to bursting, Anne gestured to Blue and saddled Chopin. The three went off at a slow trot, stamping their path through the early morning haze.

Chopin knew his way, and Blue was well-trained to run alongside. Choking with sorrow, Anne searched through her gauzy vision to find the exact spot where she had always spoken to Alex. *"After I left you in Mallorca, do you know how many times I saw your face in every man I passed, how my heart jumped with the possibility of you everywhere I went... for years, until I couldn't see anymore? Which told me that I would never get you out of my heart. But I had to get you out of my life. I thought I'd managed that… until you reappeared.*

"In the pace and splendor of your world, would there have been the room that Nicholas would have needed? I took it upon myself to answer that, to justify not telling you about him… which I had no right to do. Alex, I promise to take care of the son you loved from the moment you two first met—the child, I am convinced, you would have loved more and more with time. I will keep your image alive for him." Sadness beyond endurance found release in tears as Anne's heart ripped inside out. She cried for more than an hour, unable to stop. When there seemed to be no more tears to shed, she raised her eyes to the trees. *"Rest in peace, my love… and don't forget us."*

The zephyr that ruffled the leaves was set to music, in overture to "The One Horse" capturing her mind. And she heard, "Not… a… chance, Annyee. Not a chance."

The trio circled a patch of light that followed them back to the paddock.

———

Anne was brushing her hair when Charles entered their bedroom. He had been at the hospital all night. "Is the spaniel alright?" she inquired, her voice weary.

"He didn't make it. His little heart couldn't take it," Charles answered heavily.

"Sorry." After a long pause, Anne said, "Alex didn't make it either. His heart …"

The need to explain was curtailed by Carney's hand over hers. Pan had informed him. Eventually he said, "The hospital in Ottawa called my office. You are to be flown in immediately and prepped for a transplant. There's been a donor."

Charles knew that the excitement this news would have brought earlier, would be minimal right now. Anne broke through the quiet. "All this time, you've been standing by, and I wasn't listening;" she said from a valley of thought. "I wasn't listening to us, wasn't seeing us. You are my strength and I've squandered so much of it over the past… my past. Though it is so much a part of who I am, I had no right to use up your dedication, your life, and you, my dearest friend, with all of that.

"Though everyone has a past, which I'm sure you do, Charles, you handle yours better than I did mine, and for that you have my respect. From the time I was very little, you have always had my love.... Right now, my heart is breaking... but if I can say I love you at a moment like this, I know that I do."

Charles' eyes leveled into hers. His voice was hushed. "Maybe it's a new life for us, Anne. I'm not an expert about a lot of things, but I'm open to learning.... Though we might not be intensely aware of it, in our years together we're managing to write some music of our own."

———

Anne asked that the bandages be removed at King's Meadow, where she felt the presence of Hap and Jessie. She wanted to be surrounded by her family, her home, her animals.

Nicholas placed a single rose in his mother's hand. As the bandages were lifted a layer at a time, she held tightly to it. At first there was nothing. Then nothingness broke into gossamer strips, their slivers melting in the light.

A mirror was placed before her. All at once Anne recognized the diamonds in her eyes.

Deedu

I COULD HEAR HIS voice though I couldn't see his lips moving yet. My heart skipped. "That's Deedu! He's looking for me!" Deedu was coming up the sidewalk with my parents. His smile gave me springs. "P-r-r-a-a-ncie!" he laughed. I broke away from my nanny and leapt into the strong arms that opened wide to catch me.

My name is Francie, but I liked better the way Deedu said it. With a rush of joy I exclaimed, "I'm high up!" I looked to my mommy who always smiled that it was okay. Daddy gave in. He couldn't scoop me up from a running jump like Deedu could, and I was too young to know what that cost him. I only knew that my daddy was always partway: partway glad and partway sad. He worked very hard and kept saying that there was "no rest for the wicket." By doing things to make him laugh, I sometimes kept him from his gloomies.

"Wot is sis?" Deedu bellowed. "A kiddy-cat? I newer see a kiddy-cat like sis!!" His sound was like the gravel under the garden gate with some brown sugar mixed in, husky and sweet to my toddler's ears, though a little more quiet today I could tell. Sheer giggles rumbled up from my middle, uncontrolled. Deedu was big and kind. He had crinkles that were always jumping at the corners of his eyes. I loved him fiercely.

"Hold on, wis all yewer might! Look everybuddy," he said in a loud whisper, "look wot's heppening now!" Besides Mommy and Daddy, there was nobody near, except the bunch of people downaways in front of my Zaida's house, who surely couldn't hear us. But Deedu and I were always pretending. Happy as a magpie, I shinnied all the way up on his shoulders to the noblest place in the world, then promptly shinnied back down.

"Wot yew come down for?"

"Sh-a-a-st!" I cautioned in Russian, imitating his loud whisper. Now and again I would parrot some of the old man's language, especially for what I thought were important moments."Wait a minute!" I ran for my paper telescope, a treasure from my Uncle Abie who imported junk from Japan. When I returned, they had joined the small group of aunties and uncles coming back from my grandmother Charna's funeral. They looked very frowning. Somebody laughed as I hitched up the straps on my overalls for another flight, revved up my legs like a pair of pistons and beat it back up into the arms that lifted me. Not yet ready to settle, I proceeded upward like a frog, with a hop to one shoulder, a zip to the other, to take up my position around Deedu's neck, with my chin resting on the crown of his battered hat and the paper spy glass fixed to one eye.

My Gramma Charna had just "passed away." And my daddy was pretty sad about that. I'd never seen anybody who'd "passed away" before. Daddy said it meant that the next time he'd see his mommy would be in heaven. That was pretty awful, and I hurt in my stomach to see my daddy looking so sorry. I would check on it; I would take a good look through my spyglass to see if I could spot her maybe "passing" this way. Then I could call her back and everyone would shake hands all around and be happy again! I spotted an elderly figure down the block. I leaned my elbows on Deedu's hat and exclaimed in a big voice, "I think I see my Gramma Charna passin' away down there!"

That earned me several odd stares. But once I'd begun, I had to go on. Pondering only for a moment, I looked my daddy full in his face and canted, "If Gramma passes away, and you let her get passed, she isn't yours anymore, Daddy! If I'm finding her, finders keepers! So if I want to give her back to you, I can!" This is where a sixth sense told me to wind down like a broken gramophone. "Or... I guess I'll have to be your mommy."

Daddy turned aside. He took out his hankie. I must have said something dizzigusting to make him sadder. I was just then learning about manners, and a new word, "in-dell-ee-cat." Maybe I'd forgotten the manners somewheres. I eyed everybody with wide-eyed uncertainty, not sure where to go from there.

As a child, I felt that my mission was to make everybody laugh. But they weren't giving out any laughtering that day. Even my Zaida—his eyes were laughing, and his chin wiggled like it wanted to, but he wasn't doing it. Instead, he invited everybody into the house for lunch, so they just went.

I shook the dark curls that were almost to my waist, and continued to focus my slanty brown eyes importantly on the next subject that might bail me out of the mess that was certainly my doing, though I wasn't sure what it was. I was embarrassed, but I wasn't a blusher. And anyway, my not-quite olive complekshun had already turned red gold with the sun. I shifted my skinny arms, chubby legs, and little pot belly. "She will be an athlete," predicted one of the aunties.

"Yeah, a pole-vaulter!" agreed cousin Issy. Deedu patted my back so's no one else could tell how I was feeling. I promptly re-checked my spyglass, pretending further interest in it, but really to hide some tears that came up… at least for one eye. Luckily, the old woman wasn't in there anymore, and the hunt became a memory.

I really do believe that I was in love with that Deedu… truly in love at four years old. I followed him around like Toy did, Bubbah's little collie dog. He was my dear old person. And this is what he looked like. He was a tall, skinny man with very long legs and arms. His face was narrow, and over each ear there was a puff of white hair, like snowballs under his crumpled hat. A bunched nose, creased down the center, bent over a wide mouth where smiles stretched out on either side, to ride all the way up to the corners of his twinkling eyes.

If you put together Gary Cooper, Danny Kaye and Yul Brynner, you would have Deedu. In summer, he was out in the sun so much he looked like a freckled lion whose skin was always peeling off… only with blue eyes and white fluff on each ear! He wore denim overalls with a bib that came right up to his chin and with cuffs that sat way above his polished boots. You couldn't ever hear his boots. Deedu had a kind of floatiness, like he walked inches from the ground.

He had to be very old, I figured—at least thirty. He smelled like spices. He was my Zaida's "lontsman," which means countryman… even though they hadn't ever known each other in Russia. In those years, when immigrants came to Canada, synagogues rescued misfortunates like people rescue kittens and puppies now, by taking them home. He learned to speak a broken Russian-English with a Montreal accent, influenced by our closeness to New York and the broadening of their vowels, my parents said.

When anyone asked where he came from, Deedu would answer "Imsk near Pimsk." We never learned if such places were for real and we never cared, because our childhood love of sounds demanded repetition. To our immense glee, over and over. "Imsk near Pimsk! Imsk near Pimsk!"

He never was annoyed with us; only when frustrated with some really difficult English would he rap with his knuckles or poke with his elbows like my Zaida sometimes did. Maybe it was a Russian thing. But I can tell you, whenever I heard his joyful "P-r-r-a-a-ncie!" I truly felt the pounding of my heart. I chattered, he listened, and sometimes his words joined in softly... always softly at first. There were sunbeams in every note of his laughtering. In his eyes I always detected a shining, and as it spread over his face, his voice grew.

My daddy wasn't thrilled about my running to Deedu, and him scooping me up. I didn't understand why he should be unhappy about my chin resting on a moth-eaten hat. He watched, sometimes sad with the goings-on. But he didn't say no. I figured he realized—the higher I got, the taller I was, the more I could see!

Not only was I fascinated with Deedu, but from the stories he told I was entranced with all things Russian, imagining a land of ice castles, their roofs plopped upside-down like scoops of technicolor ice cream, with their striped cones piercing a cold sky... and skating in its center on a glassy lake, an ice princess decked out in white satin and fur.

———

The head of our family was of course my Zaida. He was not a pious Jew. He was a leader and a doer, he said, making a clear distinkshun. He lived for his family with his own kind of religion: "Pay the mortgage, feed the mouths," (in this case, six daughters!), and, "I give the Bubbah five dollars for a new hat every time she gets a little cross!" He was certain that a man wasn't a man if he was afraid to get his hands dirty. He was a foreman at the CPR roundhouse, where he made a decent living for the times, uninfected by the stock market crash of 1929 because, like most people, he hadn't enough left over to infest. His daughters were his "jewels." Zaida was a most contented man. It showed in his face, which was bright-looking, with sharp blue-gray eyes, a spready nose, and a smile that boasted two rows of his own pearly teeth. He wasn't tall. He was full of little muscles, in such a nice arrangement that he could have been a bald-headed doll. He seemed always in fierce concentration, but forever with a twinkle. Whenever I hear the words "Good Humor Man," I picture my Zaida.

Bubbah never sat. She hovered, making sure that everybody had enough of everything. She hovered with "krimma feese," feet that were weak, sore, and barely supported in ugly long black oxfords. But oh, how her love of all of us gave her the strength to be on them from morning till night, cooking the meals that we would gladly stand in line for!

Bubbah's and Zaida's house was a duplex on a heavily-treed street populated mostly by workers with blue collars, also laborers, many of them first owners with married children living on the same block and, in the order of things, with grandchildren crashing in and out all day. There were small family stores on all corners; their keepers knew everybody at a time when most lived "from hand to mouth" and bought most needs on credit (though not my Zaida. "Never!" he would say.). The whole street was like a big bunch of family.

Unlike most homes on Jeanne Mance, where rows of steep iron stairways on the outside led up to the second stories, Auntie Sophie's upstairs apartment was reached through an inner vestibule that needed a key to enter, then through a French door with glass panels on the right that twinned my Zaida's on the left, then up a stairway. Auntie Sophie lived there with my Uncle Abie, cousin Issy, and cousin Boots, who was very pretty but a little bit shy. At the end of the day, Boots looked as clean and starched as she did in the morning; not a shiny curl had shifted, and she probally didn't sit on the floor much to play with any of the amazing junk her daddy brought from across the big buddy of water called the Pass-if-ik.

Us cousins hung out by the garden gate when the weather was nice. Raffy was the oldest. He was our "pie," always sweet, with a voice so soft he could be a teddy bear. But I never said that. His sister Laya was tough. And I guess she was my first best cousin. To me, she was like a magnet, always with a story about how she managed to smart-out somebody, but in a fun way. Even at four, I knew her tales weren't all true, but that they were as she figgered them. I was attached to her like Elmer's glue.

Rachel was the smartest. Even before she was a grownup, she liked to work... always orkanyzing my Auntie Isobel's house or my Uncle

Yank's dresses business. "Yank was a dreamer," everyone said, and if not for Rachel with her smart managering, "he'd have gone down the tube." (It was hard to imagine a tube with enough space for Uncle Yank!). Jelly-bean, Rachel's sister, was just like her name sounded: a roly-poly funny kid with ears like teacups and wide spaces between her teeth, but always with jokes, lots of fibs and a grin like that devil picture with horns and a big fork.

Boots was Boots. She always had that name. I never knew her real one. Her brother Issy was "all ears," earning their size by picking up all the juicy stuff in the neighborhood. And Esterel, my sister? She was my friend, my protector. She was five years older than me, but with her gentle ways, was sometimes like another mommy, she was so nice. It was easy to make room for me on that gate, I was so little. If not right beside them, I was under an arm or between somebody's knees. I was a squirmer. The adults called me "*pre-petch-oo-wal mo-shun,*" which sounded very important.

The uncles and aunties conjugated in the dining room, the center of my grandparents' house, as they did most every Saturday and Sunday of their lives, when everyone was welcome to best everyone else with their stories and ideas! The only thing formal was the setting, around a big oak table with my Zaida always at its head. Under it, I could hide and listen in—especially to my Uncle Abie, the best teller of tales, who bewitched everybody with his egg-saturaded antikdotes—along with Toy, who would sit bird-like beside me, waiting for scraps, both of us being very much in on what was going on without anyone seeing we were there! What a chattery group! Today I wonder how that cluster of personalities got along so well.

I loved that room and I loved them. Most times there were eleven individuals with eleven laughing faces, eleven separate opinions and as many different ways of shouting them! Auntie Ada, with hair like steel wool, peaches-and-cream skin, and a voice like a foghorn, was the oldest; so after Uncle Abie, she said the next most. Auntie Rita was quieter but very thinking, and would always start with, "Well, you see …" But by the time she could explain what she wanted everybody to see, someone else had already butted in. Auntie Isobel was fashion-plated, always very busy. She spent her time copy-catting very esspensif dresses in time for Uncle Yank's lines each seasoning. Sadie was the youngest and was slow, they said. She just listened, but she was kind, and wore a flower in her hair at five o'clock every day when Uncle Harry came home from the factory where he worked. Auntie Koki had a fine figure and many boyfriends. A year later, she would marry Uncle Yank after Auntie Isobel died, because he wanted to stay in the family, and marrying a sister was a mitts-full, he said, which was supposed to be a good thing. Auntie Sophie had fine ideas about how to spend money fast. With my parents and grandparents, that made eleven.

I loved the ambulance in that house, the lace curtains that hung like vanilla colored ivy over the windows, the fuzzy wallpaper, and jolly Persian carpets that were so soft for sitting. On the other hand, I wasn't too sure about those pictures of the old-folks-left-behind-in-the-old-country, all heavily framed in a collekshun above the mantle, their sternness spooky in the soft light of a chandelier that looked like a wheel of seashells turned upside-down, with a long chain for clicking it on. Pull-chains operated all kinds of ess-en-chuls—fancy things, like the one closeted in a room by itself with the sink and bath next door in a separate room. I enjoyed pulling that chain, listening to the roaring flush in the bowl and marveling at the stormy whirlpool that might take out a little girl if she didn't jump off in time! Can't say that I didn't throw the odd paper doll in there, to watch it swim... or one or two alleys to learn that they didn't.

The house was full of love and life. Children were welcome in every room, even beyond the French doors and into the parlor, sunny and warm with the lemony smell of furniture oil. Thick carpets sat on polished oak the color of honey; rubber plants stood like soldiers beside the big bay window; little doilies protected the arms of chairs and sofa. And in the center of it all, the reason for my venturing: a player piano! The day it arrived, I was beside myself with joy! I quickly discovered the music hidden in its bench, in paper rolls full of holes that played enough to keep me happy for hours. All I needed to do was pump the pedals to fill the whole house with the loudest and finest of music without having to read a note—unlike what my sister had to do when practicing her lessons! (Her nature was patient. But how I hated the little black heads and curly tails that danced their misschif on the rungs of each musical score!)

In that room, I could pedal all day if I liked. I could imagine myself as the world's greatest piano performer bringing an audience to its feet… or maybe I'd be twirling round and round, the most famous ballerina on ice! My poor grandparents never said a word. It was all so unfettered… as long as my little legs could go! Drama was my constant companion, at the mercy of a thriving imagination bouncing ahead of me all day long. My parents must have hoped that my effort and ambition would some day rise to meet it!

———

Deedu lived in the basement. There was an old rocking chair there, an iron cot, orange crates for books, and a row of wooden pegs where he hung his couple of shirts and things. He would come up into the garden from there, through an outside pit, like stairs from somewhere under the earth. He would pretend to be a jack-in-the-box, but he looked like a popping-up scarecrow! We called this place "Deedu's Garden," which of course it was.

Sometimes I would come upon him mounding leaves at the curb, always in small piles instead of one big one.

"Why are you doing that, Deedu?" I asked, the first time I saw him light a match to one of them.

"Coz we hef to do sis careful, we dowanna make it big fire, sat blow away an ketch everysing up."

"Why can't we jus' rake 'em up into one big castle… for us to jump in first… like you do in the back sometimes?"

"Coz sey stuff up sewers on street. See down sere? If wind comes an' leaves slide in, se water can't go down an' we flood it," he answered.

"Why?"

"Coz, when somesings get wet, sey grow bigger."

I thought about that. "I don't," I announced with chagrin.

He looked up with one eye almost shut, like it wanted to wink but got stuck. He said, "Yew keep drinking yewer milk and yew will!"

That's partly why I loved Deedu. He knew everything.

Summer could be pretty warm in Montreal, when we had to open the windows at night to get cool and got up drenched in the mornings. Deedu had the coolest place in the house, so he still put on the same checkered shirt and blue overalls. And of course, the same old hat. Winter or summer.

He didn't eat with the family. Bubbah cooked for him, but he liked to take his meals in his own repartment. He would lay a pillowcase—washed each night and hung by the furnace to dry—on top of the orange crate which sat on its end, so he had place for his pointy knees. He washed his dishes in the laundry tub before bringing them back to the kitchen, which Bubbah washed again when he wasn't around. Not that Deedu wasn't as clean as a whisper; it was just that wash tubs were not kosher.

Sometimes Esterel and I slept over at my Zaida's if Mommy and Daddy needed to go out. Before bed, after my dose of Neo Chemical food to fat up my skin and bones, I'd steal downstairs to see what Deedu was up to. In winter, sitting beside the furnace was the same to me as sitting beside the coziest fireplace. I loved it best when it was blizzardy, watching the walls splotched with dancing flames that peeked through the grate on the furnace door, listening to the fizzing-up of the coals, as the wind whistled and tried to gobble up my Zaida's house.

"You want?" he would ask, shoving a plate at me.

I never had an appetite, not because I didn't like food: I just hated to be still for as long as it took to eat it! But this was different. Snacking beside Deedu's fire was an aventure. I would help myself to a piece of cheese and sit importantly on the guest bench, a shiny stretch of wood held up by giant gray blocks at both ends, and with a pillow on top. My size.

All was very tidy. If I got up early enough in the morning, I would knock at the top of the cellar stairs as I had been taught, so that I could come down and watch Deedu make up his cot tight as an elastic. He bounced a nickel on it once, like they do in the army, to show me; it was so smooth, it bounced very high. One time I came upon him tucking in a sheet, and asked in my squeaky voice, "Can I do it, Deedu?" His laughtering was like a trumpet. He poked me gently in the rib with an elbow, which meant that I tickled him rosy. He let me try. I couldn't pull the sheet all the way straight. Deedu liked it anyway.

Major, my daddy, wanted to make a rule that I could only visit with Deedu outside the house. But I overheard Mommy raisining with him. "God and I keep an eye together… if not me, then Pa. But I trust the old man completely." I wondered for a flying moment what kind of an "I" they kept… a capital, or a small one. My daddy read to me a lot and was teaching me the ABC's, so I was learning how to spell some words. But at four years, I couldn't get to know them fast enough.

Mommy made regular visits to wherever we were, often with glasses of tea. I thought she was checking my behavior, if that was what *caw-shus* meant. She knew Deedu would never lose his temperature with me; he was my protector. And on some days, when their kids were there, one or two of the other mommies and daddies would wander down to listen and sing songs against the giant furnace thrumming with its flames and embers, as noble as any fireside on a winter night.

I was warm, sheltered, and full. I loved my family. But you know, my mommy would never say "I love you" when I said it to her. Instead, she would get a funny shine in her eyes, grab my arm without any telling, and knowing what was coming I would plead, "Mommy, Mommy! Please don't bite me!" After the painless gobble on the soft part of my arm—right or left, she wasn't par-ti-kalar—I felt loved-up, right to the middle of my tummy. Mommy was sooper stishus, you see. The menshun of love might bring an evil eye, but a bite would definitely harken my guardian angel!

In Montreal, children under twelve were not allowed into the daily movies because of a fire some years before that had caused a giant tragedy. We were allowed only when accompanied by a grownup, and even then only into kids' films, like ones with Shirley Temple, and sometimes for that new cartoon mouse called Mickey, who looked like the comic papers and was very funny. When we went to see those, we also saw prefews of what was coming next, films starring Mae West or Greta Garbo or some others. I only had to see something once, and an idea would come into my head!

Mommy owned a lending library on Sherbrooke Street. Sometimes my nanny Ida and I would visit, but I couldn't read the books—they were too growed-up. On Saturdays, though, I got to perform my imitayshuns which got a nickel an act from the book dizcussion group around the table, big and round as a moon, that was my stage. I would begin with Mae West—"C'm up n' see me sometime," drawled with a wink or two, got great preesheeayshun. As Shirley Temple, I sang and tapped "The Good Ship Lollipop." My best was Greta Garbo, stricken with the vay-pers and mewing like a kitten, "I vant to pee alone." They laughed pretty hard at that, so to make them laugh more, I did one of Charlie Chaplin, waddling flatfooted with walking stick and derby hat, and a paper mustash hanging from my nostrils. My audience, made up of Mommy's clients, wailed that their socks wouldn't ever dry! Why was that? I wondered. There was nothing wet that I could see.

I would always test out my acts on Deedu and could depend on his clapping to be the loudest of all. He would rap his knuckles, slap his sides and bellow, "Oh-ho, P-r-r-a-a-ncie!" When it was my turn to listen to Deedu practicing his harmonica, "*Per-fek*!" I would say to the Russian immigrant who played "Oh, Canada" so passionately!

One day, Deedu's nose looked bunched up, crookeder and redder, pushing his eyes closer together as he smiled, "P-r-r-a-ncie! "Panimayish... pay attenshun."

He was making a spotlight by taking the shade off an old lamp. And with his fingers he was forming shadow figures on a basement wall that would have fooled a pack of puppies. One had a long snout and pointed ears. Another showed a pug nose which Raffy named "Duke the Boxer." A bunny shadow wiggled its ears. The one with a slanty forehead, a berry at the end of its nose, big teethful mouth and long tongue was called "Rolf the Wolf." Deedu said that was a name he "plocked out of a hat." Couldn't have been his hat; I looked. There were no names in there. When us kids wanted him to repeat any of those animal shadows, we asked for them by the names we gave them, many after the carr-ok-ters found in books.

"Where did they go?" I demanded the first time they disappeared off the wall.

"Say are chust sink-ups."

Astonished and distressed, I persisted, "But what happened to the think-ups, Deedu?"

Deedu pretended to poke a finger into my tummy. "Sey wasn't effer sair!"

"Why?"

"Coz som sings are chust sink-ups." To satisfy my curiosity, he quickly proceeded to weave a story around one of them. Even with his very broken English, we kids could fully understand every word. Years later, I realized his stories were all likely true because most had no endings, you see; probably about people he must have known and had to leave behind.

Some days Deedu would doodle in a scrapbook, and come up with funny drawings. At which point we would yell, "Again, Deedu!" Happily he would rip off one page after another to fill the blank ones underneath. All efforts looked like that Mickey Mouse, only with different ears and noses!

In summer Deedu could always be incountered in his garden. He belonged there as much as the gate and the flowers and trees, because he was always digging, planting, or cutting. One afternoon, to get a big lot of work done, Deedu was hoeing piles of weeds in a hurry. Tomorrow was the single day he didn't work in the whole week, when he would visit his lontsman, he said.

He never told a story about that one. Deedu kept him a secret. As a madder a fact, to the cousins, Deedu was one big secret. As time went on, when he would answer none of their innocent questions, he became one big *delishus* secret! Was it possible that the lontsman was a lontslady? they asked each other. Lucky the garden gate couldn't talk like they did! It was there that her image became imprinted on my secret mind… old like Deedu, with a puff of frosty hair over each ear, and a flower growing out of her battered hat.

In the garden was a patch of dirt saved for me. Deedu tended his garden while I dug. But where had I put my little hoe that morning?

He turned from a patch of peonies busy with bees. "Lost and fowend?" he suggested. That was a wood box built by Deedu at the bottom of his stairs. We never knew what we'd find in there. We had a 'spishun there was more to be found than was lost! Sure enough, I found my hoe and some wonderful pieces of shiny paper, some glue and a few crayons. This was a game; hiding something so one of us would find the latest treasure.

"Spaseeba," I said, convinced that such bounty deserved a Russian "thank you." Then I asked, "What are the bees doing?" as I dodged them with alarm.

"Sey make bee-lines!" he chortled, slapping his side and planing his right hand to dive and swoop like I'd seen boys do when pretending they were airplanes. "Steady! Steady! Up! Down!" And into a dance he went.

Well, he knew that wouldn't satisfy me, that I'd come back to it again. "P-r-r-ancie, hokay. Chenerally sey take some powder from here," he explained, sifting a bit of pollen between his fingers from the middle of a big red peony, "and sey pud it sair," into the middle of a white peony.

"Is that sharing?"

"Ya... sharing." Deedu scratched his head, waiting for the question he knew would be forthcoming.

"Why?"

"Coz."

"Coz why?"

"Seeds in powder, see?" With weary understanding followed by a dawning, he challenged, "You plent seed. Den wot heppen?"

"Flowers grow."

"Ya! Yew smart gerl!"

"Yep."

———

But that didn't plant *the* seed in my mind. Not yet. *It* happened at the garden gate, with the cousins. Raffy, Rachel and my sister weren't there, or it wouldn't have happened. They were "the elders" of the gang, the keepers of our parents' code, kind of; but they had gone off to see a Spencer Tracy movie at the Lido.

The rest of us lazyed around the gate, swinging and jabbering, when I learned what happened when ladies and men "slept" with each other—in those words. I was so mad, I spitted out, "My mommy and daddy wouldn't do that!" Protesting further when informed how babies were born, I shoved myself up on the bottom rail of the gate and shouted, "If your mommy doesn't want that to happen, she should stay woken-up, that's all!"

There was a squeak in the gate when cousin Issy raised his chin on the top rail, and with his own peculiar sound, which cracked an octave above everyone else's, his giggles poured forth in shrieks. He had the biggest ears, and they served as two giant scoops for informayshun from miles around. No one knew how he managed this, just that his ears seemed to pop up wherever there was something "juicy enough" to be heard. His words.

"Golly, you're stupid!" his adenoids proclaimed at my outcry.

"I'm not!" I sobbed. "And my name's not Golly! *You* stupid!"

There at the gate, I received a course in botany, sex, showbiz, gossip, and the beginnings of a very passionate vocabulary. This was home—as home as one could get. And the roots were very deep.

Deedu liked to read the Russian newspapers. When he fitted his small glasses on his nose, he looked as serious as my daddy. He would buy them at the Five and Ten, and made him look much more importantly into my face whenever he chose to repeat, "What yew want to be when yew grow up?"

I liked picture books, so I said, "I want to look at pictures." He would hum for a minute, like he was putting my answer away for a while, then ask me the same question a few weeks later. Always quietly. Indoors, he didn't joke as much as he did outside, where he would holler his words "like a Shakespeeryan Bowlshavik," my mommy said.

Sometimes I got *asasperated* when I wanted him to be serious. I finally complained, "You're always making jokes, Deedu!"

He had a needle between his fingers and he was threading it. He didn't like to be missing a button and was sewing one on a checkered shirt, essakly like the one he had on. "Da. I make se funnies, but I'm not choking all se times! I'm meaning stuff, too," he whispered, thinking hard and rubbing what looked like a fresh bruise on his jaw.

Deedu really didn't need to say anything. A smile, a twinkle, a shrug, would do; and we would know. Which was much of the wonder of being with Deedu. And we didn't need to worry about what he was thinking of us. He was part of my Zaida's house, where grandchildren were uncondishunly loved without the need to esplain ourselves. But he always watched for how things infected me ... with a twinkle in his piercing blue eyes, under brows that were like two shaggy white shelfs.

"Shast...." A baby chick had somehow fallen from the chicken man's truck one morning. Deedu constructed a box out of an old crate with enough open slats for air, but not large enough for the fluffy little bird to escape. We made a pillow and blanket out of my Zaida's old long johns, thanks to Bubbah who couldn't help getting in on it. We three each had a turn running our fingers over its downy body, and watching… "for se neck to get longer, and se fezzers to grow."

We were poor as church mice, as the saying goes. Though Mommy was the prettiest of all her sisters and my daddy was the handsomest of his brothers—you can't have everything—so we ended up being the poorest of the lot. I say this because my mommy told me we were poor. I didn't know that. I thought we were rich. I felt rich… in warm and laughtering love, lots of attenshun, good food, a roof on our heads, and my wonderful big sister who I loved and who loved me. Whenever I fell and skinned a knee, which I did pretty often, I got lots of symphony. I was a most happy child.

Until. "We are moving away, Deedu."

He was bathing Toy with his spectacles on, probally to see the fleas. With soapy hands he lifted them to his forehead and said, "I sink about sis," then slipped his glasses back over his eyes, but not before I noticed a really dark circle around one. He began to brush the dog before giving him back to Bubbah, and said little more to me that day.

I loved to travel, especially on the trolleys, to see my daddy's family. But this looked to be a journey of a different kind.

"I'm gonna throw up!" I warned, not trying to blink back my tears. Was this the end; were happy times all over? It was one thing to walk a few blocks from our place to my Zaida's house, but quite another to have to wait to visit from a faraway land! At such news, I kicked up a corner of the carpet I was standing on to demonstrate my feelings.

Daddy took my hand with a partway look in his eyes. We were going to a fine place called Toronto, he reported. His new job would make lots of money, so we could have a nice new home and come back to Montreal offen. I snatched my hand back and cried, "I'm not going to that place there! I'm already here!"

"Toronto is where I might make my fortune," he struggled.

Just like how the Three Little Pigs got started. I would never want to hear that story again, and wished my daddy hadn't got their idea. I would hide where no one would ever find me. Or wear a "For Sale" sign, and maybe Deedu would want to buy me as his helper.

But there was no talking or crying them out of it. We were going, and that was all.

Later that day, I made off with Toy in tow. We trudged to the end of the street, then turned a different corner than the one we took to get to our repartment. I was running away. I was brave. Following an unfamiliar trail, shined by moonlight instead of streetlights, my mind stopped guessing the way. As the sounds of the street faded and it got really dark, I started to get afraid.

I knew I was crying, but there was nobody around to hear me. I sat on the wet ground and gathered some pebbles. If a giant or a ghost came by, I would hit them with stones. Suddenly there was an awful shaking of the ground and the sound of a million garbage cans rumbled closer and closer. Not one giant—a million giants!

A great yellow light zoomed alongside us. "Shoom! Shoom! Shoom!" We were bathed in yellow! I grabbed Toy by the collar, but was not strong enough to keep him from bolting as an ear-shattering screech took out our hearts. He pulled me away with him, his body trembling, then he pulled away from me. The last thing I thought was "Don't let them catch me ..." before I went out on a bed of wet grass.

Toy was not very good at sniffing his way back to me. When he arrived at my Zaida's, everyone feared the worst. A police dog found me before morning, fast asleep a few feet from a railway track.

No words were said about it, except that my parents held me a lot after that, and decided to keep that "I" again. The night before we left Montreal, my mommy tied my wet hair in rags for bottling my curls in the morning. "Just like Shirley Temple," she bribed the actress in me. The perfume of Sen Sen on her breath had always been comforting, but not tonight. I didn't want to be cuddled. I was more sad than I could ever remember. So why gussy up for a kalamity?

The next morning, as we were leaving, I looked up at the sun hiding behind a gray cloud, and thought maybe that's why Deedu's eyes had turned so gray—from the reflekshun. I saw his lips say "Pomish"... remember.

The trees were shedding their gold and crimson dresses. Everything was bathed in a pink morning—the houses, the trees, even the cars parked overnight on the street—familiar friends. trying to be comforting. But I squeezed my eyelids shut to keep them out of this terrible espeerience while the tears ran down my cheeks. Inky, our visiting blackbird, sat on Bubbah's clothesline, motionless. Toy licked my hand. It was a Sunday and some bells were sounding out my sadness from a nearby church. I was going to the land of "never again." I held tight to Deedu's hand before getting into the taxi that would take us to the station.

Until she made the best friends of her whole life, Mommy didn't like our new home much. We lived in a flat, which meant a flat square building next to a flat sidewalk, flat against the road. The neighbors did not seem so friendly at first, just curious. My mommy cried. And for us, there was no garden gate, not even a garden. And no cousins, no grandparents, no aunties or uncles. But Toronto was where my father was going to make his fortune, so Mommy was doing the dootiful thing.

But there was a limit to Major's opportunity. He would find it hard to triumph over what the doctors had already diagnosed as ALS—a mistake, years later found to be post polio—but all the same claiming his energy and enthusiasm from age thirty. As a young man, Daddy had been a champion tennis player. Now, with "drop foot," he couldn't ever play tennis again, and too many of his dreams would never be filled.

On the other hand, we were lucky to have a dad so strong in other ways. With society trying to get past the Great Expression, how he struggled to keep up! He never gave in. He managed a menswear store from early morning until very late at night. And he built things, too—cupboards for mommy's kitchen, a kid-size ironing board for me (sometimes borrowed by Mommy for pressing out sleeves), a desk for Esterel; he even pitched a tent in a nearby park for us to play in, where he right away fell asleep. He worked six days a week, ten hours a day.

When his head ached, as it often did, I would slap a cold cloth on his forehead, sometimes dripping wet. He made much of that. So I continued to do it, taking in all that comforted and impressed him. Sometimes I laid my virtues on a bit thick, like "You don't have to buy me new shoes, Daddy, they're so esspensif,"... even though I might be pining for them! They loved me for that. I wondered if they knew I lied.

———

Zaida had a lifetime pass on any CPR train, to go anywhere in the country. So did Bubbah. They both soon came to visit, then only Zaida because Bubbah couldn't walk anymore. When Zaida came alone, he came unannounced. Ekcitement was at a peak. He came with a suitcase full of useful presents from all the aunts and uncles, but the best were the toys and junk from Japan sent by my Uncle Abie. My grandfather would drag his belted, overstuffed valise from the streetcar, haul it up the front porch and into the hallway, then proceed to shove it up sixteen narrow stairs before calling out, "Chana! It's me! It's the Pa!… the Zaida!" We all shrieked and cried at the same time … especially Mommy.

But I was never as ekcited as the day we returned to Montreal for our first visit. Mommy smocked a pale blue pinny for me out of one of Daddy's old pongee shirts. (Bubbah had smocked dresses for the Czar's children, and handed the craft down to her daughters.). We packed up for the train. We were going home! Poor Daddy probally never felt suxessful at making his family as happy as he'd set out to. In leaving him behind, I had to figure out what to do with my tearful throat, but quickly got over it as we neared Montreal.

The family was all very happy to see us. The great part about visiting was we were staying at Zaida's house, which meant we could be together with the cousins every day. As soon as we arrived, dear Deedu appeared hat-first from his gap in the earth. I pretended great surprise, so he shuffled along like a clown, then turned to me with his own astonishment.

"P-r-r-r-a-a-ncie!" I must have cannoned into him! He grabbed me by the waist and flung me like a rag doll up into the air, then caught me as I screamed, "Deedu! I'm here again, Deedu! I bet you didn't know I was coming!" Bubbah and Zaida laughed, and so did my aunties and uncles—like they hadn't seen anything like it!

We unpacked and settled in. I went into the garden to find my friend again. He was leaning on a spade. He had a scar beside his eye that I hadn't seen before and a blue mark under it. I slipped my hand into his, and he turned sunny. "P-r-r-a-a-ncie!" Then, "Look, look!" he exclaimed softly, and pointed to Bubbah's clothesline. "He is greeting yew!" Sure enough, there was Inky perched and cocky, like the very vain blackbird he was. "Caw! Caw!" or maybe "Haw! Haw!" this time. I liked the thought that he was as laughtering and happy as we were.

Deedu led me toward the summer kitchen, and pointed to a nest stashed in one of its eaves. He cautioned with a finger to his lips. We were both very still, and in time to see another black bird fly into it with something wiggling in its beak. "It's a worm! First, she chew it, zen givit to babies," Deedu explained.

So... that must mean... "Blackie got married!" I concluded. A mommy and a daddy for those baby birds!

In the past year, three of our cousins must have thought about being older than the rest of us down under six. So they and my sister took off more in their own puffed-up direkshuns. And the feeling with all of them wasn't essakly the same. Since we moved, they'd done their things without us; it was hard to take back my space at the gate without bumping one of them and getting a toler-rating smile. Even their colors seemed different... sharper, and they had borders. Maybe I was seeing their individualies, instead of a mess of cousins.

At first, they were very very nice, and I wasn't liking that too much because it didn't feel true like before... as if they had practiced being nice, and got frozen in nicey-ness. None of them had thought up any aventures, not even for my Uncle Abies's cucumber pickles—but that's another story. It was like it was them who'd moved away... and just when they stopped being nice and were my real cousins again, it was coming on time to go back to Toronto.

So I tried speeding all of them up like before. "Ice man!!" This made them tear off to the back of the ice truck to gather the preshus bits into bowls made from our shirts or pinnies. Cool treasures, especially dillektible when the iceman good-naturedly played his part in shooing us off! Or I would yell, "Shmatas!" Street music it was, as the driver of the horse-drawn cart answered with what sounded like the same song. He was not selling, but collecting: bottles, wire hangers, old metal, all kinds of used stuff. Bubbah always gave us something for the poor man. "He has eight children," she would say each time. We rounded out our aventures by following the stone-face knife sharpening man

ringing his big brass bell and crying out with all of us, "N-A-A-FS!" all
the way down the block.

Know what? Visiting wasn't so bad. It meant treats, even though
there were *acayshuns* when I had to wear dresses sometimes instead of
overalls.

Like the day Auntie Ada took us to the top of Mount Royal. At
first it appeared very steep, but the horses easily pulled our carriage up
the winding road to the Chalet at the top. I pushed my head over the
stone wall to see if I could spot my Zaida's house down there, or the
repartment where we used to live.

Though it looked lots different from up there, when pointed out,
each familiar spot brought wings of gladness: I was flying back, to
nest once more in my Montreal home! I could see Côte-des-Neiges
and Sherbrooke Street, and if there weren't so many trees in the way,
probally Outremont a little further down, and on into surrounding
meadows that stretched far and around. From up there it was like a
dream... I could see so much at once, scoop it up like a movie picture,
and make it mine once more.

———

Our next visit was planned for Hanukka. Because of a giant
snowstorm we were running late for the train. Daddy bought our
tickets. At his command, Esterel grabbed my hand and the three of us
flew down the ramp where direkshuns and skejules were pasted on a
wall, then tore through an archway to our train. "Wait! Wait!" I sobbed
to the conductor who waved us on. "My Daddy, he can't run! Please
don't leave him! He can't come any faster!" I pleaded.

A hiss of steam told us we had just made it; the conductor didn't
answer, but held his hand up in the air for some minutes. His shrill
whistle announced last call to board as my daddy reached the platform.
I felt the trainman's kindness in my inside soul, as happiness swished
through me like warm fudge. I smiled my feelings at him; he put two
fingers to his cap, then looked both ways for an "All clear!" and with a
loud "Yeeup!" came the thrill of the doors thumping shut and the train
beginning to move... through the yards, the houses and buildings, and
into the countryside. Daddy would be with us just for a couple of days,
but it made my world just fine. And the kid with no appetite was soon

digging into a fifteen-cent tomato and cheese sandwich bought from the newsy. A luxury in that day.

The storm followed us east. Snow banks lined the ice-rutted roads of Montreal, only wide enough for a single car, stretching their peaks to mountainous heights in my vision. We arrived by taxi because nobody owned a car in those years unless they were very rich. Our boots crunched over earlier snows that had piled and caked to a thick crust. Frosty bites grabbed at our faces, especially at our ears and noses. The trees were thick with ice in an afternoon sun not very melting. Layers of snow coated the pointy roofs. Icicles hadn't dripped away like in Toronto. It was so very cold. But there was that smell of damp wool and chimney smoke that belongs to Montreal in winter... and I blissfully breathed it in.

Everything on the street looked the same, though there were always new people moving in. A few balconies were hung with stiff washing, soon to be removed by a new-formed neighborhood delegayshun "always at the ready," we were told as soon as our eyes swept them in.

This time Deedu was leaning on his shovel, talking to my Zaida, but with his eyes surprised by me. "DEEDU!" I yelled so loud it echoed down the street. Seconds later, those muscular arms caught me from a breathless run unhampered by my snowsuit and buckled boots.

"Pr-r-r-a-a-ncie!" His ruddy face was alight, and his pipe tumbled out of his mouth. How I laughed when he tossed me into the air, winter gear and all! My daddy raised his eyes to the sky. I looked. But there wasn't anything up there that I could see, except more snow coming down.

Still skinny as a bag of bones, I was growing taller. "We build a bigger snowman to keep up wis yew!" Deedu announced. Right then he pointed at a big pile of snow already gathered for it. "An' we put face on him."

"A punkin face?" I wanted to know.

Ah, Deedu. "Okay, we put on punkin face."

So we right away set out to the corner store. We had to settle for a large squash because we couldn't get a punkin after Halloween. Instead of carving it with a nose and eyes, Deedu circled one side with crayon numbers, starting with the number one and ending with twelve.

"Where's his face?" I demanded.

"Right here, see? Clock face."
"Oh, silly Deedu! You got no numbers on your face!"
"No-no P-r-r-ancie, but clock has."

That's how I learned to tell time. And that's how Deedu taught my daddy how to make learning fun.

———

He was downstairs fixing a pipe—listening with an ear for where the trouble was. I dug into my bag of treasures. "Here, Deedu!" In it was a week-old Russian newspaper, some tobacco for his pipe, a corncob for Inky who didn't need to excape the Montreal winter, and a can of sardines for Toy, who loved them even though he wasn't a cat.

"Oh my gewdness, such nice sings!" he exclaimed, getting up and wiping grease from his fingers on a rag that looked essakly like the checkers on his shirt.

I also brought a bag of alleys, my favorites, to show Deedu, one by one. But something got into me, and before I could do that, I grabbed a piece of cardboard for a slide and sent everyone of them shooshing down all at once, pretending they were skiers. But I hadn't calkalated right. Too fast, before I could catch them, they finished the slide and rolled down into the drain on the basement floor! I think Deedu would have got as excited as I was at first when they started to shoosh. He would have clapped and clapped, and roared with laughtering. I loved to make him laugh. Joy is what we did.

After my skiers fell into that bad place, when I got my tears wiped and Deedu fished the alleys out of the drain trap, I chose joy over sorrowing, especially with the smell of Bubbah's bread a-sailing! While it baked, I watched her in the kitchen, leaning on her iron to press Zaida's shirt for the meeting at the Synagogue. She used two irons, taking the hot one from its warming place on the coal stove and putting the cool one to hot up in its place. A giant kettle puffed steam out of its snaky spout. At the same time, I could smell burning sugar from a great big pot. Bubbah asplained that it was "carmelizing." When she dropped a little water in, bubbles hissed just like the train in the station! But this smelled much better, like candy. Loud rumbles came up from my tummy as I watched her add vinegar, cabbage, grated apple, beef bones, cans of tomatoes, some water, a "shmenya" (bit) of kosher salt and pepper, all sweet and sour a-sailings, "that would simmer into perfekshun the rest of the day... and announce to the neighbors that Bubbah is making her borscht," my aunties reported.

Now I have to tell about my Uncle Abie's pickles. Uncle Abie used Zaida's summer kitchen because he didn't have one of his own. This was where his pickles were. I know why they called it a summer kitchen, in winter, it was best as a 'frigerator. But anyway, when us cousins wanted a pickle we would steal in, one by one, until we were all together in a bunch. It was like being in the army. Laya was sentry, keeping an eye on Issy who was our "tellijence" posted in the diningroom, knowing way ahead if someone was coming. Raffy was the planner, so his job was done with real thinking. Rachel calkalated to make sure we didn't fish out too many, so that Uncle Abie wouldn't be 'spishus. Jelly Bean? She scrunched in with her roly-poly-ness, and all she did was tease, "Someone's coming!" every second till nobody believed her anymore. Boots stood in a corner with an espreshun that maybe meant she didn't like pickles.

My job came next. The older ones would hold me by my socks over the tall barrel so I could reach for the pickles fast, like I was rescuing everybody from starving. (Later in life I would shiver when thinking about the plunge I might have taken into the brine!) To top it all, not more than a couple of cousins really could tolerate the hot pepperies of my Uncle Abie's pickles—but it was an aventure, you see.

Those were weeks of happiness. At Hanukka, Zaida would light the eight day menorah. Deedu was begged to sit with the family. But Deedu couldn't sit for long; he had to be doing something. Little by little he came into the room, and little by little—after standing by his chair and very slowly tippy-toeing his way to lean on the door frame for a bit—he left. Like he couldn't make up his mind. Strange ways to some, but children can assept many ways. I would carry his latkes downstairs, and shyly, he would thank me with his shining Deedu eyes.

He was very serious about his jobs. In winter it was to keep us warm. So maybe he decided that sitting at Zaida's table meant forgetting that responsibility. Well, right away he got to sifting ashes and raking embers. I watched as he saved the live ones for the next load, bedding them just right to kindle the fresh lumps banked on top. He stoked the coals to let air in, opened the dampeners, and waited for me to return up the stairs before going at his potato pancakes. He was shy about taking, but not about giving.

"Somesing for yew," he said, when I went down to get his plate. In a hand-size glass globe, snowflakes whirled around a cluster of colorful castles, each with onion-shape towers and ice-cream-cone spires.

"Again!" I commanded in my zeal see a repeat of the snowstorm in all its fury. This had to be Russia! I had thrilled to enough tales to know all about the colors and candy cane stripes on those roofs. I held the globe to my chest like one would that famous Hope Diamond, with total faith that an Ice Princess would soon make her appearance in there. One just had to be payshunt.

Snow was piling up. Cart-pulling horses flounced ahead of automobiles stuck in icy ruts. Even in a city so used to such weather, things were shutting down… including stores and deliveries. We were stuck in Montreal a lot longer than Mommy had atipsipated. No better place to be stuck! The wonderful smells of tomato and rice soup, bread baking, apple strudel, oniony brisket, and the constant parade, the warmth, the fun, of familiar loving faces.

There was time to listen in on party-lines, to make nonsense calls by dialing any numbers that came to mind, and "tele-teasing"with them. And there was time to be with Deedu who, in my mind, never slept. He was always up first thing, shoveling or stoking, or reading by his furnace with his spectacles on when I peered down the stairs to steal my first or last sight of him at the beginning or end of my day.

When we had to leave for Toronto, I found him in his room, drinking a glass of tea through a sugar cube and eating a piece of mandelbread which my Bubbah had pressed on him. He was looking in his books, and showed me one with pictures of Russia. A faded snapshot fell out of one of its pages. "Is this your little girl, Deedu?" I asked.

"Nyet." He was sulky. "Yew are."

He'd made a house for me out of popsicle sticks, along with a few dried crabapple faces stuck on sticks. They were the people for going in and out. "Do svidaniya… Goodbye Deedu! I will see you again soon," I promised, so sure that fresh excitement would be waiting here for us.

I'd made a crown for him out of silver cigarette papers. I sat it on his hat. It made him happy. "Ti kraseeva devushka, yew... yew beautiful little girl... a Russian princess! Always use zis up here." He pointed to his head.

"Ok! I am a princess... an Ice Princess," I corrected airily.

He bent down and placed a kiss on my hand... the singular one in my memory.

"P-r-r-ancie, we best friends, ok?"

"For sure, Deedu," I pledged, with freshly aching heart.

"Pomish... remember, yew can be anysing you want to be. Dyew know it yet?" he asked, as though my answer would keep us together.

This time I added a little more. It would be our secret. "I want to have a movie place, to let little kids in... and maybe they can come up on the stage and sing and dance afterward. I like to do that when I come home after a movie, don't you, Deedu? Or you can come and make animals on the big, big screen, with different noses and different ears so kids can guess what." I folded my arms and nodded my head for Deedu to know I was most certain of my decision.

His eyes lighted up.

Though Mommy was still heart-sick, I was making friends in Toronto and so was my sister. My first friend was Elinor; my sister's friend was Sarah. Every Saturday afternoon the four of us would take our six cents to pay for the movie show around the corner. I was learning more big words! Searching for one to describe how ekcited I felt about the Fu Manchu serials we saw each week, I chose the newest biggest one in my growing list, "Mommy, It was simply monotonous!" A good choice. It was making her laugh again.

My Uncle Solomon in Montreal decided to marry his financy, Molly, the next September. Daddy took me to the wedding because it was his brother and he got to choose. Uncle Sol was my "book uncle." He bought me my first Anne book, *Anne of Green Gables*, and I loved him very much because he was the youngest and the most fun of my daddy's brothers, and truly "a kindred spirit" like Anne said. This time Mommy stayed home with Esterel, just for a long weekend. Again, we were staying on Jeanne Mance, where I was sure my cousins would be waiting at the gate. Would Deedu keep getting shorter as I got taller? I wondered. The next month I would be six. Would I be too big to fly up to his shoulders?

It was still like summer; he would be in the garden because nobody needs a furnace yet. I went to see. Nothing was there, not his spade, or the oilcan that killed the squeaks in the gate. Toy, who always followed Deedu around, was in the kitchen with Bubbah. The same aunties and uncles sat in the big dining room. They might have been dizgusting world politiks and fillosofees, but they weren't smiling. Maybe because I didn't live here anymore, they'd had trouble finding somebody else to make them laugh.

I just couldn't hang around in the garden, waiting for Deedu's surprise jump-up. With curls a-flying, I dashed down the inside steps to his room. In the pocket of silence, his absence fell around me like air full of dust. His bed was neat and tight under the green flannel blanket. His hat hung on its nail. I had never seen Deedu without his hat; I had never seen that hat without Deedu.

I listened for his sounds... soft words saved for indoors, the rising chuckle on seeing me there, the rattle of a dampener—no, it was summer, he wouldn't be furnacing—well then, the scraping of a rake or a trowel, or the thumping of earth flying from his spade against a basement window while digging a new garden in the back of the house.

His bed was too neat.

Bubbah's clock in the front hall bonged four times. Like a introdukshun to a performance, each time we'd heard it bong, Deedu had done a funny dance for me. But today, the stillness cried out for him. I listened for the voice climbing up and down with happiness at our re-you-nion. Had he found some other little girl to tease and joke with? Another family to live with? Those thoughts made me so jellus, my stomach turned into one big mushroom with its edges burning and curling back like poisoning.

By now I was storming the room with my eyes. Turning it topsy-turvy for signs of Deedu, I picked the basement clean until there was nothing left to inspekterate. There was his pipe—now in pieces because it had been very old and crackled—his spectacles on top of his orange crate table, and in one of the inside spaces, a scrapbook and a folded newspaper with an elastic around it: on closer inspekterashun, the one I gave him last time. On top of that sat the silver crown.

His bed was too neat—not a wrinkle—and different. It was dusty.

I started to be prepared... for something, though I didn't know for what. I didn't notice Daddy coming down the stairs. He put his hand on my shoulder and said softly, "Deedu has gone to Heaven, Francie." He was gentle but strong, not at all part-way.

Was I needed to answer that? I couldn't breathe it to my mind. I didn't know what to do with such informayshun. I struggled with that Heaven place that I couldn't yet find in my imaginayshun. Was he visiting my Grandma Charna? Wouldn't we ever see him in the world anymore?

"Why, Daddy?"

"Because it was his time to go, I expect."

"When did Deedu go there, Daddy?"

"Shortly after our last visit."

Why hadn't anybody said? Mommy always told us that no news was good news ... was that why? Or maybe they thought because we lived so far away that I'd forgot about Deedu? Or why? I was all too heartbrakened-up to ask. I just wanted to sit there, in Deedu's chair. The light was going away. I looked out the cellar windows to see if I could spot him somewheres. One green-gold window was looking into the sunset. I felt it on my face and over my hands that turned green-gold, too. The pockets of my eyes got heavy and spilled.

Daddy stayed with me. "This is what I think... we lost a good friend, and crying is ok, so go on and do it," he said. But I kept my eyes on the window and spotted the first star, and entertained the idea that it could be Deedu trying to get a message to me. Maybe to tell me to listen to what my daddy said... or maybe to announce that he'd just got lost, that's all. He would find his way back....

Like when I ran away with Toy that night and was carried back to Zaida's house, where Bubbah, Mommy, and all the aunties were wringing their hands and tearing at their aprons to wipe away the badness of their fears. "A wonder she didn't catch ammonia!" they'd kept wailing. I thought I'd get a lickin', but they forgot to give it and hugged me instead.

"If Deedu came walking down the street now, I wouldn't yell at him neither. I would just be so happy to see him as livened up as you and me, with his big smile showing he was alright. I would hug him too, even if too tight hugging made him shy.

"Or maybe he was in the hospital?

"By not getting here in time, I let my dear Deedu pass away—What had I been doing when Deedu was passing away? If only we had stayed here in Montreal!"

I didn't realize I had said all this out loud until Daddy spoke. "Deedu would never want to be the cause of this kind of sadness," he said.

———

I didn't think to ask what Deedu had died from, like adults do. He just died, that was enough. Though I knew by now that people died away, and I knew it meant forever, I'd taken for granted that someone as special as Deedu would cheat that part of it. It didn't seem right that Deedu could be "up there," like my daddy said, without giving me a sign. I looked for him in the sky… like maybe he'd been kidnapped by angels… if those angels did such a thing.

The cousins were nowhere around. Maybe they had cried enough and now it was my turn. I pictured a monster sweeping my Deedu away, and this room, where the sunlight had played, where the animals had danced, became a tunnel of tears.

All washed-out, I pleaded, "Daddy, I'm askared! Make him come back!" I took his hand and searched wildly in my head for how to convince him to use the powers so easily given to a daddy by a five year old. I knew I could say what I needed to, that at this point he was far less daunting, and I didn't have to worry about pleasing him. "He didn't say goodbye to me yet!" Only my mouth said it: my head didn't. "Deedu told me I was an Ice Princess! He said one day I would find the rest of my princessing right here, and he touched his heart for 'on his honor.' I can't find it yet! Deedu never fibs!" There seemed to be no stopper for my sobbing.

Daddy breathed despair. "He touched his heart to show you where to find your princess—in your own heart one day. In the deeds you will do, in what you will accomplish. Your heart is the best storage place for what you want to do, what you want to be. And for all the happy memories that you wouldn't have now, if you hadn't had Deedu for a best friend. We feel poor because he's gone. But we're rich because he was here." Said by a champion daddy, who was physically forced to live a lot in the back street of our lives.

My uncles and aunties were very quiet when we came up from the basement. They too must have suffered in the sharing of my first experience with death. They had no idea, nor did I, that this same little girl would remember each one of them, with all their endearings and peculiar personalities, just as they sat around that big oak table in that one meaningful moment in time.

"Heaven is a beautiful place," Daddy persisted. "I'm told nobody gets sick there, not even a sniffle. Deedu will get to do everything he likes to do. It is a place with no danger. The sun shines every day… and there are gardens everywhere. All he needs to do is ask the angels for a hoe and they will give it to him. He'll have his own garden to dig, to plant and to care for."… We were walking up the street. It was dark. "Remember how he loved to dance? The angels will clap for him, or dance with him, whatever he chooses, for as long as he likes, for one never gets tired in Heaven."

My tears stopped for a minute and I challenged, "But what could be new up there for Deedu? He liked to always be learning!"

Daddy had a smile. "Maybe he's raking leaves… of gold." he answered, looking pleased with the thought.

But I called him on it. "Real gold? Like Mommy's wedding ring?"

"Uh… well everything is touched with gold in Heaven, you know."

Daddy had forgotten his cane. We did not go all the way up the road. But he succeeded in holding my interest. "Will you and Mommy already be there when I get to Heaven?"

"I surely hope so. We'll be waiting," he smiled his kind smile, pulled me next to him and tickled my chin, "ready to hold you close, just like this. "

I looked straight at him. "Daddy, you're silly. I will be growed-up into a big person!"

"I'll remember that."

"And I got to remember to remind God to be extra extra good to Deedu."

That night I slumped down on my bed, tuckered out, but unable to sleep. I had not yet decided, to my satisfaction, how to tell those angels that they should have waited till I saw Deedu one more time.

I had taken the scrapbook to bed, with the pictures Deedu and I made. There were some cut-out snowflakes, and paper tracings we did around the shadow animals on the wall. While the reckulekshuns of doing them paraded through my mind, I couldn't help remembering what the place had been like with Deedu in it. Like the time I sat watching for him to come home from seeing his lontsman, glad that he had a friend. The times he'd have all the cousins sitting at his feet while he told another Russian story. But always he turned his head to look direkly at me... "Panamayish?... Understand?" Maybe because I was the storiest.

Next morning, I heard giggling that sounded like Jelly Bean. My Zaida was tossing her over his shoulders and high in the air. I wandered into my Bubbah's kitchen when Zaida put Jelly Bean down, put his arm around my grandmother, patted her bottom and shouted, "This is the Bubbah! Beautiful, eh?" I knew he was trying to tell me, "Francie, you still have us... and we're the same." The house was always like my Bubbah's carmelizing... warm with love, always soft and flowing. But I needed to be brooding. I even rejected the piano that had never been silent all the times I was there, though it would start to be that day... the day of my Uncle Solomon's wedding.

Daddy said I didn't need to go if I didn't want to. But I did want to, so I tried to enjoy it by hiding my sadness. That was pretty hard because pictures of Deedu kept popping up, and my eyes kept leaking. In the night, when my eyes finally got to sleep, I had a dream. Deedu was sliding off the sky. I ran under him and called out, "Don't be afraid, Deedu! I'll send a cloud to catch you!" Deedu jumped, right through the cloud, and slided into a dark hole at my feet. Trying to save him, I'd done worse. So I yelled for the angels to drag him out and off to Heaven... even if I wasn't ready to say goodbye yet. I woke up with the sun starting to warm away the shadows in my stomach and on my chest.

I had to learn about saying goodbye. Daddy helped me place a stone in Deedu's garden. We scratched his name on it with a sharp pebble from under the gate.

Years later, when in the company of cousin Issy, and having learned that Deedu had been a mere sixty when he died, I asked if he knew the cause. "Didn't you know?" he replied, somewhat perplexed. "Remember that one day off each week when he said he was visiting his lontsman? Turned out he was boxing for money. On that last day, he won a *lot*. Someone must have followed him and robbed him of his winnings, beat him up, then threw his body into the river. Though he couldn't swim, he didn't drown. The police said he was already dead."

I was stunned. I could not picture Deedu with such an unglorious end. I wiped the tragic truth from my mind, to keep him covered with gold.

———

Twenty years have gone by. I stare at my Zaida's house, now occupied by two or more generations of immigrants, and the memories flood. When people are so special in life, their legacies are forever treasured. It is natural to regret the things I should have done but didn't, or those I did but shouldn't have. But we were just children, so one day I will write a "fix" list—to make everything better for those up above who may be watching to see if I've learned anything!

I see them all so clearly: my people marching through my vision to rendezvous with our special brand of joy. With Deedu among them. Returning with my family a couple of times a year, I felt like the luckiest kid on earth... nourished by the welcome and the love.

Best of all, I can remember it.

———

"Never turn your back on anybody needing help," my Zaida had always said. "It may be an angel passing through." Deedu. The angel in the basement. My last request of him had been: "Write me a story?" He answered, "Da, I write it for yew, maybe wis pictures." His last story turned out to be a bankbook.

But first, back to the beginning. Denyu Abramovitch was the son of a peddler. He had three brothers and one sister, who simply disappeared along with their families during the Russian pogroms that scattered or forced out much of the Jewish population at the turn of the twentieth century. He was thirty when he walked alone into Lithuania and worked as a farmhand for almost a decade. He never married. Picking up work here and there, Denyu made his way across Europe for another dozen years, and eventually emigrated to Canada in 1929, with little more than a change of the clothes he wore.

A graceful man, he took his turn in the growing ranks of the displaced, but soon, through the synagogue, found a place in my Zaida's house and in the hearts of the family, especially the cousins, all ardent admirers of the "pied piper" in checkered shirt and blue overalls—in my eyes a most princely uniform! He lived with chosen simplicity, the most important ingredients, kindness and fun, with a Russian sense of celebration. No one knew why he changed his name to 'Deedu,' except that perhaps there was a little child in his past that did it for him. Though he'd decided never to go back to his homeland, he was steeped in a culture that pulled him back through mind and heart that had nothing to do with politics.

The envelope here on my desk may be the last of a score of them, sent to my attention throughout the past year. "You are doing an excellent job… handling things expertly! I salute you," is the latest report from the lawyer. "Never thought it would come to anything, frankly," was his latest verbal message.

I take it kindly. This is 1949. There's a War behind us, when women filled many of the jobs held by men. Secure in our abilities, we are coming out of our kitchens and extending our interests. Though big families are once again the trend, a great majority of women are managing to attend night school. Some, like myself, are lucky enough to be living their dream.

And the cousins? Raffy, married with a family of four, is on the road representing ladies' fashion houses. Laya is selling real estate. Rachel is running her father's dress manufacturing business, and doing very well. Jelly Bean had a nose job and lost her baby fat, to become one of the most beautiful of women. Boots looks after her widowed father with utmost care. My beloved sister Esterel chose to be a laboratory technician. Married with two children, she was suddenly wrenched from us by a disease none of us had ever heard of.

I'm not the same person I was when Issy told me about what happened to Deedu, but I am still not yet stun-proof. For I am the recipient of Deedu's fortune, saved for P-r-r-a-ncie once a week from the bruises he got in the boxing ring. It's not at all strange that he speaks to me now... familiar words that time and place cannot erase. "Se world is yewers. Yew can do anysing, be anysing yew want. Pomish? Remember what I'm saying?"

I remember. I remember, Deedu. You gave me all the right memories.

Deedu, you were a big secret ... so strong and even in every situation. You are the example of what I looked for in a man when I married. In all of my men, I have been so lucky: in my Zaida, my father, my husband, my teachers, and my little son, who, at three, is showing great imagination and appreciation of laughter and fun.

Eighteen years after your death, I signed the first part of your instructions. Briefed by the lawyers, I learned that my assignment was "to be anything yew want to be"—that in order to receive this large endowment and bring my aspirations to fruition, I must not abandon my dream. It isn't an easy assignment. It takes research, footwork, consultations, training... hardest of all, "chutzpah"—taking chances.

I review all the forms, put my fountain pen back in its case, and look around our office where shelves of illustrated children's books look back at me with colorful splendor. In this children's lending library, hundreds of fascinating authors will tell their stories to thousands of pairs of curious eyes and ears.

Come with me now, Deedu. This place is yours. We have just put the finishing touches on a small round stage in the next room and the three dozen seats surrounding it. Here is our theatre, and yesterday we signed our first performers, a troop of visually-impaired children called "The Hawks," who whistle and dance and do magical things with harmonicas. You and I have always had so very much in common, Deedu. We love life. We love to make it happen... as we will each day in this place.

Issy waves a white flag in the form of a piece of paper before popping his forever-popping head around the door. "I have another."

"Leave it for me; I'll sign that next." Almost reluctantly, for it's truly the last one, like a thread that binds us, my friend and benefactor. And Issy? He is a loyal, diligent assistant, still "all ears," who keeps me informed and organized in a thoughtful, steady way. He has saved this for the end… to read thoroughly, to savor. The final paper giving you and me, Deedu, complete ownership of all we survey, with the final addition soon to be completed—a glassy outdoor winter garden for families of skaters, under its blazing marquee, ICE PRINCESS.

We're doing it, Deedu! Ya budu sku chai. I miss you always. Goodnight, but never goodbye.

P-r-r-a-ancie.

The Road Ahead

"I don't know if I can struggle with it anymore, Mom."

"If you want to be an entertainer, it is a struggle. But for now, get yourself on that plane and see a bit of the world. By the time you get back home, you will know what you want. Oh, here's a little story for you to read… with my heart's love. Promise that you won't open the enclosed envelope until you've read the story, and made your decision."

———

Once upon a time, there was a group of actors who decided to take a trip to Paris. Their destination was the Eiffel Tower.

They started out from Rue de la Pais. Unable to afford a guide, they worried about the unfamiliar route. But curiosity was strong; they would learn their way.

Just ahead was a magnificent structure, and the group decided to join the stream of people wandering in and out. With its own share of architectural genius, the cathedral didn't need to be Notre Dame to impress those who respect amazing artistry or—more important to some—the power of prayer.

A fine beginning for thirteen young people of different faiths, who felt fortified by the quiet place.

For a time.

They headed for Rue Rivoli, but found road crews tearing up the entire intersection at le Champs Elysées, making this route impassible. They consulted their map. To reach la Tour, they would need to detour around le Champs Elysées, toward L'Arc de Triomphe.

But not Neara Lavabo.

"Me? Walk all those extra miles?" she whined. "Do you know who I am? I'm Fara Tappit's cousin and I've waited too long to get here!" To arouse the attentions of the road crew, she purred, "And I will do a-ny-thing to avoid the detour. I wish to go to the Eiffel Tower—now."

Neara was a looker. There was no mistaking her message, and the roadmen quickly grinned their comprehension. "Mademoiselle," whispered one whose intentions were indeed on the shady side, "I will show you the way. It is called Le Bon Chance. It worms its way beneath the Avenue, but is guaranteed to deliver you there."

Without another thought, Neara fluffed her hair and declared, "I'm on my way!" She brushed by the others with a shrug and a look of scorn for their lack of aggression, as she perceived it.

La Place de la Concorde was easily recognizable from brochures consulted in preparation for the trip. Shaped like an octagon, with a French city represented by a different statue on each of its corners, La Place was built on the original site of Le Guillotine, where Marie Antoinette, Robespierre, and countless others had been beheaded.

What majesty from such a beastly origin! As if to atone, the graceful lines of the Obelisk of Luxor reached heavenward, gleaming white in the sun. If not for the detour, they might have missed this famous Parisian landmark, reputed to be one of the largest in the world.

The day would be hot and humid; already the group was feeling bedraggled. Why not simply hail a couple of taxis?

Maybe it is best explained by saying what these troopers didn't want to be: doctors, lawyers, business people, secretaries, all in a hurry. The choice to be artists might present delays and discomforts, but would likely be compensated by a widening of their vistas. Collectively, their creative voices agreed that they would reach the Tower only by allowing the journey to lead them... on foot.

And so they began to sing, "Strutting Down the Avenue!" Some had very fine voices. People were charmed, and many stopped to join in or cheer them on.

Though forewarned that Anglophones unschooled in French might not be too welcome in Paris, each, with their attempts to communicate, received only friendly responses. Faith, diligence, and one firm step at a time were bringing them closer to their goal.

Perfectionism forms itself, they discovered, with little jabs of joy. Was this not perfect? They were good company for each other, and look—they were ending up in many cameras! (Small audiences at first, oui, but good practice for more exciting ones to come, n'est-ce pas?) They called themselves "Les Forge Ahead Players."

With a trailing entourage, the twelve sang their way through the lush botanicals of Le Jardin des Tuileries. They stopped for a time to absorb the glory of the famous gardens before turning into Cours la Reine.

What an experience for a sound engineer! With its symphony of peeps!!! shreeps!!! slams!!! rippling laughter, bicycle bells, expletive-deletives, and a stream of fast-paced chatter from a troop of school children on their way to La Louvre.

And for a cameraman! With its trees, stately and full, lining all thoroughfares and both banks of the Seine, like giant tour guides pointing the way through a plethora of river and street scenes. Blossoms everywhere. Wide, manicured boulevards, like square-cut emeralds, bordering the endless pageantry of architecture and superb statuary. Paris, dubbed "a woman's city," provided not only a visual, but also an emotional map for the members of the troupe.

To draw upon each experience was like opening presents, one at a time ... with varied responses of course, because all twelve weren't affected in the same ways. In order to interpret emotions, they learned that they must invest some of their own. To understand and to live them, what better place than Paris, City of Light?

Serious stuff. But today it seemed that the city was boasting her frivolous side. Her women sparkled; her men flirted; her children skipped and chattered. Paris also had her mysteries, and the band of student actors, especially the girls, were forming questions in their minds.

Such as, "Mademoiselle, what were you planning when you chose that outfit this morning? Was it to suit an occasion or your mood? Or do you simply dress in your best every day?" Also, "Why do women, old enough to be our grandmothers, look so smashing in a simple skirt and blouse, and maybe a scarf or a cardigan casually tossed over the shoulders ?" Or perhaps, "And how, because Paris also teases with so many of you crowding the pastry shops, cafes and restaurants, do you stay so slim?" The Players would not leave without finding out.

Paris is not without its sadness. The little band shared some of their dwindling funds with a widowed beggarwoman and her child, and listened sympathetically to tales of their extreme poverty.

They spent a few francs at a flower stall operated by a handicapped lady. "Smell them," she advised, as she wrapped the purchase. "Always take a moment to smell them." They might have missed the fresh, dewy aroma of fresh-cut violets on a Paris morning, as well as the valuable meaning of her words.

Musée du Petit Palais and Musée du Grand Palais. There they were, as they were described. Two members of the group decided to pass by the famous galleries, but the remaining ten could not. Perhaps the road had to include the wrench of saying goodbye to friends. "Au revoir, then, mes amis... Until we meet again."

To make something of themselves meant letting the present in, the rest agreed.

In the smaller gallery, the actors marveled at the works of Monet, Renoir, and Delacroix among a host of Renaissance painters. On entering the rotunda of le Grand Palais, much larger with its immense front porch and ionic columns, they thrilled to the splendors of modern art beneath the famous glass dome unleashing its light upon them.

Wasn't it Aristotle who said, "Hope is a waking dream"? By this time, feet were sore, hunger gnawed, and the group dragged with fatigue. But hope was lending determination. True to their name, Les Forge Ahead Players forged on.

Doubts and fears turned to triumphs as they crossed and recrossed the Seine, enthralled by the rhapsody of water traffic. Big and little bateaux, some carrying tourists, others transporting freight, were all eking out a living on the picturesque water highway where horns, blasphemy and song shared equal rights. The way is not easy for most, they learned, but nothing could dismiss the poetry.

By now, the parade had dispersed for lunch. Our actors ate theirs by the river, next to a bench where a young woman was enjoying a cup of tea in one hand and a crème-filled pastry in the other. She was very slim. Could her secret be in the way she savored the treat... in tiny nibbles? Her tailored jacket and mini skirt were elegant though not expensive. Attendez! It was an outfit that suited her personal style!

Time-out was rejuvenating, and bore out the wisdom of their acting coach: "Entertainers never know when they might be called upon, so treat your bodies well."

The group turned up rue Franklin D. Roosevelt, stopping here and there to meet people, to learn more of the language and absorb some of the culture. Discouraged by the creeping heat of mid-day and the length of the detour, two more members of the group were coaxed away by flirtations and promises. Another ran out of money and decided to return home. Setting their sights on remaining in Paris and completing the trip at a later date, one actor took a job at an outdoor cafe, his wife in a boutique.

Two began to whine: "What the hell are we doing here? Neara is at the Tower and here we are poking along like inchworms! She had the right *idea: get there any way you can. We're too hot. We're too tired. We can't go on... it's no fun." Needless to say, such dialogue was in itself frustrating. Intent on reaching their goal and with little time for self-pity, the trio journeyed on.*

"Getting there" is not easy; believe it. The process requires patience, strength and tenacity; in this case it flagged the first nine and challenged the remaining three. For them, sensitivities were developing, to be recorded in their emotional files, together with the sprouting seeds of perceptiveness.

F.D.R. led them onto l'Avenue des Champs-Élysées , and the centre of twelve radiating avenues in a busy arrondissement circling l'Arc de Triomphe. Halfway to the Tower!

But hold on. Automobiles stopped for no one. There were no traffic lights. Tourists were weaving between moving cars. Les gendarmes, peering sternly from caps pulled well down over their roving eyes, and arms crossed with authority over their chests, offered no help at all! Unaware of the underground passage to l'Arc, our three characters followed the tourists, with prayers on their lips!

Laughing at the unusual experience, they almost ran smack into the beautiful Larissa Lamour, female lead in "Le Monde," a movie being filmed in Paris. There she stood, beside a pair of giggling girls. But hers was a dark, sad face. Tears streamed from her eyes, moving the three to offer assistance. Larissa indicated a brass plaque in a row of them mounted on a pillar of this famous landmark. "Mon père, my father.... I never knew him. He died in World War Two, in defense of France. Now he is just a name among rows of metal."

The three hung in.

L'Arc de Triomphe, the emblem of French patriotism, was Napoleon's monument to bravery. Here, Larissa had found a piece of herself. No matter how successful, or how beautiful, none are exempt from life's trials, you see.

When the actress was composed, she asked her new friends to accompany her to the lookout on the roof. Where much of Paris lay before them, Larissa learned of their mission and listened to accounts of their journey. "You will make it," she declared, "because you are absorbing what experience imparts. Along the road ahead, you will use this knowledge in various ways. Oui, you will be richer for it."

What brings success? Talent? The choice of method to express that talent? Or those who recognize and support it? All three. But nothing will happen if the ambition, passion and dedication are not present. And of course, the energy.

"Experience teaches what an actor might forget," Larissa explained. "Because we live so much with fantasy, we need to be reminded to face what can be so easily ignored in the real world. Actors must be aware of what affects people, what might affect one and not another, what words and actions mean.

"How likeable... mais no, that is not correct... how memorable can you make your characters?" A wistful smile claimed Larissa's delicate features. "Glamour lives in fantasy, my dears. Fantasy is what most people want; illusions are the pathway to 'somewhere over the rainbow.' As actors, you must assist your audience there, if only for some moments... to help them forget their troubles, their daily pressures, or to lighten a load. Your role is to create illusions and make them seem real, No one must guess that your performance is the result of intense travail.

"Spirit? Let us look back, for instance, to the World War, when hundreds of movies were made. Most played to patriotism, faith and dedication. The result was a healthy, tough morale that brought people together in a common cause. Movies bring to the screen their time, place, and message; actors must capture and project the spirit of these. As we travel more and learn about others in this world, we become more skillful at doing that, my friends."

How fortunate to meet someone so expert in their field! But not for that reason only did they ask Larissa to accompany them on their trip to La Tour. The group had fallen in love with her beautiful nature and gracious interpretations of the meaning of her role.

Would she like to come along? "Mon père... my reason for being here.... I will remain for a while," she said, adding good wishes for their success, and promising to keep in touch.

Jardin de Trocadero, in the Sixteenth Arrondissement, would have walked them to the Eiffel Tower. But they decided to spend the few remaining daylight hours in the garden at its feet, to see for themselves the bronze statues and exquisite stone pools, where it is said lovers appear as soon as evening descends. As predicted, they soon appeared and happily embraced at the foot of Gustave Eiffel's tower liberating its electrified splendor over the magnificent City of Light.

With tired bodies and painfully blistered feet, the three made their way to the foot of the landmark built to commemorate the Centenary of the French Revolution. Hearts soared, then plunged when they failed to join up with the pair who had left the group at le Petit Palais.

But this was here and this was now, where magic and wonder cried out for attention. With the long road behind them, the three friends had no doubt about going the distance. One step at a time... with eyes and ears and hearts wide open.

It wasn't an easy climb. There are over sixteen hundred steps. As in life, for every dozen or so ascended, the trio needed to rest or backtrack... to recoup, rethink or correct.

So they didn't rush. With each step, they appraised what they had learned, and shared their ideas. Knowledge of another meant awareness of oneself. They had opened their minds without trashing their wisdom; they had practiced understanding and acceptance, and nourished their abilities with awareness established firmly in their minds. First lesson: hard work must partner talent, no matter how gifted one might be.

Halfway up they encountered an attendant, and asked about the actress who preceded them. Would they find her at the top?

"Lavabo? You mean her?" He turned toward a figure skulking by itself in a corner of the stairwell. Carried away by an easy ride, now trivialized and lifeless, Neara had been dumped in her very shallow, short-cut career.

Old Lavabo hardly welcomed her buddies. Used and confused, she resented their elevated spirits and happy faces. "Took you a long time," she pouted. As the travelers related their experiences, she smirked her lack of comprehension. How could inspiration evolve from so many detours and challenges? Unable to glean a thing from their tales, Neara's reaction was to turn her back on the three and hope that they would go away.

———

But Les Forge Ahead Players didn't go away. Instead, they completed the sixteen hundred and fifty-two steps, to find The Tower not nearly tall enough to express their heightened spirits! Lights bathed them in a rosy blush. They were alive with joy and wonder! They renamed the scene "City of Sky," from three hundred meters above the Earth!

No question, attainment of this vantage point was a privilege... and as such, would in turn demand much that they could give.

"That was a long hike, Spence," said the young woman.

"It surely was, Kate," he answered. "Now what say you, Laurence? Was it worth it?"

"Jolly good," responded the young man, alive with all of Paris at his feet. "My word! Reaching such heights is quite a task, isn't it? A powerful adventure, physically and emotionally, I would say. No doubt a necessary journey, for the enhancement of sensibilities... and abilities, in order to convince an audience of the songs we sing and the characters we must portray."

"We have also discovered that each of us must be true to ourselves," Spence added, *"fully aware of our weaknesses and strengths, working to improve on one and building on the other. This trip to the top is merely the beginning of the road ahead."*

Laurence bowed to his friends. "Determination brings magic in its train, as the saying goes. Agreed? I have a feeling, old chaps, that we're on top of the world.... To stay."

———

The girl finished reading the story. She knew that her mother had written it especially for her, and was grateful for its support and its challenges. Her answer was a giant "*Yes!*" She had what it took to follow her dream; and she would! As she pressed a button to dim the light above her seat, the forgotten envelope fell to her lap.

.... *"We will be going into production for the Broadway musical, Gigi. You are invited to audition for the principal role."*

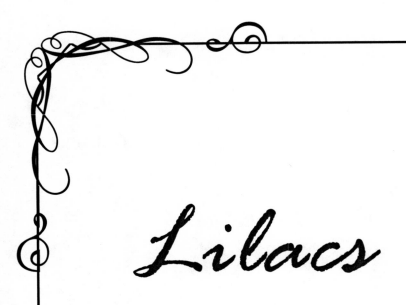

Lilacs

JORDANA STUDIED THE BLANK page on her Smith Corona and regarded the wastebasket brimming with crumpled paper. It was no use; the effort was not producing results.

But the story had to be written. Notes and jottings had been stored for years, waiting for the right time. Certainly that time was now, while memories were still alive and accurate. But each attempt to put them on paper cast the writer into a block, and she began to believe that the book might not want to be written—a book with no ending.

In her years as journalist, all articles had come together smoothly with strong wrap-ups. For months now, these notes had been picked up with hopes of retracing memories and releasing a few fears, only to be put aside when words refused to come, and the story remained stifled in its past. A daily exercise, futile to a writer, frightening to a survivor.

"Don't give up," Matt would encourage. This day, he bent to plant a kiss on the back of his wife's neck and regarded the crumpled paper already topping the wastebasket so early in the morning. "There could be something good in those throw-outs, you know. Rest your mind for a time. A postponement might clear the way, ease you into those years more as a writer than a victim." His voice was gentle and even. "If you stop obsessing, as though your need to write this were some kind of exorcism, it might all release itself by itself."

Dearest Matthew, her caring husband-friend. He was many times right. But he didn't share her past... the part she hadn't shared with him....

The Last Goodbye. A fitting title. But how could Matt be expected to understand why one moment immortalized itself above all others, when she didn't understand it herself? She'd tried changing the title, but that made no difference. The image that chained her ability to produce the rest of the story was indelible, so that escape never completely happened for her.

Release itself by itself? Oh Matt, my dear—it's been thirty years! How many more would constitute an effective waiting time?

She had tried writing objectively, a step away, where the memory would no longer pain but could still be reached... to chronicle those years as though she were writing about someone else. But he kept standing there, waving. At her.

Re-think, she decided on this Monday morning. Why not trust the force that wanted to lead her, as Matt inferred? Crash it out on the keys as quickly as it comes, without a thought to what is being written. Let it have its way. She appealed to the Smith Corona as one would to an old friend. "Oh," she moaned, "You know... that cursed war.... "

———

She was just fifteen. He was eighteen. When shared feelings had never been difficult, and both were young enough to believe that love would last forever.

Thirty years later, such feelings had no right to be there.

But they were. And if they'd never left, why couldn't they be written? "Remember the lilacs," Jordana lectured herself. "Once again, walk through a forest, stand on the deck of a ship, or on a lonely hill... to unlock whatever is hiding. Or try a few handstands to shake the traumas out," she laughed dryly, tossing another wad of paper into the basket.

———

Alain duMont suffered a restless night, tossing and turning since three AM. When he finally drifted off, the dream was the same. Her hand slipped into his. He pressed it gently, then woke up, looking for her. With the dream's increasing frequency, the touch of her hand was beginning to feel very real.

Tired, he swung both legs over the side of the bed and took a moment to study his surroundings. He disliked hotels: they all had the same plan, identical appointments, similar mustiness. This was an exception.

He tossed back the night curtains to greet a foggy morning, and passed a practiced hand over the polished wood of the burled walnut sleigh bed. No mere veneer. Quality reappeared in an Empire writing desk and in the heavily-carved frame of a day bed, lavish in green plush. The contents of The Georgian Arms paralleled those on the floor of *DUMONT ET FILS*, established in 1920, re-established in 1948, and now in1972, the largest emporium of antiques in Paris.

DuMont picked up the morning paper delivered to his suite, and turned directly to the classifieds for the notice he'd placed: *Seeking owner of half-star pendant, etched with profile and initials J.D. Paris 1939.* Box number correct. Satisfied, he ordered breakfast, showered quickly and threw on a thirsty robe provided by the hotel just as the food trolley was rolled in.

As he switched on the radio to await the six o'clock news, strains of "Lilac Time" wooed the beginnings of hope on his second day in the city, where Alain had finally traced her... across the ocean to Quebec City, through Montreal, and finally to Toronto, a place he frequented to purchase works of art. The dream had begun just a few weeks ago, with the warmth of her hand in his. Did it mean he was getting closer, or would this be one more dead end?

———

Today was their birthday... long ago a yearly celebration just as the lilacs were blooming all over Paris. At eighteen, Alain had been very much in love with Jordy, to the delight of his family who regarded the girl as his "twin"— couched in the term, but unconnected by bloodline.

"So like each other," Grandmère had repeated. The birthday she slipped identical pendants over both their heads, she crooned, "Regardez. They are engraved with your initials, but with the image of the other." She placed a hand on each of their heads and recited her benediction, "Wear next to the heart, so that no matter where you are, they will keep you safe and together."

The original gold star had been the fob on Jordy's father's watch chain. Two inches wide as it was long, cut in half, it resulted in a pair of odd but interesting shapes, each deeply-etched. "To have and to hold," beamed the old lady. The idea had been hers... the goldsmith had brought it to life.

That birthday was the last they shared. Hitler's army rolled into Paris as swiftly as it had conquered Poland. The ominous wails of S.S. vehicles could be heard throughout the city's wide boulevards, soon to vibrate with the daily crunch of goose steps.

Individuals were arrested for no apparent reason. People simply disappeared.

It didn't take long for a motorcade to blare its way through the gates of the duMont estate, casting the housekeeper, Madame Fournier, into a role as savior... a dangerous choice. Quickly she herded both children down a back stairway mocked by the delicate fragrance of two giant lilac bushes that concealed the door to the wine cellar, where it was dank, dark... and silent.

———

Jordana waved her children off to school and began tidying the den, gathering the last evening's newspapers, plumping sofa pillows, and removing all evidence of TV snacks. She chatted with herself.

"Great kids. And Matt's so wonderful... understanding, caring, protective, and fun. He supports all of my projects and compliments my achievements." No question, she deeply loved her family, and would behave like a she-bear if need be, to keep them protected and together.

Jordana went back to her typewriter. Maybe she was feeling obligated rather than inspired to write this book, agonizing with it to where she robbed it of its development. She was a writer, not a sob-sister. Why couldn't she simply delegate each memory to its chronological place? Perhaps she needed a good lead to get past the stubborn flashback that had likely distorted itself over the years.

But the pages stared back empty. No use, no use.

She needed a walk.

She made a face as she applied her lipstick and considered what the mirror had to say. Not too bad for forty-seven, she thought, pleased with the truth of that. She liked the chin that seemed shorter now with the resetting of her nose. Wishing to forget the accident, when she'd gone head-over-handlebars on her bike and broken her nose in two places, she was nevertheless pleased with the result. Surgery had heightened her cheekbones and erased a few frown lines. She lightened her hair, and the effect suited her.

Lending playfulness to it now with an Afro comb, she fluffed it out, and with a Frenchwoman's flair for accessories, tied her favorite scarf to her belt and was ready for what the day would bring.

She snapped a lid on a tall coffee and headed for the garage with her current column tucked under her arm, "How to wrestle your pillow into a good night's sleep," reported with the usual wry humor. She would drop it into the office before taking her walk. Then pick up her dress at the cleaners, to be ready for the birthday celebration that night.

———

Alain chose a black sweat suit for his morning run, and thought back to what took away his youth. War. Its menacing claws stretching and sucking... to twist, wrench, and violate, forging memories that were like pustules, relieved only slightly by recollections of their escape from the fear stalking Paris, and calmed somewhat by visions of underground sympathizers, the chains of their hands grasping and leading through endless dark forests with their strings of hiding places as numerous as beads on a strand.

Jordy. Throughout those silent journeys, shafts of moonlight would play upon a tearful face and raven waves framing dusky, frightened eyes. He would protect her. They would stay together... forever.

Alain and Jordana reached safety on a farm near the village of Amiens, owned by relatives of the Fourniers, where they remained hidden for weeks—until the sounds of battle drew near, and they were ordered to take separate routes.

Hand-in-hand, they climbed a hill behind the old farmhouse, where they could look upon the entire village and remain unobserved. For a time all was quiet. Clutching their necklets, they fit the stars together one last time. A warm sun, announcing its superiority over all, struck its golden light upon them.

How one moment could turn the world to darkness! How a word of farewell could banish youth! Gone from him. How could Jordy be wrenched from his life like that? She was still warm in his arms, but already he ached with an emptiness, the kind that instantly turns to anger. As the rumbling of artillery grew louder in the distance, young Alain's heart hardened to stone.

———

Sweeping away three decades, Alain relived Jordy's parting words: "You see, mon cœur, the sun sends us on our way with its promise."

He watched her pull away. "I will always love you, Alain duMont! We will find each other again. We must!" He saw her go, swallowed up in a black sedan.

But that was more than thirty years ago. Alain laced up his Rockports and sighed with futility. A worn-out, saturated story, cocooned in history; one tragedy out of millions that came out of the war.

He checked his itinerary. An appointment at one with an art dealer, then nothing. It was just past seven AM. He'd grab a cab and run the familiar trail, along the city's Harborfront. His plan was to spend a week: time, he hoped, to trace his latest lead.

The morning was heavy with mist when Jordana left the newspaper office and crossed Queen's Quay toward the open spaces bordering the lake, planned for the development of restaurants and antique markets to serve the trends of the nineteen-seventies.

It was still early, and pleasant to have the area to herself. The sun was struggling to gild a layer of cloud threatening rain. Jordana checked for the waterproof cape folded in her handbag, and walked on.

Eddies of curled leaves that had drifted around all winter, rattled against each other like fragments of china. The clouds began to blush; the city turned rosy with the reflections of dawn. Jordana's eyes circled the lake where a lone sailboat cut its thin wake, like a cone of thread unraveling on top of the water. High above, a flight of geese booked its destination north with "Awk! Awk!" and just above, "Greep-greep!" accompanied the very close sweep of a gull.

Noticing the flotsam along the shore, Jordana marveled at how a brew of dead fish and slimy weeds could possibly produce the fresh, pungent marine smell that she found appealing. She laughed at a cluster of birds, a half block away, falling over each other with alarm as a tall man tore through their ranks. Something about the way he ran… She turned her head and called upon her peripheral vision to track his approach.

Which was swift. She settled on the end of a lone bench and slipped the morning paper to her lap. There was no one else in sight. She would watch him run by.

An errant breeze tossed her hair like wheat, and the corners of the newspaper kept time to their rhythm. The bench teetered as the man planted one foot on the end of it. "I am... am taking... a... breath," he gasped with a light bow from the waist. "May I... share this place... pour un moment?"

Alone on the beach, Jordana should have been opposed to such friendliness, but she recognized the dialect and the words playing hide and seek with his English, and relaxed while maintaining her guard.

He had to be a dedicated runner. One could tell by the way he moved. He was comely, attractively tanned, sporting a full but well-shaped beard dotted with silver, which brought him to about her age, give or take a few years. He reminded her of someone... Gregory Peck in "Keys of the Kingdom!" Yes, that was it. Majesty in a sweat suit... not just because of his good looks and the color of his habit, but for his grace and noble carriage, which set him above plain gorgeous.

Sweat beaded the man's brow. With a continental air that screamed of a life of comfort and sophistication, he stepped to the side, repeated his bend-from-the-waist and smiled, "Okay?"

It was unwise, she supposed, to befriend a stranger on an empty stretch of beach, but there was something both innocent and heartening about the man's manner. So she simply commented, "As long as you feed them, they'll follow, you know," masking her caution by casually referring to a pair of waddling buddies snapping at the last crust of bread from the runner's fingers, their feathers ruffling with excitement.

"Do you mind the birds?" he queried with concern.

Jordana turned her gaze to look fully upon him. A network of wrinkles framed gray-blue eyes; wisps of gray woven into layers of fly-away hair, accented their depth. Her heart gave a leap and she stammered, "N-Not at all. Often my wish is to be one, just for a day... to... to simply take off over the bay!"

They both laughed at the rhyme. At the same moment the waterfront sharpened with the blues and greens of the June morning, and sunlight bathed the pastel cones of a row of lilac bushes with vivid mauve. Their scent was delicate and sweet. Alain looked directly at the woman beside him... twice... lowered his eyes, was silent, and gently shook his head as if to shake out an error.

"Oui, to be that gull up there!" he agreed, lifting his gaze to the sky. "To fly, to flee the pressures that challenge our chance to rest, to relax! Oui, Madame, I comprehend your wish!"

Jordana digested the soft baritone of the man's voice, nagging her with something that struggled to come alive....

"Mais, alors," he said, addressing the hungry flock. "When they see I have no more for them, they will become... how you say... friends in fair weather?".

Jordana bit her lip to control a smile. "Very close... fair-weather-friends," she corrected, remembering her own difficulty at first with expressions foreign to her. "Same as some people!" she laughed openly.

The man nodded. "Sad for them, no?" He turned his attention to the newspaper on her lap. "You are scanning the classified section. May I inquire, for a job, an automobile, or a person...? If my question is too personal, I will withdraw it," he added quickly.

A gray cloud blocked the sun for a moment, then sprinted off to chase some others. The symphonic blast of a lake freighter merged with the hum of an awakening city. "I don't mind," she answered, surprising herself. This stranger was reading her newspaper from his end of the bench as though he were perched on her shoulder! Maybe that explained his love of birds; he's a hawk! Her voice turned cool but polite. "I'm a freelance writer, always looking for inspiration. Tipped off years ago by one of my teachers to try the personal column when in need of an idea, I was just turning to it."

"Ah oui, a writer. One who enjoys her work, correct?" he responded with enthusiasm.

Discipline was abandoned. "Most certainly," Jordana answered eagerly. "But the marketing part is not so enjoyable. There's a profusion of writers out there, loads and loads of them much better than I."

"But you persist, no?" he softly interrupted, charmed by her lack of pretension, and calmed by a creeping quiet within.

Nagged once more by something begging for her consciousness, Jordana turned her head to the lake and watched the waves that were folding under themselves. With the soft winds coming off the water, a row of elm trees lining the shore was shaking off its morning laziness. Despite the breezes, Jordana was feeling a warmth. She turned to face him, "Oh, I keep at it," she answered. "I have a deadline looming for an article about teenagers becoming adults, baby-boomers leaving home... what is currently termed 'the empty nest syndrome.'"

"I know what empty nest means," the man responded, with a curt edge to his voice. "There are many kinds, many reasons."

Involvement in an issue she'd obviously touched upon did not appeal to Jordana. She chose another route. "Today, I have the urge to write fiction. Wrestling and agonizing over characters often serve to reveal oneself to oneself... frightening when grappled with, yet so worth the emotional risk." Was she sharing too much with this stranger... looking for a suggestion, a handhold from one who appeared so level? How silly! With the intention of parting company, Jordana folded the newspaper under her arm. But she didn't leave.

Like two figures activated by the same switch, they rose together from the bench. He was quiet. She was reflective. They wandered for a while in silence toward the part of the beach where the sand was like cinnamon and sugar. They rested their elbows on a large boulder flaunting its Pre-Cambrian patina, and watched a ferryboat bearing its cargo of city workers.

Alain broke the lull. "Expect reality to be more complicated than fiction."

His statement, more like a lecture, might have annoyed the writer had his tone not betrayed a sadness. Something rose up to forgive it. "I doubt if there's a story written that isn't based on a measure of truth," she ventured.

Desperate to hold her attention, Alain found himself hitting recklessly on a reply. "The personal column, numero huit... eighth on the list. Would you care to examine what you think of it for a topic?" Women are messy with newspapers, he scowled, as three sheets glided to the ground and would have scattered in the breeze had he not caught them. And for a writer, she was a very slow reader. "Something?" he demanded anxiously.

It was strange to experience a chill on such a warm morning. Jordana could scarcely breathe. Her face paled, and her response took a long break. She searched to uncover the youth beneath the silvery beard. She looked for her childhood in the depths of smoky eyes framed in faint creases. She spotted the chain at his neck, though the pendant was hidden. She checked the urge to grasp for hers, then remembered that she no longer wore it... having tucked it away on the day she married Matt.

All was quiet. I've always been good with faces, thought Jordana. Especially with those stored in such memories. Despite the years, she should have recognized the streak of hair that had always been unruly, the questioning lift of one eyebrow... his friendliness and his smile beneath the growth of beard. Yet recognition had to come from a newspaper notice held in the palm of her hand! Forgive me, Alain.

Alain! But she did not call out his name. Instead she thanked the light tracing the precious form that stood before her, as though it were God Himself. You are alive. You are well. And here we are, as though we'd arranged to meet. What brought you to this spot, on this, our birthday? What brought me? She lifted her gaze to heaven, but felt prompted to keep her silence.

There was splendor in Alain's smile. She ached to reach out, bury her face in his chest and feel his arms close around her. But lifetimes held her back—his and hers—lifetimes of intense searching for lost love and dreams of finding it; those adolescent dreams that had ruled her heart until she put them away as one would press a corsage in a book.

And now, she was unable to determine how the inside of his heart would accept reality. They had escaped the horrors of war, only to be faced decades later with the weeds of war... wild memories and built-up uncertainties... which could be exactly that: built up. Could this be the reason for her silence?

To give herself time, she said, in a voice she hardly knew, "Did you just come across this ad... or did you place it? " He hadn't recognized her. Time and surgery had done their work. She said no more, while her heart pounded inside her ribs.

Excitement swept briefly across Alain's face. He sensed a quick mind and possible interest. They walked on, found a fallen log and stopped there. "Oui, that short notice is my placing ...but the story is long," he answered. Dialogue with this writer was dispelling his sense of futility. It was like not being alone anymore; in generating the interest of another, that long-ago time was coming closer as he talked.

His voice was much deeper, but still like velvet. "Mais, as the saying goes, 'thoughts serve best when they are thoughts together.' I mean that my ability to find her must depend on her willingness to respond, not so? If she is committed to another life… which is most likely, she might not want to be found. Then I will never know, though I have spent so much of my life hoping for her."

Hoping for her. Jordana heard the words at the top of her head, and struggled with the feelings that loosened a string of memories. A fourteen-year-old in a party dress stitched with satin roses to add dimension to her bosom, and yards and yards of pleats to round out her hips. Their last dance.

And sweet recollections returned by themselves.

As they moved more slowly along the beach, Jordana searched for an excuse to make a quick departure, which she knew she should take, but didn't want. She paused to feign interest in the leap of a grasshopper and a flutter of butterflies. But she wasn't seeing them. Her unlocked past continued to journey her back, frame by frame.

———

She was six years old, left in the care of friends that day, when Mama and Papa were called away to her grandmother's funeral. "A car accident," was the heartfelt explanation for their total disappearance from her life. Alain took her hand as Mme. duMont instructed, "Jordy is your sister now." And to her, "This is your home, little one. You have our love. Do not be afraid."

The duMont family was loving and wise. Jordana grew up with little of the emptiness that can accompany the loss of both parents. They filled that void simply because Jordana was young enough to totally accept them. Though Catholic, they raised the girl in her family faith, with attendance at synagogue on Saturdays, and the study of Jewish history and culture after school during the week.

Consistent reminders of her father's patient teachings and her mother's devotion anchored memories of her parents. The little girl treasured pictures of a tall, sunny man who wove dreams with her at story time, and a pretty lady with a hearty laugh and love in her eyes. The meaning of those pictures might have faded in time, but for Grandmère who, when Maman duMont was taking her nap and Papa had retired to his study, took the children aside after tea one day to bestow The Gift. Jordana's half of the Star of David, recreated by this grandmother, would remain for the rest of her life, a tangible reminder of her roots.

Years afterward, she would vividly re-live the inevitable parting from Alain… together with visions of arduous treks through endless dark forests more terrifying without him, and other hands and faces revealing themselves in the shafts of light. She carried no identification on her person, no clues to her parentage. The pendant? She had been warned to leave the religious artifact behind, but had scooped it up at the last minute with her belongings. If anyone were to ask questions, she would simply say she'd found it. She had no doubt that, with Grandmere's benediction, it would continue to keep her safe.

Faith is power. It sustained her as the air filled with the threat of advancing artillery, and breathing became hushed. Desperate arms opened to them, so many faceless children holding onto each other to form a vulnerable chain. With faith, Jordy soothed the littlest ones. "Do not cry. Everyone is here to keep you safe," she promised, while witnessing one tearful wrench after another as families, many of whom would perish in the death camps, gave up their young to be shepherded away from the depravity in Europe.

Smuggled through paths ominous with weird shapes and shadows, the children emerged at last into vast open fields sloping to the Channel. With the boat in sight, they dashed and stumbled in their rush to reach it as though wild animals pursued them.

The crossing was smooth, but heavy with sobs and nightmares rejecting all attempts to comfort. In Southampton the weary troop was quickly herded onto a ship sailing for Canada, where the children would be placed with foster families for the duration of the war.

A Quebec family opened home and heart to the teenage Jewish refugee from Paris with two major partings in her young life, sensitively aware that Jordana was too old to be raised as a child, yet had to be as needy as one.

Jordana knew danger. She knew fear. She was afraid to shut her eyes at night, afraid of her memories, afraid to let them go. But she grew to love and trust both family and country that welcomed her so openly with their sincerity and warmth.

In time, the nightmares faded… except for the parting from Alain. With the threat of never seeing him again, Jordy grieved in the dark of every night. Was he alive or dead? He kept waving goodbye. Would she ever know?

She was one of those kids who loved school, and she did well. In her third year at Montreal's McGill University, she met Matthew Strauss and married him not long after graduation. The postwar years were full of growth and excitement. He had studied law; she, journalism. At first they traveled. Though much of Europe was still rubble, other countries beckoned, and the young couple backpacked for a couple of years before settling down.

Matt was sensitive and loving. Content with her life, Jordana nevertheless protected Alain's place in her thoughts. Where was he? Had he married? Did he still think of her? How could she help but think of him?

And now, a lifetime later, beneath a radiant sky, her words were withheld as his brought the years of separation to an end.

Jordana studied the horizon. When one has a dream that goes on forever, the dreamer can be totally unprepared if—when—it becomes a reality. Her lip quivered. Her heart was wrung, yet she couldn't find speech. Though she made every effort to discipline her face, she was powerless to block the tenderness that flooded from her heart into eyes catching the sunlight on raven lashes.

A team? But that was so very long ago. On accepting their pendants, they'd promised to stay a team. But teams disperse, people change and need to go on. Am I letting the team down, Grandmère? Or is it time for that, too, to change? Guide me with your wisdom.

Worried about the woman's lengthy silence, Alain felt compelled to break it. "Does my story inspire you some?"

His concern beckoned caution. Was he picking up on something? Her breathing remained labored. He had gone to such lengths to find her—surely he deserved an answer! But think again… think about what a reunion could bring.

When the war exhausted itself, Jordana could no longer pretend that the parting was not forever. During her first years in Canada, the Red Cross attempted to locate the duMonts, but she received no word from or about them. The memory of Alain waving goodbye had stamped itself on the final page of her youth so that whenever she tried to write about her last years in Paris, she was unable to leaf back from that memory, or ahead to those that followed.

Guilt. She had been swept to safety, had left Alain behind, and for that he might have been killed. Clearly it appeared that she had abandoned all those who loved her, not knowing if they would survive; and if they hadn't, it had to be because they had rescued a Jewish girl. A death sentence.

Without fully understanding why she'd had to leave the country and Alain did not, she had obeyed. Later she'd learned how dangerous it was to be Jewish in Nazi dominated France. Because of the love and concern of those who'd protected her, she was safe in Canada, and over the years a growing awareness of the dangers she had escaped fed the sense of guilt as effectively as water fills a sponge, until her mind had become saturated with it.

With understanding taking shape, some of the lead lifted from her heart.

It occurred to her that she had always been very protective of Alain when they were children. It seemed important now to ask herself why. Because of her deep love... and an eccentricity in him that she had sensed needed defending.

His insatiable curiosity. He could never know enough. He would continue questioning and questioning until people would lose patience and she would spring to his defense. She suspected that he might be feeding that need now.

A lovers' reunion? Her cry was silent. Dearest Alain, too late for that. There can be only one waltz; we cannot choreograph another. Impetuous conduct would doom them both; though the link between them had weathered more than three decades, it was too late to renew it unrestrained.

She had to surrender the youthful romance... and, with hope of setting the old ones free of guilt, create new lines to be written. She would always be in love with Alain, but their love had to survive one more parting, because once again, there was no place for just the two of them.

Captivated by the writer's deep reflections, Alain continued to feed them. "My parents were killed in the war." For a reason not known to himself, he left out parts about harboring a Jewish girl, and the tip-off by a neighbor to the Gestapo shortly after Mme. Fournier and the children escaped.

"In Amiens, I joined with the French underground; then after the war, gathered together what was left of properties and funds, and re-established the family business, all the while searching for Jordy through phone calls, letters, cables to various agencies. Many records were lost in that war. Still, I could not imagine that she had not survived. I tried to forget, though I knew I never would.

"Her whereabouts remained elusive, until two months ago when I was informed of the name of the vessel that carried her to these shores. Through that information, though somewhat complicated, I have finally traced her to this city. But the last mile always seems the longest, so I must not get discouraged."

"Did you re-establish the business immediately after the war, with no years in university, as, uh, many young people had?" She almost added, "As you'd planned?" but thankfully checked herself.

"With the help of the Fournier family, I was able to complete university, while they, as you say, 'minded the store.' The Fourniers, I must tell you, were honored at the Yad Vashem Holocaust Memorial in Jerusalem, for their bravery in the face of personal danger in wartime.

"I married... was married for twelve years, and am a divorced father of three girls.

"I could not get Jordy out of my mind; all the while, thoughts of never seeing her again continued to distress me." Alain related the dream. "She is near. I am certain of it. But I feel locked up. I am not sure what finding her will mean."

Jordana watched a spider spinning its web between two tree limbs, where an ill wind could destroy it with one gust, and wondered why God would commission His subjects to deeds that proved so futile. A knot of sorrow stilled her voice. This man standing before her occupied a total place in her past, but what place in her present? "Is there no one you care to share this with?" She heard herself ask.

DuMont raised an eyebrow and smiled. "I just did."

Her heart lurched. She swallowed. "Well yes… but I meant …."
They arrived back at the bank of lilacs. Their heady perfume rolled
back the span of time unable to be shared. As the past was wrenched
out in painful segments laboring to come together, warnings flashed
themselves across Jordana's innermost thoughts like words on an
electronic billboard: *Say nothing; he will not link you with that child-
woman.* But was this brave… or cowardly? Was this noble, or brutal? At
last she said, "You are sure you have traced the woman to this city?"

"If you would like me to remit to you all information, I will be happy
to," Alain responded with enthusiasm. "I will send the information, if
you wish to write the story. I am sure that Jordy has changed some, as
have I… just as I am certain that she could not help but be my same
beautiful Jordy."

Your beautiful Jordy will have cut, lightened and tipped her curls
ash blond. The resetting of a broken nose will have shifted her features.
Her figure will be different—thankfully still slim, but different. Her
accent will have disappeared, along with all gestures that might reveal
her country of origin.

Alain… you are living in a different world.

"Regardez: my key to her!" he exclaimed with the interruption of a
fresh thought. Extracted from the neck of his sweatshirt, the whirling
pendant caught the sun's majesty… as it had that day, high on a hill
overlooking the village of Amiens. "She would have the other half…
with my image. You see?"

"Yes, I see," whispered Jordana, wondering what her life would have
been like had there been no war. But there had been, and it exacted
many a price, in numerous cases cutting to pieces the choice, the right,
or the wisdom to reclaim… anything.

What if she were to tell Alain who she was …only to throw their
lives into upheaval. She would not, though the longing for him clung
to her heart.

What was real? What was true? Tough and sensible, was she not?
As if to emphasize her confusion, a maverick wind converged on her
helter-skelter thoughts, to dance them about like the tree tops that
whipped back and forth in answer to a sudden weather change.

To interrupt the pause that filled both pair of eyes with their
separate torment, Jordana undid the scarf from her belt and tied it

over her hair. "Do you write at all?" she asked Alain. Her heart spun with memories of the poetry that had tumbled so easily from his pen a lifetime ago.

Alain watched her tuck some errant curls into her scarf. Without taking his eyes off her, he appeared to think about that question. He paused for an answer, regarded the woman by his side and lifted a brow. "Years ago, as you say... with 'the inspiration.'"

Poetry that she could recite back to him, line by line. A story she could retell, word for word... current now, in these last hours.

One didn't need to remain in the thick of war to be hurt by it. Those lost in its holocaust had been her family, her strength. Though waged in fields thousands of miles away, the evils of war had followed her across the ocean to rob her of the power to express them.

How many thousands of refugees were suffering guilt simply because they had survived? For Jordana, the inability to totally accept freedom had blocked the telling... moving her away, keeping her apart within its crippling fist.

Write objectively? There's no such thing; and it's the motive that decides the morality, she determined, with the release of guilt opening the hidden recesses of her soul. I still love him, dearly and with passion—and I'm not afraid of that.

"The promise to Grandm—your grandmother," she stumbled, "you have kept it, you know, Alain."

His gaze pressed deeply into hers and lingered there for more than a moment. He took a deep breath and replied, "Are you trying to suggest, Madame, that I should leave things as they are?"

"I shouldn't wish to tell you what to do," answered Jordana, tearing her gaze from his to pick up a pinecone and run her fingers over it. She could tell him that love wasn't always in the winning. It often meant walking away. She could say that they must put the past with its bruises behind them. But the words stuck in her throat.

There would be pain in the writing, as there is pain in birth. Jordana considered Alain's involvement with her in the creation of the book; weighing how much, when inevitably tying in her own feelings, might be too much ....

How amazing this love between a boy and a girl that is timeless! She nodded her head. "I think," her voice took on strength as she held tightly to the folded newspaper, now dear with its notice in the personal column. "I know that I can write this story." Pain faded from her eyes, and they filled with promise.

Alain nodded sagely and plunged on as though he hadn't heard her. "You see, I needed to find my love again. I needed to know above all else that she is well." His tone was strained, but shades of sorrow had cleared from his face.

Jordana noted the shift in his statement to past tense. What you needed, Alain, was someone to share in it... so you could retire the past to its proper place. It was her turn to interrupt: "And you have been convinced that wearing the pendant all these years has helped to keep her so. That is beautiful."

Alain looked directly into the face of the woman, and peace softened the lines beneath his eyes. "You have a delicate mind." With but a moment's hesitation, he added, "If you write this, I have the trust that you will bring to light a... superb rendering, as warm and compelling as... this sun at noon." Jordana looked up. All threats of a storm had scattered.

Alain's mention of the sun at noon was like a thunderclap. It was the same sun, but it shone differently this time, as if to acknowledge and to cap a promise, and she could barely respond. "Even though..."

"There seems to be no ending?"

A soft nod.

"For some, the war is not over. And love? That kind never ends. But I understand your meaning. In such an event, you have my blessing... to finish the story as you think it must end."

There is such vulnerability in love, Jordana concluded, as she struggled to grapple with what lay before her, both stressful and heart-heavy from all that they had been to each other. Captured in another time, Alain might again be a youngster looking for a teenager with long dark tresses and a Scarlett O'Hara waistline. A sure sign that memories must remain memories.

For instance, that moon up there... meant to light up the night. Though it can be seen in daylight as well, its function fades. So it is with all things touched by change. Is this not sensible?

As they walked toward the parking lot, Jordana looked to the lake where the sailboat had been. Its wake hadn't disappeared; it was still there, but in someone else's line of sight, no longer in hers. The vessel had moved on. If it were to turn about, its path would cut through the original wake and change it. This had to be the wise way to reason.

And this newspaper rolled tightly in her hand is no longer just a newspaper. It depends on the part it plays and for whom: for some, an editorial, an exposé or a lifeline; tomorrow a fly swatter, a paper hat, or used to wrap a catch! Those are truths: each truth has its time and place,... and when time for it is over, it is over.

Jordana shared an affinity with the lake, especially on a breezy day, when its playful surf had always beckoned to her with its caprice. But now, it was rushing and sighing, "What is lost today, will reappear tomorrow... with changes. Go on... go on... you need to move on..."

Her voice was little more than a whisper as she toed a shallow pocket in the path. "Wherever she is, sir, I am sure that woman still has love for you. How could she not, with all that you shared! Yours is an agonizing story, but gently magnificent, and if you will allow me, I will attempt to tell it that way... with Jordy's torment on a parallel with your own.

"But because love challenges with its various choices, the story will have to write its ending. If you will allow that, it will. For me, it is necessary to leave my readers secure in the knowledge that you will not endlessly keep looking. Can we agree on that?"

With a significant pause, Alain drew himself up in a courtly manner. "Oui, Madame." His smile brightened and he fished into his wallet. "Here is the card for my business in Paris. But, I haven't asked, how will the book be signed?"

Jordana pressed his card as one would lips to be kissed, and reached for her own scrolled with her pen name. "How about a book by Alain duMont with a little help from Joyce Douglas?" she said lightly, extending her hand.

He held it and was still. "I cannot ask for more. I look so forward." He consulted his watch, "Ah! It is already afternoon!" He bowed with her hand in his. "With regret I must make my departure."

The pressure of his grasp made her tremble. She regarded his wonderful face with painful thoughts asserting themselves. Among them: someone else will love him... differently.

Through all of life's difficulties, she had called upon faith, and she did so now. She would look upon this day as a healing, the day she began to forgive herself with freedom found to recapture her life. She breathed in a promise of renewal, and sensed Alain's sudden strength, his startling support, akin to being wrapped in his arms. Ah, the body might age, she reckoned, but the heart never does!

As they walked slowly toward her car, the effects of parting once more stabbed like the blade of a knife. "Goodbye," she said, easing away from their simple handshake.

———

"Has everything been satisfactory, sir?" the room clerk hovered, concerned with Monsieur duMont's sudden departure.

"Très bien. Excellent, but my business here has ended."

Or it's just begun. That funny little way she had of saying her s's... how she cocked her head to one side to listen... the inflections in her voice, responses in her eyes. Wisps of the familiar that fluttered around inside him until she dropped his name before he handed her his card, and he was sure. She is beautiful. Changed, but as beautiful; this time with refinement. A woman. Someone else's.

As the 747 lifted and circled for direction, Alain looked upon a city bathed in sunlight, and ran his fingers through the chain around his neck. "As you predicted my dearest Jordy, we did meet again, and under the same golden sun. Alors, we will keep it in the writing. You and I, Jordy, together in the writing. Always."

The Paper Boat

THE CHAMBER DARKENED AND tipped from corner to corner. An angry room, like a clumsy cube tossed by a raging sea. From a window high above, a shaft of light floated along webs of mist seeping through its tightly-closed sash, with gauzy shards breaking away like predators prowling for their target, to spiral toward a young woman crouched in a corner in fear.

The room was chalk white and frigid, with no fittings other than the stretcher beside her and a row of them along a wall. The girl struggled to comprehend. What strange force dragged her through those double doors? A force beyond her control, or her own damned curiosity? Never had she found herself in such a peck of trouble!

Her mind spun. The crypt-like enclosure groaned and trembled like the very earth was crumbling.

Suddenly it stopped.

Slowly the room tipped back. As though no quake had occurred, all was still. And bit by bit, recollections of an ER reporter with a habitual lack of discipline, led by a compulsion to lay eyes on a killer—to stand this close to him—crept back into focus.

With her wings so clipped, the quandary was not so much about what had enticed the girl in, but about how she was to get out.

Nothing made sense. Searching for anything that might, her eyes traveled from the cadaver to the row of them swathed in spotless linen, angle-parked at what appeared to be some kind of loading station.

The lady reporter held onto a newspaper clipping as one would a key card: "*AFTER WEEKS OF INTENSE PURSUIT, CABBIE SHOOTER FINALLY GUNNED DOWN BY POLICE.*" Data in hand now trembled with unbridled fright. It had undoubtably lured her in here. But it wasn't programmed to get her out.

No longer the rookie of a year ago, Robin Dinofrio, whose beat was the hospital ER, was earning recognition for a style that partnered straight reporting with social conscience. "Unusual," her editor had commented, "but you've got something that people want to read!"

For that, Robin credited her writing teacher, who had groomed her for more than straight reporting, "You have a way with words, Robin. Use it. Get out there. Research… again and again. And don't forget your own point of view." A lesson learned, now cloaked with regret.

Convinced that there was more to this morning's headline, Dinofrio had set out to discover it. But pursuit of that extra had landed her here, as though in another time and place, surreal and terrifying.

———

It all began with her tendency to be headstrong, that had somehow got out of control. Following the trolley to the morgue, she'd stood outside its double doors and considered what might be gained by entering, when a sudden energy that seemed to come from nowhere powered her across the threshold. A most irrational occurrence; not one this reporter had ever before experienced! When the doors clicked shut with a loud metallic sound, her remaining fortitude dissolved in a centrifuge of panic. Despite one desperate shove after another, the doors refused to open.

She was locked in.

Confusion ferried dismay. Alarm surged through her like cold steel. The staff had seen her enter the cooler. Why were there no answers to her calls for help, the pounding of her fists?

Change of shift. That had to be it. But… if there were no further admissions, she might have to remain all night… in the cooler… with them! Robin's eyes tested the lineup steeped in eerie light, ashen and still.

Her skin pricked and tightened. She took deep breaths in an attempt to control romping heartbeats and jellied limbs struggling to rise from the concrete floor. With no way out, to take her… where?

In fear, Dinofrio succumbed to the quivers that ran through her body, rendering her helpless. Her head whirled; she sank back on her heels and covered her face with her hands.

A rustle brought a rush of air, an icy caress. With it, a strong odor: gun smoke! Robin detected some movement. It seemed she was not alone. Looking about, she saw no one, and heard nothing. But—there it was again, another stir. And colder.

Her cry was faint. "Who's there?" In answer, the snick-snick of tree branches brushed at the window as they looped and swayed in the wind.

And a hollow voice thundered, "Come out of your corner! You are seen!"

Which drove Robin further into it. Through lips that hardly moved, she stammered, "Wh-where a-are y-you?"

Except for her thumping pulse, silence prevailed. The girl's eyes strained through the mist. If this was some trick, there was no laughter.

The smell grew more pungent, the chill icier. The rustling strengthened like crackling glass. A torrent of rain dashed at the window. Tree limbs leapt and arched, their shadows terrorizing the room.

From her position on the floor, Robin looked up to locate the voice. Through the darkness, her eyes singled out a lumbering shape on the stretcher closest to her, twisting its body and sniffing at the air like some animal. With the speed of an arrow, a pair of tormented, blazing eyes confronted her through the haze.

The voice fired like a cannon. "You said I was vile! 'A monstrous distortion of humanity,' you wrote!" It had one green eye and one yellow eye. Its bindings were smeared with blood. And on its head, a sudden ring of... flames?

Robin froze with horror. This had to be an illusion. *It's scowling at me, yelling at me.... It's that murdering stiff! A moving, talking, supposed-to-be-dead stiff!*

Posed like some sultan, the creature on the gurney rose through a cloud that washed its head in milky light. "You may well cower in your corner, lady! So, 'death is too good' for me, eh?" Roars of manic laughter, "Caw! Caw! Caw!" bounced from every wall.

Crowned with spitting incandescence, the mummy-shape crackled and crooked its burnished head while croaking its furious admonitions. Its eyes, oscillating in their dusty pouches, sharpened snake-like into Robin's that were veiled in terror. "No!" she sobbed. "Someone... please!"

"No one here but you and me... and them!" snapped the cadaver, pointing its ashen chin toward the lineup. "And they have gone on."

"You're dead. You know you are! I-I saw you there, d-dead." Robin's wail, in its shakiness, hardly seemed like her own.

Its mouth gave an icy twist. Its answer was a growl not human. "Not yet, girlie. This beast dies slowly. Mortally wounded, it continues to haunt." Its voice clanged like a bell in a fog. "Revenge comes next. This time from the Reckoning Zone!"

Gripped in this nightmare, the girl attempted to marshal threads of logic. She managed to piece together that as of now, Robin Dinofrio, ER reporter for the *City News*, sat huddled in a corner of the hospital morgue, blabbering through chattering teeth at a ghost stationed on a gurney squeeking like hell on wheels a few feet above her, where, as one impatient to jump off, it was making slow but determined progress in its attempt to writhe and roll out of its bindings....

She rediscovered some of her voice. "Re-ck-ckon-n-ing... Z-zone?"

"Where even a bad person has a right to be left alone!" The cadaver regarded her with distaste. "Where the trip from Life to Death is not as quick as everyone surmises, though the body might be cold.

"I was promised solitude!" it squawked. "I was working hard at making the complete Crossing when your irksome condemnations interrupted my process!"

It had a sound. Snarling and threatening; the sound that comes out of a loose cannon with serious issues, whose solutions are determined at the end of a strong arm—or weapon.

It had eyes, furious eyes, as terrifying as those behind the weapon at the end of the arm.

Yet this setting—not a dark alley or a school corridor, nor any of the currently not-so-safe places she might have touched on in her reporting, then absently filed away—hardly fit a crime! This was the morgue, the curtain call of human existence, where all actors, good or bad, permanently surrendered their occupation!

Or did they?

It stretched. It assumed an alarming shape, arms flung backward, perpendicular to its torso, and chest lifted to arch its back. Its head pivoted toward the reporter. With a war whoop, it shrilled, "What's so upsetting about those doors? Everybody locks their doors in this millennium! Here, they lock after what is judged an intrusion."

Hours ago, wasn't it, since her life had begun to tilt along with this room... since she'd bravely stood on the threshold and been forcefully welcomed? Fortified by how a bullet could transform a devil into a harmless nonentity, she'd boldly throttled her judgments over the powerless form. "Murderer! Death *is* too good for such as you, you fiend!" Loathing for a crime so extreme had spun itself into a tornado that could, at times, be Robin. That was before she discovered that the doors had locked behind her.

Now, it seemed, *she* was the one being judged.

Robin pressed her fingers to her eyelids to banish the fiend's merciless glare. Not unlike that of some surveyor, its gothic posture swung to where she cowered, and it stormed, "Get up off your knees!"

Under the lingering pressure of her fingers, Robin's eyes fuzzily attempted to focus on the thing sitting higher than herself. "I m-must be in the wrong place! But I'll be happy t-to leave!" Unable to rise, however, she remained where she was, her kneecaps in pain from the floor.

The small chamber echoed like a rotunda with the dead man's reverberations. "As it happens, you are certainly correct! Not only do you meddle with my Reckoning, but you are also trespassing!" Enraged, it slammed a hand to its head, which served to rattle the sparks spilling crazily from its phosphorescent crown.

"R-r-ight!" gasped the girl. "It must be... very unc-c-common for anyone to ch-choose to be i-i-n this place."

Its brows crossed like daggers; its eyes plowed into hers. "But didn't you just choose to do that, girl? Uncommon, you say? This place? Caw! Caw! Not so very. It's common enough... everyone gets to be here... eventually. Caw! Caw!"

Robin could not put a color to the face that rippled its ravaged features in time with its sulphurous crown. Neon red one moment, shadowed in gray the next, to be sullied in sickening chartreuse as it clattered its torso toward the window heavily stained with streaks of rain and mud. Twisting back to her, its face now white as parchment, its mouth curled with contempt as it shifted to inch its way nearer.

With nowhere to move, Robin stifled a cry and her chest tightened. Clearly, the killer's evil was not done.

She regarded the looming apparition with stricken syllables, "Go back!... I won't, I promise I won't interrupt your r-rest— uh, your process— any more! Oh please go back! I w-won't bother you... ever again!" Courage was discovering its limits.

Wildly, Robin's eyes tore into every corner of the room looking for another exit. A hush fell. It knew what she sought. She knew it knew as pain flared from her door-pushing wrist. Further efforts to get out, she was being warned, would be futile.

The chill in her spine resumed its journey and her flesh began to creep. It wasn't real, this. At any moment the creature would disappear in a vaporous puff. Robin shut her eyes and reopened them. Still there.

Was this some kind of ritual, or could it be a rehearsal for something? Maybe she'd suffered a blow on the head! In this holding place for the dead, where everything but her own attire was white, Robin found an excuse to be gone. *Red outfit: unacceptable and disrespectful. Even this monster would agree.*

She looked up hopefully for a response. There wasn't one.

Wake up from your delirium, girl. If someone were to suddenly turn on the lights, all this would probably disappear. If she hid herself, buttoned away inside herself, the creature might be unable to find her. *What a dumb thought!* Its shark-like gaze plucked her from the shadows like a fish would its bait.

She had to be in hell.

It grit its teeth. "You listen!" Two eyes glowed red, so coupled together as to scowl at one another beneath its twisted brows. Sharp cheekbones narrowed knife-like to craggy hollows beside a mouth sulky with a petulant droop. It looked as old as eternity.

Its next sound echoed like a war cry: "It's Judgment Day!... Mine. And you have arrived in time for it!" Eerie strips of moonlight marched the figure's grisly shadow along a back wall, resulting in two heads that loomed and quivered, four hands and four fists that clenched and unclenched. There was no other light except for the strange halos surrounding two withering skulls.

The gallop of Robin's heart tramped its way to her head.

Despite her warning, her vision strained in search of a Push-to-Open button. *Every pair of hospital doors has its button, pad or switch... on a wall behind the doors, or somewhere nearby.... But there's nothing like that here!*

And she heard herself beg, "Whatever you want! What *do* you want?"

Spank! Spank! Like it was some kind of count-down, the fearful spectacle smacked its trolley. "I was shot dead in the street!" it hissed and jolted as one sitting on a bed of spikes. "Twenty hours ago, earth time... twenty years in this Reckoning Zone!"

That place again. Madness! Here in the news, right here in my hand, is the madness that landed him here.

Like a trumpet blast, the voice of the cadaver blared from all corners of the chamber. "We're all insane! No matter in what state—rage, love, lust, greed—manic or depressed— all humans live with their own kind of madness!"

"But I only thought—I didn't say—"

It swallowed her words and viciously spit them back. "You! Don't! Have! To! Say! You might as well speak up; I hear your every thought... every single one."

Robin felt her face flush and her lungs struggle for air. By now she was convinced that she'd lost her mind to this fiend who was taking possession of it.

Inflated with its power, the corpse fastened her with a ghastly grin. "Before I'm interrupted again by your ignorance, I'm informing you that I've already spent twenty years in what is called the state of 'Self Awareness' in this damnable place. I'm told for the crimes I have committed, I've gotta spend five times that—a hundred Reckoning years, they call it—in Learning, Contemplation and one more... oh yeah, Evaluation... before I'm allowed to Cross Over."

But this guy just died yesterday! It paused to allow her that thought, then triumphantly carried on, "In this Zone, one Earth minute is a year; twenty Earth minutes become twenty years; five times twenty, one hundred years, and feel as long in time in here as they would on Earth. Do you follow? What's ten hours for you is ten years for me... in the Reckoning."

Though faint with disbelief, Robin's spirit hadn't totally disappeared. Embers flared and her eyes grew bright. "I cannot imagine you honestly judging yourself... n-no matter how many years you invest!"

Another hideous laugh. "When your turn comes, baby, we'll check on you!" Its tone leveled but the blood-red eyes remained the same. "Like I told ya, everyone passes through here. Some have to commit longer, is all. See that guy over there with the black moustache like a postage stamp?" Robin shrank from the image that appeared suddenly on a wall. The voiceover contributed by her luminous neighbor sprang from there: "Hitler, they call him. That devil's been wandering around in here for thousands of Reckoning years, and will be for all Eternity. He'll never be granted a Cross-Over. And judgin' by the latest news, there's more like him comin' up! Can ya beat that? Battle after battle, and nobody's learned nothin'. So what's a little street war? I got to thinkin'…. Anyway, Time-Full-of-Nothin' in the Reckoning Zone, with no end in sight, is the Ultimate Punishment. Worse than Hell!

"And those brainwashed fellas in pursuit of the pleasures of the hereafter? What a brainless, fucking waste!" Its sheets ruffled with the absurdity of such a concept. "To answer you, America, all Facts are tabulated here. Everyone's Facts. There can be no alterations of Facts!

"I have no choice but to be suspended in this Zone where I must evaluate with Honesty the deeds I have performed." Its sound wavered, its echo died, and it hung its head.

To discipline her mind from running further amuck, Robin struggled and won. One thought at a time. Honesty from this thing was hard to accept, and the lack of logic fanned her courage. *How can evil be classed as "deeds?" Unacceptable!* She lashed back with ragged breath, "Evaluate? You, who took a life so easily! To have committed such a crime, you must be bereft of any ability to evaluate, sir!" There it was… she'd given the stiff a title!. Would that cancel out her refusal to think of it as ever being human?

"Shhi-i-i-i-t-t-t! You insolent broad!" With waning regard for her own safety, Robin had managed to provoke a resurgence of rage at the end his short fuse. His eyes ran redder than a bloodied river. A hideous grin displayed a mouthful of crumbling grinders. "For the purpose of your column, America, I suggest that you start with this in mind. There are only two senses in this Zone. Two. A sense of Right and a sense of Wrong… but not necessarily in your terms."

"Oh, I do believe that!" she cut in, shooting her gaze straight into his. "And my name is not America!"

Ignoring her objection, he continued his reign of terror. "Here we must face Truth, America! There can be no cheating, no distortions, no absence of Truth."

Insane!

"Nevertheless what you must hear!"

Robin detected more than anger. The ghoul was expressing a need. She bristled.

"That's an assumption," he corrected.

"And what does that mean?"

Wasn't she testy, though? "I am not in this room for this particular experience, America! I assumed *you* were!"

"For argument's sake," she snapped, "let's say I'm not having a good one!"

"Get this right, baby.... For argument's sake, let's imagine you're here to learn something—or more clearly, let's assume *you*, who dropped in on *me*, are therefore under *obligation* to learn! What's more, let's conclude, America, that you will put your learning to some *use!*"

He was right. She'd chosen this road. But where had it taken her? *If I were to write about this, they'd lace me up in a straight jacket in five—*

"Results come from Choices made on Earth," he chose to continue. "Choices influenced by Circumstances and People. Get that through your pretty head! And I'm just comin' to Checks and Balances... ah, and Justice!" With his growing irascibility his static increased. "Stripped of worldly goods, status, and power," he cackled, "all Souls are judged equally, and must Reckon under the same Rules!"

Hah! Sinner turned preacher! What a crock of—

"Go on an' judge me... any way you like," he grinned slyly, reminding Robin once again of his entitlement to her thoughts. "I'm not rakin' in a fortune performin' some religious act for you. Some of those guys who do, end up puttin' a lot of time in here, prowling the Zone in search of Redemption, comin' to terms with their ordinariness, no matter how powerful they seemed on Earth. Material rewards don't exist here: one can only score by facing the past squarely. That is called Reckoning, America. Some cannot ever; for those who can, it might take longer than life on Earth."

His savage expression turned baleful. "It's bitter work. We worry our minds... right to the cartilage. We study the teachings of those who have gained back their Souls, enough to Travel Through. There's a reference Library in here, where we're compelled to spend at least three hours each day in more than one area of Study. I've read through stacks of Books since you decided to drop in. I converse with a growing Knowledge, you see. "

How does one rationalize an encounter like this? Robin agonized. *A dead murderer using his trolley as a lectern, like some philosophical troubadour?* But anger triumphed over confusion. She made two fists, and despite the fury hammering away at her heart, fought to keep her voice level. She stood up.

"Well now, looky here! It's on its feet!"

"In case you haven't observed," sniped Robin, "I'm the only one in here 'on its feet'! And while we're on the subject of me: why, may I ask, do you keep referring to me as 'America'?"

He howled. She crammed herself back into her corner. "You are a journalist, girl! You influence America's thought processes! To do this you expose yourself to all sorts of situations in order to write what you judge to be truth! You like to think you're fearless? Rather, you are heedless in your self-righteous pursuit of justice! But we'll get to that later...."

Pinning her with a prismatic gaze, he rasped on, "I've just completed some research on you.... You are loyal. You love your country. You get along with your neighbors most times. You make quick decisions—a characteristic, I must say, which does not always speak well for your wisdom. However, a lot of generous people are heedless.... You are an idealist, America! But you are caring and open to learning.... You are free to write what you believe. You are America!"

And for tomorrow's headline? HOTSHOT JOURNALIST IS FLATTERED TO DEATH IN A MORGUE....

On that note, he vanished.

Where to now?

"Not only are we given license to read into your mind; we also have the greater power of vision!"

So it's hide and seek! Robin spun around and found him pasted to a wall. Or was that maniacal pose just another shadow?

With a smirk he broke into the silence. "This happens to be Vision," he reported through the milky light.

This happens to be warped, drug-induced trash, I'll bet!

His eyes ignited and his tongue seared, "Aren't we smart!" With a grasp on each side of his stretcher, he attempted to straighten. His knuckles were large and bony, surely to be avoided.

Discipline. Think, rather than act. From one with his background and no apparent conscience, his rationale seems too thought-out, and hardly fits my concept of the criminal mind. No doubt about it, there'll be more mischief in this unlovely chamber!

Suppose... suppose... I've somehow met my Maker, and this cooler is really my last trip... and I'm part of the lineup on my way out, with no recollection of what snuffed out my life! Think about it, Robin: when death is instant, are people granted a final moment of awareness?

What if this is not dialogue, but some kind of Crossing for me, too! To draw upon some applicable knowledge, Robin mentally searched into past experience as a writer, but came up with a zero. Science fiction had never been her area of interest.

She shuddered. Might the words of that venomous beast be her eulogy? Had she lapsed into some kind of mortal funk, or was she not going anywhere but insane? Slowly, Robin took stock of the bodies lining the far wall. Among them, perhaps a few unacknowledged champions, all having influenced other people's lives, now shrouded and waiting for admittance to the final show of all.

Her roommates? Should she count herself among them? Wishing she could be somewhere else, she stood before the ghost. His face was like crumbling plaster. *Okay, I haven't uttered a word about what I'm thinking. So, if you're so tuned-in, answer me, you devil!*

Like it was a receiving line he planned to introduce, he waved his bindings toward the string of stretchers and wailed, "I would like to. But you don't *Listen* like they do!"

This time she didn't run back to her corner. *Dead people don't do this. One cannot talk to dead people. He is talking to me. So it's true, I've got to be dead, too!*

As though she'd just pressed *play*, his response was immediate. "You aren't dead. Not yet anyway!... I get some choices up here, see? To frighten you to death, or to transmit to you directly what I learn, as I learn... and why I need to." Stiff fingers fumbled as though for an inner pocket. "If I had a cigarette, I'd offer you one... to relax you while we go through this next exercise."

The impulse to sneeze away his suggestion was irresistable. "Achoo!"

"G'zunt."

"Fuck off!" Anger unabated flashed through Robin. She drew herself up. "If you know as much as you pretend to, you ought to be aware that I gave up smoking months ago!"

His lip curled. As swift as a whip, a leer cut across his hideous features. Zig-zagging pupils lit up like instruments on a flight deck. "Pretend? Why the hell would I pretend when truth itself can be so outrageous! As for you... I know more about you than you know about me, America!"

Sharing cigarettes. Sharing *anything*... with this monstrous bird? Generosity was most certainly out of place here. She preferred the wiseacre attitude that fit his profile; one she could anticipate and believe. He was watching her closely. "So now that you know everything there is to know about me, would that be my cue to depart?" she snapped.

"Wouldn't you just hope! Unlike me, you've got a life to improve, sweetheart. In your bailiwick, reporting how you deem fit—with social awareness, tenacity, wit, or even humor—you've proven yourself to be a pretty good journalist. You reach a lot of people. We should give it a whirl... to reach some of those people with what is here before us, don't you think?"

A whirl? With a stiff on my dance card? Robin threw back her head to focus a look of repugnance fully upon him, to defeat with a laugh such a suggestion.

It was she who was defeated.

Ravaged by rage, his voice took off like a fire alarm."My oh my!" he shrilled, while all parts of him fought to move together, lifting and folding. Just as suddenly, his tone weakened like one drowning in grease. "Nothin' can pain this pig anymore... not anymore. Sorry, lady. Moreover, I'm allowed one contact with the world I left—only one," he bleated. "Just like the single phone call to one's lawyer... before I'm trundled on."

"Why pick on me?"

"Let's just say, sweetheart, that not many others stop to chat."

He faded into darkness, with only a hint of light remaining in his crown. Willing herself not to weep, Robin appealed in a small voice searching for reason. "What is the point of my being here? How long must I be in this place with you?"

"For as long as I need you to be."

With diminishing hope, Robin regarded the hollow echoes of their dialogue, with their weird exchange of words and passions, as if they were lines in a play.

Based on what?

Confusion struggled for direction. For some puzzles, she knew, there were no answers. For many, she'd learned that answers were feared, disregarded or denied. Then there were those followed by the need for more questions and answers. Robin remained as silent as the thoughts that were raking her mind.

As a departure terminal from a muddled world, a more unlovely station could never be imagined. Robin stole furtive glances along the covey of strangers, and froze as the next notion thundered into her head. *What if all are Eternal wanderers, and I am surrounded by... The Forces of Evil!*

As if to shake the wheels off his stretcher, the dead man clamored, "You don't have to be evil to have bad karma, America!" Toad-like, he shaped himself into a triangle. His distorted features transmitted waves of anguish. "Nothing can justify my action. You are right about that. I didn't intend to kill that cabbie; I just wanted to rough him up because of what he did. As a present to myself... for the part he played in robbing me of the little bit of goodness in life that was mine.

"I escaped the scene of the crime, but I couldn't get away from the running, forever running... dodging the cops, knowing that it was just a matter of time. Anger that can't be controlled needs only a few insane minutes, and you're on the run for the rest of your life. I don't remember starting out bad; it just happened... and it went from bad to worse."

"You want sympathy?" queried the reporter, her frayed nerves not hidden.

"Pull in your claws is all I ask. I'm not looking for sympathy, America."

"Good!" was the terse response. "Because you don't have it!" *Where are you, Lord?*

"He ain't here." Cadaverous eyes continued to glitter. "Understand this, America. I repeat, I am not looking for your sympathy."

Robin's temper flashed with her eyes, but she didn't utter a word and tried her best not to think of one. At least her hands could hide from him, even if her thoughts couldn't, she determined, as she pocketed the memo in hand, the report that said—oh no. She must not recap, she must not think....

With no further admonition, Lucifer adopted a tone of introspection. In a courtroom manner and with an unreadable face, he began to present his case. "They named me Luc, for Lucifer—after the devil, I guess. My stepfather preferred the name Draggo. meaning a drag, unwanted. A noose around his neck, ya know?" Lucifer's mouth contorted as he spat out his memories. "You thought you'd find a story here? You will if you listen! You have kids?"

Scalded with fright, Robin snapped, "No!" But he would know that she had two, at this moment in the care of her mother.

He did. "You care about them. My parents didn't care about me. That can make a big difference in one's character development, I'm finding out. In your line of work you've encountered stories like mine: Stepfather a bully, always drunk; finds his daily fix in beating up on his wife and her baggage. In our case, Maxie and me.

"'Have a good day!' You say that to your kids. Our parents never worried about either of us havin' a good day. A good day? Ha!" Like a caged leopard, Lucifer began to wrestle with his confines, shaking the guerney closer. Robin paled. He slowed down, as though out of recollections.

With a giggle he grew testy. "My poor mother never had a day without a curse from her husband's mouth or a blow from his fist." A manic giggle was followed by a sharp cry. "We could almost tell the time of day by the number of her bruises!" Lucifer faded to no color, resumed his ghastly green, and loomed over his jury of one. "Ma was always shrinking away from stuff... like you are... in your standing-room-only audience of one!"

He stomped on his stretcher. Robin's heart beat like a triphammer. She lifted both palms and took a step back. "Stay away from me!" she screamed.

There was no sign that he heard. With outrage increasing, he attacked with scorn, "How would I know back then what it meant to adjust to society's expectations? I'd already devised my own method of survival on a street that had only one side: a hostile side, for the purpose of survival. Deprivation offers few choices. Get that, America?

"Black kids cry discrimination. But I've learned that's not the biggest problem. It's where poverty places you in society that nails ya to a wall. If the cards aren't dealt fairly, why play society's game when you can invent one of your own? Mine was formed by the gang on the block. Most important to me as a kid was acceptance, like it is to every kid. Hence my entanglements."

With his head bent almost to his chest, Lucifer could barely be heard. "At that place called home, we had no guidance, only meanness. I felt the boot of my stepfather for whatever I did or didn't do." Grim lines deepened around Lucifer's mouth. Like he'd opened a book and was reading from it, his voice strengthened. "But when that old man, in a drunken fit, raped my kid sister, I knew I had to get us out of that so-called home... permanently. I was only fifteen, but big for my age. Maxine was thirteen and very scared. I robbed a gas station for a starter, and the starter became an occupation... to keep us fed and on the move.

"When we finally got to the east coast, I figured we were far enough away to begin life over. Maybe I could get a job that wouldn't keep me lookin' over my shoulder. We got a nice coupl'a rooms where no one asked questions, and Maxie bought some decent clothes. She looked real pretty, and for the first time, she was happy." Again Luc stopped, then grunted almost to himself. "One day she never came home. She was run over by a taxi."

Robin's hand crept to her throat. Raw nerves broke into her voice. "I'm sor-sorry." She meant it. "But surely you can't hold all taxi drivers accountable....."

The flash of Luc's eyes matched the spikes of his head, as he raised both with a jerk. "I blamed everyone and anyone! I blamed the entire world! I blamed humanity with its blind eye, for where we found ourselves! I blamed the lack of caring and support, along with the rot in our home."

In the course of his outburst, Robin thought she detected moisture in one eye, but tossed the thought. Luc carried on, "I never used the word 'love' because we'd never known any, my sister and me... except what we felt for each other and never put a name to. It was more comfortable to hate. First the taxi driver who was high as a kite when he hit the kid. Mostly, I hated myself, responsible for her being there... and for being alive when she was dead!"

Maybe people don't know when they're dead, thought Robin. *Like me, maybe, right now. They go on living with the same people, only in another time zone... as though nothing ever happened. Or maybe life is all imagination... and there really never is anyone else.*

Luc grunted his approval. His eyes darted sharply, but he lost some of his abrasiveness. "At least you're thinkin', which is a step up from opinion-formin'! You might just be approaching the point where you'll keep an open mind and allow experience to tell you something.

"I would say up till now you've been convinced that facts of importance are hidden beyond the average person's ability to grasp them... when most times, they're out in the open for all to see, it says here in the Encyclopedia of Behavior. But you have to *see*, America, not just *look*! You have to *listen*, not just *hear*."

Lucifer cupped his chin with a crumbling palm, in a teacher-to-student pose. "What did you hope to gain from this encounter? You tell me, Mizz Dinofrio! On second thought, disregard! Let me help to answer that. Please take notes....

"Dislike of oneself makes the ability to hate others much easier. I got that in here from another book on psychiatry... and it's true. It became normal for me to cultivate my hates: hate for my parents, hate for Children's Aid, called in once to examine the neighborhood, to 'assess risk' they said. I guess we didn't make the case list because we didn't see any of them again, or maybe they just couldn't put a name to our plight. I hated the neighbors who turned their backs... especially the time my stepfather sat me on a stove element that hadn't yet cooled. Or maybe he'd turned it up especially for me, d'ya think?"

She was unable to answer. In the waiting stillness, Robin experienced a lunge in her stomach and felt she would surely be sick. How to get through this death song which she no longer wanted to research, yet had to accept.

Luc twitched and writhed, fell silent for a moment, then relentlessly continued, "The neighbors? They just stood there, gawking. 'A bad boy,' they kept saying. I wasn't quite six years old. But my old lady came alive for once and actually started to scream! Ma was scared and got a move-on. She got me to a hospital after peeling me off the stove. I can still feel the pain searing my little balls before I passed out. Lots of scars among my souvenirs, you bet." As if to fortify his story, fresh bruises covered Lucifer's countenance like lumps of dough rising in a warm place.

Robin's guard dropped. The sight was ghastly, but repugnance defected in favor of the commentary that left her as cold as the room. *Lord, how could anyone rise above such cruelty! Memories loom to rule another day.*

Or was she being taken in? Despite her uncertainty, she couldn't help saying, "It... it's so shocking."

As if they were etched in black ink, the creases around Lucifer's mouth grew deeper, more grim, haggard and forbidding, with no trouble discharging their rage. "Still suspicious of my veracity? I've told you and told you! I can only Reckon here with Truth!" Sections of his distorted frame seemed surely about to detach and his anger erupted. "'Too shocking?' Is that all, baby girl?" He mimicked her with cackles: "Shocking! Shocking! Shocking! Life *is* shocking, America! You're a reporter; haven't you noticed?"

Luc reared himself to a lofty height. "Did you ever go hungry?" he challenged, squinting his eyes to warn Robin that only Truth would be tolerated.

For some things perhaps, or more correctly put, she might have felt a yen, or maybe suffered a few pangs because of a delay. There were times when her family of seven had to stretch the stew. But no, they had never been "hungry," in the continuous sense.

After his escape from Cuba, it had taken her father a few years to get on his feet. And he'd had to learn a language. He hadn't much in his pockets when he met her mother and started to raise a family in the late seventies. She did remember some bills mounting in a bowl on the kitchen table: the local grocer, the butcher, the pharmacy. But the family was always cared for, and somehow those bills got paid.

She remembered the shopping excursions every Saturday night with her dad after he'd spent twelve hours on his feet as a department store sales clerk. Mother was home with three littler ones, and this was his way of helping. She loved to food shop with her dad, partly because he always kept in mind his little girl's need for a treat—a piece of chocolate, maybe an ice cream cone. In her family, love revealed itself in many forms.

"Gives one pause, doesn't it?"

He wasn't going to quit. "I never went hungry," said Robin.

Luc's brows knit. Like a sorcerer contemplating his next brew, he rubbed his hands together and continued his inquisition. "Were you ever cold, meaning without heat in your barracks?"

Robin's memory leapt. Our "barracks" were above a store. But they were responsible for heating both floors, a condition written into the lease. By the grace of a friend, they had coal that day, lugged in two heavy buckets by her mom along a busy sidewalk in full view of the neighbors. They'd run out of fuel and money. Daddy was managing a store in northern Ontario, the only work he could find that earned some decent dollars to send home, though not quite adequate for raising a family in comfort. But they didn't tell him that. Mother had good friends because she was a friend. Friends helped each other. Robin had never experienced Luc's kind of cold. "No," she repeated.

Lucifer examined her recollections along with her answers. With shoulders humped and a glare like two beams in the snow, he snapped, "Were you ever sick with no one to care if you lived or died?"

Oh, he had a mind! Skillfully, he'd manoeuvred to what were her comfort memories. The warm ones, like spring rain, lying on the floor on Sundays to read the funnies, her own garden with its patch of dirt under the back stairs, behind the store...

Games and hot soup brought to her sick room belonged to those memories. Mother and child re-bonding as two tented heads, not just one, bent over a steaming pan of Friar's Balsam. Her mom, her buddy, still. Such memories were easy to recall: Robin would always feel emotionally aligned with them. "There was always someone to care," she had to admit.

Obsessed with his quizzing like a cat with a ball of wool, Lucifer twisted his lips as, minute by minute his voice continued to lift and plunge. "Did you ever fall asleep in school because you had to spend most of every night searching for junk, like empty pop bottles to swap for pennies that would buy anything with alcohol in it to keep your old man happy?"

She was attempting to answer when Luc chopped in with his laughter. "I hated school. I suffered from exhaustion, malnutrition … and my own hostility, and I wore all acquired grudges on my person as if they were medals! Disinterest was my protection against rejection. I hated myself; and anything that represented goodness, I equated with being nerdy."

Because Luc hadn't blinked at all, it was hard to imagine him sleep-deprived, with a need to shut his eyes. And he didn't seem to want to shut his mouth, talking his heart out all this time—his dead heart that kept on living! It struck Robin that she, in turn, was feeling the need to respond by reaching back to those years, to compare....

Luc's last question presented no difficulty. As a teen Robin hadn't liked school much either, finding it confining. She hadn't fallen asleep at her desk, but might as well have, for she'd done a lot of daydreaming, with scant appreciation for learning until she went to college. But this poor wretch with no rainbow in his life had nothing to salvage.

Scornful titters from the occupant of the gurney broke the stillness of her thoughts. "Now you're gettin' it, sister! You've finally decided to listen!" Encouraged, Lucifer's queries gained momentum. "Tell me, did you ever lie or steal, you pretty little thing?" He clicked his tongue to mock the innocent answer he anticipated, and the gully between his brows deepened.

To Robin, this was a jungle in purgatory: impassive with Lucifer's malevolence, choked with the brambles of her resistance. Pulling together one more answer, she found her gaze drifting beyond the hideous corpse and up toward the light deserting his badly pocked face. She had to think. Reporting news, she reasoned, meant keeping one's head. Though she might be fantasizing, she might not be, which meant that she must find a way to get back on course. Despite this resolution, her next statement was hopelessly undisciplined. "Your talent for drama greatly surpasses mine, sir!" she blurted. Now why, at this precarious time, had she chosen to provoke him!

Like a delayed firecracker, Luc stared at her, incredulous, then spurted his response. "Answer the blasted question!"

Robin jumped and her muscles prepared to defend. Her spirit returned, and she wondered why she'd weakened. How to escape this damaged, miserable soul! Panic and fear are one's worst enemies, she reasoned, but fear often triggered a plan. All at once, she swished her mind of opposition. She would go along for now. Could she bluff it out?

To answer the question: did she ever lie or steal? Like drums in a jungle, memories of some real whoppers sprung up with little effort. But they'd been innocent little fibs, hadn't they? Fibs that served to test limits, when telling the truth would have been much simpler, and likely more believable.

But steal? No way. She would have been too afraid to try. Her father was a proud and honorable man with "Thou-shalt-nots!" high on his list. Thoughts of Tammie frisked through her memory, the stray terrier she'd been allowed to foster while awaiting its rightful owner. Her father could hardly afford the classified he placed in the newspapers.

Reunited with its owner, the puppy had to depart, not without a whine or two or three and a lick around Robin's chin. She hadn't got to keep the puppy, but she'd gained something more precious: The value of honesty, along with the welcome to visit Tammie whenever she liked. And times did get better for them.

Recalling the years when they'd had to do without, Robin knew that because they'd been morally rich, they had never been poor.

Luc's sheets twisted tighter in his excitement. "How about opportunity?" he hissed.

He's writing his own obituary by comparing his life with mine! concluded Robin, as the ghostly figure coiled its bony frame to skulk at her more closely. But her grit was fast returning and her voice rose along with it. "What *about* opportunity? I thought we addressed that!"

Parts of Luc's face, shadowed by his shifting crown, were lost in eerie concentration. "You're a princess!" he decided to trumpet. He coaxed an arm out of its tethers and with spreading fingers, pretended to shade his eyes from the royal entitlements of her class. "I'll bet the most you privileged kids ever did for money was selling Kool-Aid on a corner!"

"Is that so!" Robin retorted with cooperation forgotten and opposition racing. *He has more than one act to equate him to a serpent!* But it all came flooding back: her Saturday job at K-Mart, secured for her by a floorwalker who was a family friend; a summer job at Charlton Stores, easy to get because her father was highly respected there; and, topping the list, her first published work, inspired by her husband and her teacher, two champions who believed in her enough to cheer her on.

Support.

The irises in Luc's eyes disappeared. The blanks zoomed out on their victim with glowing precision, "Get the point, sister? The right *time;* the right *place;* or *know somebody,* right?" His wink was atrocious.

His pupils rolled out like a pair of stoplights. "If I hadn't had to split with a dealer, I could have made more money in one hour than you make in a year, Sweetheart. So you see, there *is* honor among thieves! Honor for the Laws and Codes that prevail!" His eyes were hooded. "But that's not a good recommendation for an honest job, is it?" Another wink.

"Car-jacking, now that's good training. Taking them cars for joy rides, like we did, could have qualified me as a car jockey!" Luc's eyelids lifted like a sliding roof and he pouted, "But I didn't wanna go there.

"So what did we set our standards by? Our so-called breadwinner was never around, and anyway he had nothing to offer in the way of a fine example. 'Out lookin' for employment,' he would report. Having nothin' when everyone else had somethin', now that hurt bad.

"Like shoes. We wore other people's when we could steal them, or we wrapped our feet in rags and bags." Luke slumped, then rallied, "Hey! That's what we were. 'Rags and Bags!'" he shrilled. "That would have described us, don't y' think?"

Thinking gets one into trouble.

Meantime, this nasty was in no hurry to let up. With a further release of rage he shouted until her ears hurt. "I put a face on! I put a face on! How else can you live with your pain hangin' out all over ya? How can you meet it or defeat it? Did you know, America, that it's the kid who pays? When your old man likes to practice his brutality on ya, it leaves ya seething! Mistreat a kid, you create a piece o' work, and trouble forms its own street."

With anguished percussion, the cadaver continued to rant. "I didn't know Luc very well; I'm getting to know him here. I'm finding out you have to belong to somebody; even if there's no one to love you, you're way dead if you got no one to love. Livin' with a drunk, learning that there's no one minding the store, you become like a stick of dynamite, exposed to the guy's lack of mercy, unprotected, ready to defend or blow, twenty-four-seven. Without a safe place in the world, how can a kid feel safe? If you're alone in it, don't never expect nothing. So much for, and I quote, 'a healthy perspective.'"

Mindful of his lessons in the Zone, Luc attempted to rectify his street talk while growing more introspective with each confession. "Teacher said if we worked we would get somewhere. I did. I worked nights and got right into trouble. With no opportunities, you see, because we still had to eat. Lacking direction," he glumly rattled, "my priorities, you could say, weren't admirable. I stole to buy booze and food, in that order. That was my work, America. The dad was always 'on hard times,' and I lied when he grilled me at the end of the day. Had I turned over every cent to him? 'All of it!' I pleaded under his fist. But no way did I. I stashed some under a baseboard I loosened—for my own needs.

"Which turned out to be… let's see now. Cigarettes when I was nine. Later, the stuff of big boys. Those are the things I grew up with, America. My training in the workplace? I peddled stuff for the big bosses, to the poor shmucks who stole from rich and poor alike to pay for their habit. It wasn't long before I joined in. I ripped handbags off chicks and old ladies. I did lots of things you don't wanna know. Above all, I respected the street code: 'Do-What-You're-Told-or-We-Break-Your-Neck'.

"Pain was the result of disobedience. So you had to learn to defend yourself on the street. If you were good at it, you gained a reputation for being tough. It replaced the power that was beaten out of you at home; becoming a fighter was a requisite for survival.

"The politically correct term for drug dealing became 'underground economy,' which gave it a certain level of, well, dignity in the workplace! Whatever. It filled the gaps in our pockets.

"And then… came the weapon," Lucifer tone softened from years of respect. "One's tool of the trade on that one side of the street, *A-mer-ica.*"

Luc retrenched to focus more sharply on the purpose of his dissertation. "Pop kept pocketing the money I brought him, and stopped asking questions. He was too drunk to figure what actually paid for his suppers. Still, with my habit and all, we lived on the sharp edge of hunger, and spent more winters than I care to remember shivering with cold. Because I was a big brute, at thirteen, I tried to join the army—mostly because the army issued shoes… to fit.

"But it isn't poverty we have to be most afraid of, America. It's having little knowledge of what's rich."

From the mouth of a "bum," this conclusion was staggering. Tuned in her line of work to heart-rending disclosures, Robin had never been privy to such a measure of self-analysis, with its levels of layering and peeling back, its openness, and its eventual disquiet. To stir her readers, she had taken many liberties.

But this?

Physically and emotionally, the abuse of Luc was beyond imagination. Not to be allowed to strengthen, to mature. No gestures of love or shimmers of light; not even a pet turtle. No books with stories and wonders. No childhood dreams. Never to count on a need being met or even to own shoes that fit. Kids poking fun. To wake up every morning with dread, and close eyes at night in fear. A life of nightmares, with no time out.

All piled up in one kid. Inconceivable.

Robin's memory harkened back to first grade. She'd ripped her dress on a nail while straddling a fence on the way to school. Her teacher had pinned it together until she went home for lunch. But kids find such things hilarious: to young Robin's chagrin, the waistband of her panties had peeked through. By the time the kids belabored its telling, the story had progressed to the absence of them. Kids. She'd forgotten the incident until now because she was able to. Her memory, unlike Luc's, was not trapped in pain.

Nevertheless, Robin couldn't give in. Throughout history, others had lifted themselves out of the burning. Granted, to do so required a strong inner quality, and a caring other to influence a child constructively, however slightly, however vaguely, for a start. Helping a child to surmount life's obstacles required an ability to respond… and to trust. Nothing like that for Luc. There were too many betrayals, too many scars.

Robin's sense of justice spoke up. "Yours was not an act of self defense. That's a fact, and such facts cannot be dismissed! There are a lot of excuses out there, for those who make a practice of using them. It's clear that your short life spanned an angry road, but *no one* has the right to take another's life."

She stopped in case Luc wanted to say something, but he didn't, so she tapped a finger on the back of her hand and went on, her own voice jolting her with its strength. "Weapons ruled for you, and you took that life. For that, there exists no acceptable excuse that I know of." Aware of the futility of her next words, she uttered them anyway. "You failed yourself. There is always a choice… to be a man."

The wait for an answer seemed like an hour.

"I thought I was one."

"A bad man is a flawed man. Not a man at all."

But all the while she thought: *How can a mere E.R. reporter know exactly why one kid turns into a brute and another doesn't? She just reports the news. Right?*

Not right. On the horns of her dilemma, honesty reared. *Incomplete reporting is not honest reporting, though I always researched as much as I was able, way back then,… before I got caught in this cockeyed squabbling of intellects!*

But it hadn't been thorough enough.

Robin looked out at the black of night, taking comfort from the familiar patter of rain, a sound she knew. To solve what she considered menacing, she should convert it to strength. If only she knew how to define it.

Spurred on by the girl's growing awareness, Luc refused to slow down. "Good!" he grunted from his hallowed spot. Furling his scabbie brow, he pointed his finger at her. "I'm not going to ask if you had dreams for your future, America. Obviously you followed some of them. The only dreams I had were nightmares, even to me, where I was always fighting for my life!"

This time Robin interrupted him. Shaking with indignation, she lifted a fist into the air. "What about the innocent cabbie? He didn't have a chance to fight for his life! You hit him from behind. A father of six kids!"

Luke burrowed his eyes into those of his adversary, forcing his trolley back and forth like one stealing up on someone else's parking space. "I didn't know anything about the man, other than that he drove a cab. But do you think it would have made a difference if I had? A father's worth had little meaning for me, having no way of measuring it. I wasn't too in control of myself. But from the moment I took out that cabbie, I felt stranded and lost—not triumphant, the way I thought I should. It would have been better had I finished myself off at the same time. Survival is not always an enviable state, America. There are many ways that life continues to destroy a person.

"Here in the Zone, we pore over our mistakes until they don't pain anymore. Once past Anguish, we move into Learning." As one pointing out facts on a notice-board somewhere above him, Luc raised an arm and snapped the tips of his fingers. "Learning sometimes tells us that the more obvious a fact seems to be, the more it might have to be re-examined."

Unlike the predator he'd first seemed to be, Luc no longer came across as threatening. Instead, he was teaching! Nevertheless, a thin smile played around the girl's lips. "Your past record re-examined by *yourself*? In your dreams!"

From his dais, Luc's face flushed with anger. "You do have a way of undoing progress!" he bawled, meeting her stand with a display of departing teeth. "You came to *me*, girlie," he grinned. "It's that simple. You're here, in *my* space, and I'm doing the *best I can* to communicate with *you*! But you're such a smart-ass, America, I doubt if you can ever learn anything beyond the walls of your *Judgmentalism*!" Luc's hair stood on end like he was plugged into a socket, while he licked his lips at the intelligence of his latest word.

Robin was too angry to reason. "You are evil... ugly... and stupid!"

"Choose one," he ordered. "Evil, ugly, or stupid."

She winced. *Robin Dinofrio is the object of a dead man's third degree!* She felt the creeping damp and her bones ached. Certain that things couldn't get much worse, she duly answered, "Evil, if I must choose. When we were kids living through a recession, some of us had to make our own fun—out of nothing—because most of us had nothing. But we weren't so resentful… we didn't take things into our own hands by …" She stopped because the comparison was too ridiculous.

She thought about priorities, how they differed under different circumstances. Her mind flipped back to shoes. She loved pretty shoes, and would put them first on her wardrobe list. Yet she always loved going barefoot! They called her Huck Finn as a child. Even today, she preferred to toss her shoes off as soon as she got home. But that was from choice. Checks and Balances.

Pieces of Lucifer's lectures were drumming themselves into her head. "Pain was my friend," he continued, ignoring her silence. "It made me strong. It made me run amuck. I figured that was how life had to be.

"Like when I was ten. The old man landed a job driving a cab. To my surprise, he asked if I would like to go for a ride… to a boy's school, he said. We were to meet somebody in the lobby. After just a few minutes, when that somebody didn't show, he told me to stay where I was; he'd come back for me. He never came back for me."

Was it murky in this morgue, or was Robin's vision swimming? *That wretched, wretched monster!*

"I'm not done yet," Luc growled softly. "Turned out to be a storehouse for retarded kids. I refused to utter a word the whole time I was there— almost two months, so I was labeled a 'go-back.' Too retarded. But not before receiving some 'special attention' doled out by the resident pedophile. Believe me, America, that was no 'Boys' Town.'"

As though Luc had just placed a barrier between her and her trust in the system, Robin ached with the tears shifting into her heart. Depths of loathing yielded to waves of pity, as she started to believe Luc's story as it was told… with expanding self-knowledge winning over anger. What was the source of such fortification? She had to know.

Like one whose neck just unhinged, Luc nodded and the nod drooped to his waist. Immediately he realigned, honed his gaze, and continued to pour out his tale. "I was the product of my stepfather's cruelty. Unaware of any choices, I perpetuated his honorable mission in life, which included the need to cause pain. In this Zone, I'm required to study the sources of my anger along with that need.

"I'm workin' on it. I wasn't born with violent inclinations. I simply lived a life with no affection or purpose. I knew they existed in some families, but not in mine, so I looked for approval in other places." In a circular shunt, as if to illustrate his luckless search, the joints in Luc's body crackled and clamped.

Robin fought to get air into her lungs. "Where is he now? That stepfather."

"I pass him in here now and again. He don't even look at me, so he ain't—isn't—finished with his Reckoning yet. Been here seven hundred years, Rec time. Got hit by a train, him and his cab... him drunk as a skunk. He never broke his pattern, see.

"But this will kill ya," Luke emitted a gleeful giggle and slivers of his disintegration floated into the light. "I'm required to hold some kind of memorial service for him in this Zone. Can y'beat that, America? Good or bad, it's the rule! But even in this place, I can't get nobody to come! Wanna come?" One shoulder heaved in invitation.

With dry mouth and eyes as large as saucers, Robin bypassed Luc's invitation and stammered, "Your mother. Wh-what happened to her?"

"Married again. Same kind of guy. Some are gluttons for punishment, aren't they? She up and left. Never heard from her again. Can't blame her much; she couldn't ever handle things—me, especially."

The man is dead... yet discovering himself! As the thought settled in, Robin perceived an element of justice in the confinement of such offenders to a 'Reckoning Zone' as a pit stop for addressing their wrongful acts.

Clearly, her sarcasm hadn't proved to be an asset, so the reporter trashed her lack of enthusiasm and began to filter in small amounts of Luc: the odd unselfish observation, his personal assessment, his growing strength considering the guidelines he'd never had.

On he rowed in his sea of troubles, ploughing and ploughing, as Robin inched toward the doors for one more try. "I never knew what it was to aspire, so I didn't acquire any strength... except in my cocky attitude.

"I didn't set out to kill anyone. My mind got all screwed up. That cabbie who ran over my sister, and my old man... to me, they were look-alikes. The two of them ran together in my mind. I had to get even with the scumbag who put his cab in reverse when he meant to move forward, crushing my sister against a pole. I was flooded with the loss of Maxie and loss of my own purpose in life. With no knowledge of how to recover, I chose violence… my way of getting revenge." In the ghostly light of his headpiece, Luc repeated, "Without Maxie, it wasn't much of a life, see. There was no sense in what I did. That cabbie was innocent. I was relieving his vehicle of some of its trim when he stepped out of a building, so I pretended to be waiting for a ride. I was his first fare that morning. From where I sat, he resembled the guy who killed Maxie; his head bunched in back just like my old man's. I got mixed up. By that time I was in another space, unaware that it wasn't the same guy, wondering why he wouldn't admit what he did to Maxie. So I shot the poor bugger."

Robin stayed fixed to her spot.

Like one undoing knots in a string, Luc's revelations filled the cold cavern, then sharpened to a keening as he continued his requiem, "I'm told that writers get rejections sometimes. How d'ya feel when you do?"

Pretty let down. But they all come with words of encouragement.

The exchange was worse than unsettling: it challenged her beliefs, troubled her nature, rendered her convictions unstable. Something besides pandemonium was questioning her safe little world. This was the Reckoning Zone, and Luc was opening the gate a crack, not for her to enter, she realized, but for her to examine.

She saw hurt in his eyes… along with what appeared to be accountability. How he was changing! How he had changed since their initial encounter!

Robin slid one foot ahead of the other until she reached the doors, hoping her progress would remain unnoticed in one more search for an escape. The dead youth's eyes were veiled as if in sleep. For sounds that would prove that there was life out there, she put an ear to the gap between the doors. And heard nothing.

There was no choice but to stay and listen.

"I never went to school. I never got educated."

Robin's heart failed its attempt to shut that out. "But you're putting yourself through the Reckoning Zone, the most important school of all, you say."

"Yeah. Since we've been arguing back and forth, I've been to the library three more times. I have to redeem myself. I have to count for something. One learns fast in here. For example, I know that you don't have to like me to listen, and that it doesn't show weakness if I ask for help."

Luc flexed a shoulder toward the doors and drummed on his stretcher with his fingers. "And I need you to know that no matter how locked in you might seem, there's always a way out... though it may not be the one you're looking for.

"We have orders in here to improve the planet we came from... before traveling on to another one. Never the same planet, which is how the entire Universe, with its millions of planets, is kept populated; for unbelievable as this may seem, there are only so many souls. We're obligated to pay back for what we were given, what we took, how we lived, and how we made it through. Those of us who have to Reckon longer because we didn't do so good still have the chance to get a better shot at the next life."

Robin took umbrage at the expression.

"You know what I mean!"

Do the others hear? Positioned like some logo on an invitation to "Tour le Morgue"—are they oblivious of this unhinged interview?

Luc sat back with a thump and cradled the back of his head with laced fingers. "For example, if one is cruel to animals, that person is born an animal in the next life. Like the pack of baby seals slaughtered for their fur? You guessed it: they were doing penance for slaughtering animals in their last life. Unable to communicate, they remembered what they did and knew what to expect. And so it goes: Cheat your neighbor, expect to be cheated. Violate one's rights, expect the same treatment. Hitler's henchmen of the 40's are in work camps all over the galaxy. The perpetrators of 9/11? They are only allowed to be still for the time it takes to watch a replay of that day's events, which is every other Zone minute, for Eternity... with no way out. Get the picture?"

Anything else in this crazy place?

"There's nothing left to tell," Luc answered with quiet control. "I keep retracing my Earth life, but very little gets resolved. Points of view are inescapable; so are judgments. But I need answers, too. If I wasn't born bad, like I'm assured in here that I wasn't, why did all those things have to happen?" His eyes widened; he looked forlorn. "If any words are spoken when I'm shoveled in the ground, what can be said of me other than... I was evil?"

Torn between compassion and justice, the girl's conscience ached with regret for calling him evil. Stranger still was her impulse to reassess the data held in her hand.

Lucifer widened his eyes. In his courtroom manner, he said, "Once you have one thought, many more follow. Who was it who wrote, 'You can never do a kindness too soon, for you never know how soon it will be too late?'" As though adding that to the notice-board above him, he pointed and lectured, "What you say is less important than your attempt to say something. Yes! I think I like the sound of that." One parchment-like limb swung free, as though heading for the door.

Luc's mercurial shifts no longer alarmed the girl. He was putting words to his feelings. She recognized seeds of remorse, the dawning of perspective, and her answer sounded very far away. "Others, who have never had to walk your path, can be unfeeling, Luc." Such horrors as this boy experienced had to be carved forever in a heart turned to stone.

Robin couldn't begin to imagine what he felt, steeped in the rejections that steadily came his way. Not the sort that one might contend with in the course of a day, but rejections personally and consistently suffered by a sensitive young person stunted by society's sleeping conscience. However, in this room she too, was facing the prospect of endless confinement, with no way out; squeezing, locking, paralyzing, forever shrouded with webs of —the worst webs of all—helplessness and worthlessness.

Had she been *sent* to experience this?

Agitated and confused, Robin shut her eyes in an attempt to push Luc out of her line of sight, hoping for some respite, praying that he would not read this from her mind as one more rejection. In the beginning she'd had such hate for him! She'd been worlds away from feeling any sympathy. Was it conceivable that she should now bother about how her attitude might affect him? All this left her weak, tormented, strangely without defenses, feeling sick and full of guilt. For him? For herself? Or for society?

Robin considered how things happen… and how things often resolve themselves. The meaning of life, she now sensed, was right here in this room.

Luc, aware that a crisis had been reached, could not release her now. Stretching and straining at his wrappings, he escalated the tempo of his dissertation. "There's a not-so-lily-white human rights system in this land of ours. I was kept around because the law required that, until age sixteen, I have a home somewhere, and there was no other place for me to go. I hung in for almost that long, with no direction, with anger my major companion. Those are my roots… in degrees, America. Results are seeded in degrees. Back there, we compared experiences and responses. Yours were acceptable to you; to someone else, they might not have been. Mine were horrendous to you, but to me, they were measured… to the degree of daily occurrences that formed my defenses, my character. I'm learning to analyze, you see."

The vision on the gurney no longer seemed savage, though his bloodied sheet was still tangled about his torso, and his skin continued to crack apart like a wall that needed plastering. But he must have had a splendid body, graceful and rugged. His countenance might have evoked passion, in a "bad boy" way.

Once released, Luc's inner rotting began to leave him, accompanied by the odor of gun smoke, called the "Purge" in the Zone. Rat-like, he sniffed the air, accepted the proceeding, and slumped into thoughtful repose. "Murder is not just a violation against the laws of a country and its people: it's a sin against oneself. I have learned that in Dante's Hell, punishment is levied according to the amount of self that's been disgraced. And the worst sins are those that violate "Man's Highest Mental Attainment"—Reason."

Robin steeled herself. There was no room for sympathy, she had to keep reminding herself. *A crime has been committed; I must not lose sight of that. Luc lived by responding in the only way he knew. But, if he were to Reckon as honestly as he claims, he could not expect to be immune to the laws and penalties that govern everyone's lives.*

Her voice regained its edge. "Let's address simple Truth. What consequences, if any, await one if Truth is compromised in the R Zone?"

"You really wanna know?"

"Yes, I really wanna know."

"No you don't. You don't want… to know."

"How can you be sure of that? You're certainly not reading me correctly now!"

"Well now, can you beat that? You're smartening up, America!" Luc bunched his arms, swayed a bit and almost smiled. "We get to be guests here for another dozen R-years… for each lie."

"'Guests,' you say?" snorted Robin. "Moments ago, you regarded such existence as a living death."

"It's a place of study, I told you! Where one needs to Connect with oneself, and Correct for the Crossing… and at the same time learn a few things and earn a few privileges! Like for asking personal questions, such as… how well do you know yourself, America?"

"What would you be learning from your unstoppable prying?"

"Doesn't anything make you think?"

With suspicion and animosity returning, hazel eyes sharpened with doubt, and Robin lit in, "Really want to know what I think? I don't believe you lost a wink of sleep over your crime!"

"I slept too well, America."

"Is there a possible way of atoning for what you did, do you think?" she sneered.

Like a bird with a broken wing, Luke extracted his other arm and rolled it limply over the first one. He hung his head. "I'm here, am I not? And I must remain here for a hundred Zone Years. That should whip me into shape. Atonement doesn't necessarily wear a ball and chain, America. My atonement is being here, working, mentally working, continually working, never stopping… in search of my Soul."

"I was going to suggest that."

Luc managed to ask himself what would be gained with more anger. So he sacrificed his in favor of further explanation. "I know you would like to consign me to Hell. During my lifetime I was convinced that no fair Planner could have created the world. But now, I am looking at my time and place in it from a distance, where I'm able to see the complete journey, from Birth to Death. What's most important: it's over… for me. And maybe, in the not-too-distant future, I'll be allowed to move on. My life was a horror, but its finale placed me here with you."

Robin lifted her head… to a ghost enjoying her presence? Did that mean he would never let her go?

"Not in my lifetime did I have a chance to speak to someone who would really listen." Luke's voice rose like a trumpet. "One must Listen, *really* Listen*!* You are finally doing that, America."

And probably the stupidest thing I ever did! What Robin really wanted was to jab at the irksome creature, wounding his conscience if he had one. *Evil and ugly cannot be separated!* But the furrow between Luc's eyes undid like a snipped cord. His mouth relaxed. His eyes lost their heat. His face was no longer a grizzly green, but pale and melancholy, a sad and withered face. He looked right into her. "I don't expect the world to change because I have Reckoned with myself."

Something stirred inside her, but Robin turned away. She must not respond to the hocus pocus this devil chose to practice. Bottom line, all his life he used poor judgment. So now, who cares?

"You do," he said.

Where had all the anger gone? Those dreadful sounds and undercurrents that were no longer? Had Luc lived, his character would likely not have changed. He would never have admitted to vulnerability, nor would he have experienced remorse. Yet it was all happening here, in this place of banishment, where his lot had been cast.

The red in his eyes was replaced with an ivory glow, and there was a possible nobility to his features. She was stunned with his vocabulary, his perception… the results of an education picked up in a mere twenty hours?

Despite the changes, Luc's face showed grave. Rather than bellow, he chose to grumble, "You sure do make things difficult. It's understandable why you majored in journalism rather than mathematics …since you can't seem to figure out things in relation to other things.

"Learning is not a given in the Zone. We earn the right by working at courses: Reflection, Insight, Consciousness, Discovery, which should lead to Open-Mindedness, a necessary requirement in order to Pass Through. We not only reckon with ourselves, but with each other, so we need what you on Earth would call a… a universal way of being understood."

He's hardly cold and he knows all this?!

"You have been informed that your hours are our years! What can you accomplish if you don't *Listen*? You don't need a sledgehammer to open those doors," said Luc, pinning the girl with a mournful glance. "What you need, America, is the Master Key... the message I'm trying to impart. "

There was little point in trying to guess. "And specifically what might that be?"

"You're the journalist."

Robin checked her temper. "Look, I'm not insensitive to your miserable childhood—"

"And adulthood!" Luke snapped. "Deprived! Deranged! Damned! Three D's, America! Allow me to offer a bit more information on the place where my father dumped me.

"In what was supposed to be a home for retarded kids, all of us had surprisingly normal mentality! It was eventually exposed as a holding place for unwanted kids, where any damned pedophile could party to his heart's content! 'The Program' held all kinds of surprises... all sorts of doings. Hey! What kind of product do you think society could expect out of that package?

"Want to know what ignited my rockets? That cabbie was scared, just like I was in that 'school,' where I developed hate for my own cowardice because I had no power. I remember the hate bursting inside, begging for release. Instead I pretended that it was all happening to someone else, and I was just standing by, watching and waiting.

"In the same way, I transferred my weakness to that cabbie, subconsciously ridding myself of it. And I mocked him. To my mind, only a wretch would shiver and shake like that. After thinking that, I recall nothing. I was stoned out of my head.

"You curious about what happened to those so-called homes and the people who had the run of them? Or what happened to the kids who came out of them? There's a starter for you. It's called 'Searching for Justice.' And if you don't know what message I'm trying to send back to the world I left, go out and play, small girl! Just don't entitle yourself to be judge and jury over anyone, living or dead."

Robin bristled at being so scolded, but she didn't try to disengage. "Why me? How do you believe I can change any of this?"

"To compensate for the evil I did, the messes I made, I see my chance in you. You're a writer in search of a story. In here is a story for you. Why *not* you?"

If he reads my thoughts, does he detect a shift? In an attempt wipe it away, Robin took herself in hand and abruptly backtracked into wariness. *An innocent man was murdered in cold blood, and this man did it! That is fact, and spreads its own judgment over all. Society dictates that he must pay.*

"I am paying."

With his life. Robin recognized the totality of that. Like with the seal hunters who turned into baby seals, by way of the officer who gunned him down, and the years of Reckoning that still lay ahead. But this Zone... it seemed too sheltered for the Final Restitution, worked through with the necessary measure of Remorse. She remained defiant. Families in mourning know that the Ultimate Penance is never enough.

Albeit, what more was there to give? Though no earthly nullification might exist for his act, it was impossible to be dispassionate about Luc the person. Everyone in his life had let him down in the creation of a case history unbelievable in its degrees of neglect, rejection and cruelty. Such thoughts brought the writer dangerously close to pity, and she had to will herself to remain outside of it.

Lucifer stayed calm. "I am ashamed of my blind urge to hurt," he confessed miserably, "because at this point, I feel myself elevating from rage to deepest Remorse."

He read that word from my mind! Harboring shreds of rebuttal, Robin found safety in cynicism. "Let's see now. *REPORT FROM THE VALLEY OF THE DAMNED*, by Robin Dinofrio. How shall I write my lead?" She regarded the wan figure at the root of it all. Hard lines had turned to mere creases, hair was graying before her eyes. Fact: Luc's "years" in the Reckoning Zone were aging him! More incredible, this loathsome, appalling, odious insult to humanity was finding a place in her heart. *Impossible!*

Maybe she should try to summon one of the "others" the way she had encountered Lucifer. Perhaps there was one here still with some Earthly sense, who would know that she was an alien in this place, who might convince Luc to release her from his mission. Balefully, Robin regarded the lineup. Any takers?

Above the fragments drooping from his ghostly frame, Luc's eyes were looking past her, unseeing. His voice seemed to come from far away. "I thought you were smart, but you're disappointing. On looking at the damage I did, you would say I'm lucky to be here... in other words, lucky to be dead." He focused eyes that were no longer vacant. "What was, was! That's what I'm trying to tell you, girl! What will be, that's what matters!"

Robin shivered. *What meaning does 'will be' have for the dead?* Skepticism returned in full sail. *One more requisite for the next life?*

"You are most assuredly right!" exclaimed Luc, rejoicing with his powers of expressing the proceedings so nicely, and with Robin's acquired concept. "I am learning that brains and brawn don't always need each other. In The Reckoning Zone, it's all cerebral: each challenge I meet is a punch in my ticket to travel on. In this Zone, as penance for my actions, the final punch is to make a contribution to the planet I leave behind.

"In addition, it's my chance to see the Big Picture, the sides of life and the choices on Earth I never got to know about. In here, I have an opportunity to choose, and it is my choice that you direct your efforts to deprived and battered children. In childhood I received the most abuse. In childhood I learned to be abusive. *You* have to perceive. *They* must perceive how and why that happens!"

"Exactly who are *They?*" Robin mocked, not yet ready for that fellow-feeling, though she knew who *They* were.

Us.

Luc's message is for Us... and concerns everyone of Us.

"If you handle it right, you can reshape the future for some desperate kids. It could make good press. You can do it! "

With Luc's prompting from beyond the grave.

"Seize a time. Seize now! "

The concept was loaded. "I always believed in the goodness of people," Robin reasoned aloud. "Maybe with me it was some kind of denial, for I'm not what one might consider naive. However, in my years as a journalist, I've learned that too many people are afraid, and cautious, to the point of inaction. You, who were so seriously mistreated and let down, can attest to that.

"Luc, if misfortune doesn't fall directly on certain folk, they refuse to act. Not because they mean you harm. For such victimized children of society, those people whose priorities lie with themselves, not untouched by your struggle, but forgetting, in their safe place, what is essential… such inaction hardens the victimized with resentment, rage and often violence."

In the process of consideration, the chain of responsibilities lengthened, adding to Robin's turmoil. Kernels of truth were rooting. Luc's pain was becoming her pain. And a new level of learning how such pain could lead to a road of reprisal gave the two of them a meeting place.

Robin crushed the memo in her hand.

There should be another flood, to cleanse and reboot the world. "Call Noah!" she cried out, not without realizing how ridiculous she sounded. Of what use? "Two-of-these" and "two-of-those" were already contaminated.

"There is less as well as more to consider," Luke corrected, hiding the alacrity that threatened to eclipse his growing level of wisdom. "One may be innocent of this, yet guilty of that. Aren't we all products of innocence and guilt, the trial and error that precede results, good or bad? Can one ever be considered innocent? Values must be based on Degrees. Results that depend on individual minds and hearts hang also with being at a certain place at a certain time. That's called Luck, America. Be honest. Write about that, too."

"It will always be there, Luc. The street with one side."

"Hopefully dotted with choices, not just shadows."

"All things have beginnings and endings."

"To themselves, yes, but an end can herald a beginning for someone else. You won't be saving my life, but you might be in time to save my spirit… for the sake of others." While his eyes screened her response, Luc lifted a corner of his mouth, then threw out the hook: "But not if you're afraid to deal with it."

The ultimate insult! Impossible to ignore!

Luc's bindings turned snowy white. His crown was so bright that whatever was casting its light on it had to be sitting above. He stretched a smile around his next proclamation. "The World needs a caring society. And attention must be paid, not to some scale that singularly measures deprivation, but to all children whose Rights must be protected from Year One. It is crucial that all of them be valued."

Once more, the room tipped, then leveled, as though punctuating Luc's sermon. He broke the bindings that still hung on him like peeling skin. His crown, which was not a crown at all, but a circle of barbs, shimmered and lifted. His torso straightened; the knots in his fingers disappeared. Though pallid, his face was cleared of its disfigurements.

"You might need a referee," he offered.

"Who?"

"To be discovered…."

How shall I begin? What shall I stress? There is so much to say! What will enable me to inspire urgency in my readers? And how was she to put this before them while remaining in here, unseen?

"You hit the nail on the head when you wondered if this was a rehearsal. This *was* a rehearsal—or your chosen assignment. Just remember: '*Cause and Effect,*' America…."

Robin lost the urge to question anymore. Truth was, she felt expansive, privileged, as she did with the most challenging assignments, but in this case, more strongly swept up by the cause. She had come here sensing an extension of a story. *So listen and learn. Don't resist. Absorb what Luc has said; imagine yourself in his place to the best of your ability, then write what you know and feel. Trouble those readers into Thinking. They will feel it. And I will be doing my job… for Us.*

Lucifer bawled, "Don't make this a campaign for some conscience-easing donations!"

With purpose, Robin answered, "It's not a *Gift* from me, sir! It's a *Responsibility*. But before the message can become universal, it has to be *mine*! You ask for no donations? It might be fitting for you to realize that in this world money is necessary in the formation of any legislation or group of people training or volunteering for public service. And that will come only if I can get the message across!"

"The funding! The funding!" Luke twisted and trilled from his creaky trolley, "I don't dance; I don't sing! I don't play music or draw pictures! I never got the chance to strut any stuff. Nowadays, looks like there's no other way to get attention!"

Robin's insides rumbled at the thought of a floppy mummy campaigning for donations! She wiped the thought as soon as it occurred, and said, "Cutbacks on school and community programs have crippled many options. Professional money-raisers appeal to greed, making the essence of the cause secondary. And there are far too many pundits to keep listening to...."

"Talking heads," Luc agreed. "They pop up everywhere: on the internet, in the papers, on the tube, in the mail—all over the planet, growing in number. What are they actually saying, and is any of it taking hold? If not, why not? You've been elected. You've got to make people *LISTEN*!"

"I'm scared," Robin stated simply.

Luc answered gruffly, "I know."

Resolute about this challenge, Robin found herself rising completely to it. "To the tears you never got a chance to shed, Luc; to the issues no one addressed, when and if I ever leave this place, I am going to unlock some doors. A crime brought us together. But it's just the beginning. You will Cross Over, Luc... with Enlightenment in your wake... and I will write your eulogy."

Open them, Robin. OPEN THE DOORS!

A soft light surrounded him. "A visitor lost, has found her way... way... way ...," he echoed. "*Selected*, America, you have been *Selected*. Thanks for dropping by." With a sigh, Luc collapsed to the gurney.

The doors swung wide with a whoosh. A streak of light invaded the room.

"Oh, sorry!" exclaimed an attendant coming through with a stretcher. "I wasn't aware anyone was in here." He wondered why the heck Dinofrio was here, in the dark, alone with the stiffs!

It was blinding, that light. Doing her best to adjust to its glare, Robin stood immobile in the light of its freedom, as the doors exposed a very busy corridor where a large wall clock above the ER announced the time. Thirty-two minutes in all.

Robin followed Luc's stretcher, trundled down the hall on padded wheels. Whispering feet, assigned to hospital sounds, led her past the ER, to a door where a hearse sat waiting. She lifted a hand to wave, but Luc was already quietly shut inside.

She thought back to their encounter, with his eyes blazing back at her. That Lucifer was long gone… to be with Maxie.

Listlessly, Robin continued down the corridor until she found the doors leading to the Sculpture Garden. It was a star-filled night with nothing but stillness and no signs of an earlier rain. The moon poured its silver light along the rocky edges of a little man-made pond. Once outside, she felt relieved though weary, and remained for some moments listening to a chorus of crickets greeting the night as if it were Luc discovering that he could sing.

She smiled. Sure it was. He wouldn't abandon her until their mission was done.

A row of orange blossoms cast its fragrance over the pond. There wasn't a breeze, but something rippled the water. As though in greeting, a paper boat floated to where Robin stood. In the fading wail of an ambulance, she thought she detected echoes of laughter… from children checking the vessel for seaworthiness before sending it afloat, then delighting in its performance. The sight of it brought a rush of sorrow. "I am playtime," it seemed to say, "the laughter, the innocence, that Luc never had."

Was it too late? Robin bent down. Gently she set it sailing, "Noah, this is for you."

Noah. Why did she call Luc that? Like he had called her 'America,' probably—with staunch expectation of a triumphant voyage, begun by two connecting souls on a mission to stem the current of ignorance, flood out cruelty and abuse… with hope as the tiller.

Wanting to know had started this journey. Needing to know had launched it. And it had been no trick of her imagination.

Clearly, she had this commitment. "I must awaken society to its responsibility for every child born, advantaged or disadvantaged, collectively everyone's children. Collectively, society must stand guard," she told the little boat.

Imagine a child with no one to want him, to put an arm about him, to show approval once in a while, or cheer him on! With no one to talk to or look to for advice, no one to count on as friend! In a tortuous, hellish childhood filled with fear, Lucifer's scars had been deeply imbedded by too many scorching degrees.

It is said that the mind constructs its own defenses. On what, with no standards, could Luc have based his? Other than the relationship with his sister, in what decent thing was he able to share?

Such a sorrowful house, with its absence of heart, respect, or even a single treat. And at six years old, to face such beastliness with no defenses! To impart the pain of that, she must not tidy any of it away.

One might say that Luc paid for his crime with a life worth little on Earth. Only Robin knew that his debt was not yet fully paid. That payment was in this mission, And if successful, perhaps some measure of glory would yet be his.

There was more to life and death than one could hope to understand. One day, beyond those gates, she would see for herself. But now she knew her job. Her mind leapt. She would use her one real talent, as Luc intended.

It wasn't simply a matter of reporting an incident. Certainly, the one in the morgue would be impossible to believe. Nevertheless, Robin Dinofrio had been *selected*… to awaken the collective conscience of a new Millennium. Selected. By a dead youth, or by The One Most Powerful?

No matter. Let's get to it.

For a starter, an exercise: "Wherever Luc's name appears in this article, please substitute your child's name, or your grandchild's name. It's Luc's story, but it could be that of any child trapped on the street with one side."

She heard it now, through her mind and voice… or was it his? "Hit them with it, America. By Degrees. Then make it a Ten!"

She stuffed some paper into the feeder of her printer and looked up toward Heaven as the clock in the hallway struck. Ten AM. So loudly this time that her ears sang! She'd been here all night, though it seemed like mere moments since she'd typed her first words:

America, Where Are You?

Reminding herself of those famous words, "After the Reckoning comes the Crown," Robin lifted a peace sign to Luc, and with fingers lightly touching, began his eulogy.

America, Where Are You?

How many of us have used the expression,
"There but for the grace of God go I?"

How many of us have actually encountered its meaning?

This is the story of Luc...

The
Mantilla

IT's A QUAINT HOTEL between the Avenues of The Reforma and Insurgentes. A renovated mansion really, one of a handful which claims "an ambience as authentic as the Spanish Conquest itself." Walled in by a mini-jungle extending its tropical breath through an interior rich with mosaics, giant tapestries, and carpets which soften every tread, Hacienda des Amistades provides a snug but palatial retreat for those whose priorities are privacy and luxury, where good cheer and good service partner one another year after year with unfailing loyalty.

It's 1972, and evening in Mexico City. Cloaked in the rubescent splendor of flaming torches, guests are table-hopping within the cave-like diningroom, transformed from their scantily-clad daytime personas into courtly knights and fashionably-attired ladies.

In strict attendance, smiling headwaiters who belong to a people flowing with words, clap hands to the strains of strolling mariachis, and smack pursed lips to prompt subordinates into action.

Anticipation is high for the evening's program, but no hurry, no hurry. The lament of steel guitars weaves between tables, when all else yields to their scintillation in a setting that glows like some Spanish heaven.

Time. There is always time in this country. Take the time to slap salt from the back of the hand, to catch it on the tongue. It flavors the chaser after sipping the tequila, say the waiters who collectively hold their sides over such gullible gringos!

Time to laugh, to joke, to be joked about; to languish, and to be heard. To savor a meal fit for the great Cortez himself, and to weaken to the lure of decadent desserts.

In sharp contrast, a shabby nook in the belly of the hotel serves as dressing room for Carmelita Vasquez. Its faded walls and chipped furniture do nothing to mar the elegance of the dancer who triumphs nightly over her discriminating audience. Tonight, a sequined study in red and gold, she could rival a Toulouse-Lautrec.

It is a quarter hour before her performance. Behind her a young man drapes a mantilla over tresses the color of chestnuts, and carefully arranges its shimmering lace about her shoulders. With Prussian composure and condescending phrases, he purrs, "Two colors, blending and fighting with one another, Mia Tempesta... to suit the chameleon you are."

He bends his fair head to kiss the lobe of her ear. "The pleasure, señorita, has been mine. I leave you this gift, with my admiration... and my farewell." A click of heels, a princely nod, and the door closes silently behind him.

Disbelief registers in eyes wide as a savannah and wild as a tsunami. Unruly curls tumble over a trembling mouth. There is a tap at the door—that ass of a chico has not taken much time with his second thoughts!

But it is the call. "Ten minutes!"

Scalding tears scorch a proud mouth. One does not do such thing as this to Carmelita. Not ever, in her nineteen years of life! Not even that son of a steel magnate, likening her to some discarded piñata whose stream of gratuities has run out! It is a smudge on her campagna of conquests! Cursing the day she encountered the man, Carmelita is bound up in a rage that unleashes a viper in her bosom. She strokes the edges of the lace mantilla, and with a venomous smile, fondles its delicacy as one would a weapon.

"Pronto! Pronto!" Followed by the rapping of knuckles which would set anyone's teeth on edge, Carmelita bellows in an outpouring of verbosity. Loath to be rushed at any time, on this night especially Carmelita must show who is in control.

She must get even... slowly. To salvage respect and inflict retribution on those in whose eyes she might be a laughing stock, she will allow all of them to wait. Five minutes: "Bang!" Ten: "Bang-bang-bang!" A quarter hour or so later: "BANG! BANG! BANG!" Sending more than one cucaracha scurrying for its life, Señorita Vasquez stomps her readiness....

Once again the strident, forlorn strings of steel guitars seduce the dancer's amazing precision and glowing artistry. With undulations likened to burlesque, Carmelita stretches both arms to the heavens, lifts her slender form to meet them, and with the torches of demons festering in her soul, traces the contours of her body, setting in motion her revenge.

A tap from a red satin shoe beckons the devil. Stomping heels on a polished slate floor heed the command. The sharp snaps of castinets trooping from clenched palms echo like cracks of a whip. "Clack!" "Clack!" "Clack!"... "Clack-Clack!"... "Clack-Clack-Clack!" Finally, "Clash-clack! Clashk! Clashkus! Clachkuses!"—precipitating a hell-fire that holds the audience transfixed.

Sure of the effects of her nightly ritual, Carmellita teases with practiced coquetry and an arousing display of hands meandering snakelike around her sinuous contortions. Curled and coiled, Carmelita twists and untwists like one driven by madness, but not in the least helpless in its spell.

With a smug, knowing smile, she deviates, and to a drum-roll, ravels and unravels the components of an angry soul.

Suddenly she stops, stunning her audience like some demon renewing her energy and divining her strategy.

The devil must surely be responding to the girl's shivering torso! In the cavern's rosy glow, fingertips flail, wrists fling, eyes like a furnace flash with rage, and matching tresses tumble over an exquisite mask misted with humiliation and with wrath.

To the hum of voices, the scurry of waiters and the popping of bottle corks, such performers become immune. Tonight however, there is no need. The house sits bewitched, stilled by some evil visitation that can be sensed as well as seen.

With all guests forgotten but one, Carmelita stokes the inferno smoldering inside her; but she must not lose control of it. She bites a lip curled with rancor, and a drop of blood no bigger than a pinprick leaves its mark on the lace of the mantilla twisting across her scornful chin. She slows to a halt... smiles... and with torment in her eyes, locates him, seated at a table behind a man with ruddy bald head. Softly she caresses the edges of the mantilla like a child with its blanket. And then, with fury surpassing control, tears it from her head and swings it aloft to the drowning thrums of the steel guitars.

Adrift and on course, the mantilla is commissioned with a painful message: "Vaya! Go, you evil gift from Hades! Back to him who tosses off Carmelita Vasquez like she is toy! Take with you this curse; Carmelita's personal curse. Maldiciones! May evil dog you in its shadow!" With shrill laughter, Vasquez throws back her head, and not unlike a spinning top, pivots into the finale of her devil's dance.

But Carmelita has a curve to her pitch. Either that, or the flight is not included in the curse. In any case, her aim is off. The mantilla leaps from its target like an imp with a needle in its bottom... and onto a path of its own.

With the heat of embarrassment rising to the top of his ruddy bald head, Harold Lowenthal hopes to duck before the audience ceases its ovation and looks for the errant parachute. But his judgment, too, is off. Beyond the fringe of his table, applause for the dancer changes to rollicking laughter as the mantilla crowns the red-faced gentleman with all of its radiant glory. It has to be part of the show.

Lowenthal is a blusher, but with humor his saving grace. He rises, waves, and gropes for the thing, thanking his stars for never having purchased a toupée. Once uncovered, his eyes crinkle in response to his audience, and he bows in the expected manner. Harold is a good sport.

But his choice is to avoid more attention. What is done is done, he appeals with palms down. Adjusting his cravat back into the neck of his custom-made shirt, Harold resumes his seat, crosses one knee over the other, bites off the end of a Havana cigar and flicks a gold Dunhill for a first satisfying puff. In the flickering light of the ruby smokestack centered on his table, he instinctively rates the lace with thumb and forefinger, then offers it back to a waiter. "Please return this to the young lady," he says in rapid Spanish.

With eyes full of terror and a smile that is fixed, the boy stammers, "Yours. It is yours, Señor. Si! The lady wishes it that way, I am sure!"

"Does she do this often?" asks Lowenthal, somewhat testily.

"Uh, sí... sí Señor!" lies the servant, shuddering with images of this night's terrifying performance. He dare not report that in the months Vasquez has been dancing, never has he witnessed such darkness, even from one as tempestuous as the señorita. Unknown to him, venom from a ravaged soul.

Harold examines the delicate lace. As though reading a story there, he studies the rows of snakes and serpent wings worked into the fabric. As a dress manufacturer, he recognizes workmanship. But he is first and foremost a businessman. Such quality would price a garment way out of the ready-to-wear market.

Worth a lot of money, Harold nevertheless sits alone. Mostly from choice. But this evening he feels the absence of a woman to receive the mantilla.

He begins to fold it, but a willful corner caught by his star sapphire ring whips round the uncorked neck of a bottle of Dom Perignon, spilling its remaining bubbles over the ruby tablecloth, creating a blotch to liken the eye of a bull. A sliver of glass nicks the ring finger. Harold searches for a waiter, but none is in sight.

He extracts a note from his billfold and tucks it under an ashtray on the dry side of the table. The finger throbs. He wraps it with his handkerchief, leaves the diningroom, and presents his booty at the hotel desk. "Por favor, please send this to …" Scrawling the back of a business card, he presents an address.

A circular set of stairs leads directly to Harold's suite. He takes them two at a time, his habit in keeping fit. Pleased that the pain in his hand has so quickly disappeared, he unwraps the makeshift bandage and finds that the injury has left no mark.

It really needs a good painting. Jenny's gaze sweeps the interior of the small gallery on Lower Church Street. Streaming through the store window, an early morning sun plays unkind tricks on stucco walls that persist in splitting and flaking despite the many times they have been patched. Though dressed by rows of contemporary paintings and lavish frame samples, the place nags its need of repair.

But Jenny hums as she dusts, guiding her cloth over a counter lined with various artists' supplies. From the cash drawer she sorts receipts, bills and memos, then moves on to form some order out of a scattering of tools, nails and bits of wood that await her daily attention. Shaking her head in quiet desperation, she plucks a pair of horn-rimmed spectacles, thick with sawdust, from the work table.

"Your glasses, Sam." With a sigh, she challenges the spare man who shuffles in from the back of the store on slippered feet. "You said you looked here last night?"

Sam plays with an excuse. "I didn't see them. How could I?" he shrugs. "I didn't have my glasses!"

With arms folded beneath her ample bosom, Jenny taps a foot in mock impatience. "Sam Rashman, if you tied them around your head every night, you wouldn't know where to find them in the morning!"

Sam fixes his spectacles on the end of his nose and begins to rearrange the order of his worktable into a more comfortable kind of disorder. Though meticulous about his person, in the havoc of his workbench where he's labored daily for thirty-five years, Sam finds it essential to have all tools at his fingertips in the transformation of wood into frames of museum quality. He studies a slab of beachwood, consults with his chisel, and begins to carve.

Jenny studies her husband hunched over his task like one performing a ritual he doesn't want to share. Her man is proud, with a gentle nature that only becomes riled if anyone, including his beloved son, should infer that his skills don't profit him as much as they should. Convinced that the man makes his frames to last a millennium or more, Jenny learned long ago not to count on any ship coming in. "They'll still be perfect when we are long gone, Sam," she says, not for the first time.

As always, Sam answers, "You must realize how old some of the paintings are in the Louvre, Jenny. Some with the same frames, still."

His wife tucks a hairpin into her salt-and-pepper braid. "Which exhibit the names of the artists, not the names of the framers, Sam."

"It's a matter of pride Jenny, only enjoyed if it doesn't matter who gets the credit." Sam's satisfaction with his choice of words is to him almost palatable.

"You're right about that, Sam. Pride doesn't bring any credit," Jenny bridles, content to have the last word..

"It pays your son's university tuition, so far from home!"

"*My* son? So now Jack is only *my* son?" Argument right on schedule.

But this time Sam dodges. "Jaacov," he corrects, thwarting his wife's next move.

"Jaacov," Jenny nods wistfully, though she doesn't plan for Sam to win this round, despite his manipulations. Then again, just one time maybe it wouldn't hurt. "You're right, Sam. You're a good man and a good father. Whatever you have you share with us." She regards the man so caught up in his work. To her, father and son seem as one and she cherishes the happiness they bring. "You can be proud of Jaacov. He's a credit to his papa."

Off the hook, Sam feels expansive. "And to his mama."

Jenny is happy. When so many young people behave like everything is coming to them, she and Sam are blissfully proud of a son who chose to attend university in Israel, contributing his scientific knowledge to the country's development. So young, both of them—the boy *and* the country.

With the store still empty so early in the morning, Jenny retreats to a back room which serves as a kitchen and sitting room. Though shabby, it is comfortable and clean, made cheerful with colorful cushions here and there and potted geraniums sitting in the window. Beneath them, a chipped sink and exposed pipes are reminders of the shoemaker with no shoes. "Beautiful picture frames, but no doors for the cupboards under the sink," she laments, then admonishes herself. Would this be the morning of her discontent? Well, maybe she's entitled... once in a while.

Beside a chintz-covered sofa, a 1940's console radio still works well. On its surface sits a small black and white television set. Jenny flicks both of them on, selects a station to await the morning news, and in a pleasing voice keeps time to a melody by Lawrence Welk.

In front of the sink, where she can always see it, hangs a framed photo of Jack taken two years ago when he turned eighteen. "So, when you're a science man," the mother scolds as though he is physically there, "you'll stop playing with swords, okay? One day you'll meet a fine girl, you'll make a nice home with lots of babies, and you won't have time for fencing. You'll have a different kind of fencing!" she chuckles.

Jenny might lack her son's love of the sport, but the honor of his participation in Israel's Olympic team, with its importance to the country, is a huge source of pride.

But Munich?

Jenny hesitates over a tub of pie apples she has started to peel. Germany. The place burns with memories of its reign of terror.

"Mama, it's different now," Jack wrote. For the 1972 Games, they would have to forget what happened thirty years ago. "There is no Gestapo, no discrimination anymore. A recent editorial reported that these Games are planned to erase all memory of the political overtones of Hitler's 1936 Olympic Games…. Jews are as free there today as they are in Canada."

"From your mouth to God's ear," prays Jenny, as she willfully attacks the apples bobbing in a bowl.

Sam shuffles into the kitchen with a parcel in hand. "The mailman brought it… it's for you, Jenny." His brows lift with curiosity. "Look, it's been around the world… with postmarks from at least a dozen countries! The postie pointed out where it started… from Mexico, look. Can ya imagine—almost seven months it's travelled!"

"Who would send me a parcel seven months ago from Mexico?"

"Open and find out."

"Who do I know in Mexico seven months ago? It can't be for me."

"Jenny!" cries Sam, bursting with curiosity, "Open the damn parcel!"

Like it was breakable, ignoring the likelihood that, after months in transit, if it was so fragile it would likely be broken by now, Jenny lifts the cord and gives a cautious snip. Slowly she peels off the wrappings, then crosses her hands on her chest as she takes a meaningful breath and exclaims, "Lace, Sam! Look at this—such a gorgeous thing!"

The mantilla slides over the arm of its new owner. "That painting you framed a while ago, the one of the Spanish dancer? It's one of those wadayacallits that they wear on their heads."

"When you don't remember, I don't remember," said Sam. "But I know it; it's a word sounds like a fireplace."

"Hearth… grate… stove… mantle… mantilla!" Jenny beams. She searches through the wrappings for a card or a letter, all the while scoffing and sniffing in an attempt to conceal her delight, "What am I… a glamorous dancer? Here it is. Let's see who thinks I'm a glamorous Spanish dancer." At the single business card, *Innovations by Lowenthal,* Jenny brightens with sisterly affection. "Hershel."

Which gets a grin from Sam. "He loves you, Jenny. That's why you got such a present from Mexico. You're his sister, the only family he's got."

"But he sent it seven months ago, and I never thanked him for it... and he never said anything!"

"Probably forgot the minute he mailed it. You know Hersh; he lives for his factory."

Who else does he have to live for, worries Jenny. *After losing his wife and two children in Auschwitz, he will probably never want to be married again.* Jenny sighs, "Our door is open, but I'm not alone, Sam. I can always depend on you to make him welcome."

"Such an adornment on me wouldn't look so good!" Sam teases, regarding his wife lovingly. "Hey, with a getup like that, I'll have to take you dancing!"

Jenny blushes. "Back to work—go!"

Moments later, she peers cautiously around the door. Sure that Sam isn't coming back, she drapes the lace over hair as white as snow and studies her image in a small mirror. Demurely, she lowers her eyelids over one shoulder, then winks her charm over the other. "A swinging bubby!" she giggles, wondering where the pretty girl went that used to look back.

... *"We interrupt this program to bring you a bulletin from Munich. At 5 AM, Arab guerillas surrounded the quarters of the Israeli Olympic team. It has not yet been determined how many hostages are being held at gunpoint. It has been confirmed that two Israelis have been shot."*

Jenny regards the radio as one would a predator. *What did it say? I couldn't have heard it right!...* She appeals to the photo above the sink. *Jack?*

She listens. *Where is it coming from?* Both radio and television are blaring their alarm, *just like in "War of the Worlds!"* She turns off the radio. *It's not a movie, nor is it one of those frightening commercials.* The announcer's eyes glare with shock. *Something terrible is happening. Right now, at this moment!*

A trick? Please make it be a trick.

As reality takes effect, Jenny's attempts to steady herself fail. She grabs the back of the nearest chair and tries to control the fear and helplessness that invade her entire body like cold steel. "Oh God," she whimpers, unable to find her voice. "Sam?" Her cry is unheard. She trembles like she's made of little pieces. The floor waves under her. She must not faint. She's got to reach Sam! On heavy legs, Jenny struggles toward the door, and with all of her being, holds onto it for support. "Sam!" she cries out. "Oh my God, Sam!"

In frantic pursuit of the truth, they call the Israeli Consulate which promises to report all information as soon as it is received. So far, "the situation is vague."

"We told him it's no place for them to be!" Jenny cries and wrings her hands. "Not when they could have been safe somewhere else!" Her eyes are fixed on the television screen, looking for her son in there. The compound in Munich stares back coldly. Two gray buildings look like a prison. Enemy territory, and in there one more mobilization of innocents—scooped up, just like that! Her eyes are dry and burning, widening with fear and loss. *My child... my soul....*

Sam closes the shop and lowers the shade over the window. He and Jenny huddle a few feet from the television, looking small and frail. As if their closeness to the screen might bring them nearer to their son, they clasp hands and wait, tightly bound to each report.

"At 5:15 AM, six Arab guerillas in track suits, disguised as athletes, made their way to a three-story building housing the twenty-six member Olympic team. Inside Block 31, they forced their way into a compartment occupied by Israeli athletes and demanded to know the whereabouts of the others, holding one athlete at gunpoint. The hostage guided them to the compartment which housed the wrestlers, weight-lifters, and fencers, with the hope that these members would be more physically able to overcome their assailants

"As they attempted to force the door, an Israeli coach, realizing what was happening, tried to hold them back and yelled to the others, 'Run for your lives!' He and one other, a weight-lifter, were shot at 5:25 AM. Nine hostages are now being held. The guerillas, members of a terrorist group called 'Black September,' are armed with Kalashnikov automatic rifles...."

Sam's lips move in silent prayer. He reaches across the shoulders of his wife and presses her close. "It wouldn't have mattered where, Jenny, in which country. The order of the whole world is tangled up in the whims of the mad." He read that someplace, and thought it too harsh at the time. Now, it is ridiculous to think otherwise. Why the son, and not instead the father? "Hear my prayer; hear me please." Sam pleads for a trade.

It is all happening too quickly… this possible loss of her child. Jenny leans forward and presses the ends of her fingers against her temples in an attempt to keep her wits about her. If she loses control, wouldn't it be the same as abandoning him? She must stay alert, send her energy over the waves, touch him with her strength. He will know.

The phone rings. A reporter from the city's largest newspaper would like to cover their reactions.

"Do you have children?" Jenny asks.

"Yes." Quietly.

"Then you can report them without my help."

Reactions? considers Jenny as she replaces the receiver. *I want to wrap him up like he is still my baby and take him to a safe place. But there doesn't seem to be one.*

Jenny tallies how often, in the privacy of her mind, she prays for the safety of her son. Every day, every night. Maybe that will count. But does it actually make her more privileged than one who doesn't pray? If so, then why is this happening? Where is the protection that she faithfully requests every hour of her life?

She should be offering a more elaborate prayer, perhaps, instead of the simple words she uses. She shudders with the possibility that there might be no one to listen.…

How does one explain death? she questions. *How does one make room for it, especially for that of a precious son? How does one go on living?* There would be nothing to work for then. So much nothing.…

The minutes go by with no changes. The booming voices of reporters, the interrupting bulletins, faltering words and the shaking of heads in disbelief, all are repetitive. The hours crawl. Commentary is full of contradictions. People protest that it is no longer safe to take part in the Olympics. Everywhere in the world, Jews and non-Jews are watching and waiting, shocked by events termed "inconceivable"—but perhaps, "should have been expected."

Warnings? There were plenty, Jenny agrees, *all blinded by optimism in a 'new age.' But the scourge of anti-Semitism in Europe and the Middle*

East never leaves. It churns up like worms in a dump… and Jews need to be aware of that.

Hours pass. Each new ring of the phone is like a bomb in a field of nerves. The family doctor offers to administer a sedative. Jenny refuses. A neighbor will come by with a casserole; but who can eat?

Cameras continue to pan the square at the Olympic compound. Jenny and Sam keep the captors in sight as they guard all three floors. The tall one in the white hat covering half his face… clearly the leader, paces back and forth with pistol in hand, holding court with a woman in uniform, like some self-appointed overlord anxious to demonstrate the purpose of his weapon.

"The pockmarked man negotiating with the policewoman is the leader of the group. He has announced that he will free the nine hostages in return for the release of two hundred Arab terrorists now held in Israeli jails."

Jenny's voice is weak but certain. "There are two hundred choices for Golda… and they are all enemies of Israel. She won't release any terrorists… because Israel never bargains."

But her husband's faith is difficult to disregard. Knowing how close she must be to exhaustion, Sam holds tightly to his wife's hand. "God will lead them out of this."

Jenny is a realist. She points to the small screen. "What chance, Sam? Our son might already be one of the victims." She chokes back her despair. "If he's one of the hostages, he'll be lost to us. Israel has thousands of young to protect, which would be impossible if terrorists were set free at the point of every madman's gun. Golda will never bargain, no matter how precious each life is." With the sorrow in her eyes traveling into those of her husband, she murmurs, "Sam… how can we lose him?"

It is four hours since the initial bulletin. The next one jumps in like the crack of a rifle, setting their hearts knocking with dread. *"This is ABC news, live from Munich. Egypt's Olympic representative, Ahmed Touni, has conferred with the guerilla leader. The answer has been, quote, that they care neither for money nor their lives, unquote. The West German government is prepared to pay any price for the safety of the nine Israelis. Willy Brandt has appealed to the Arabs to allow several German politicians to take the place of the prisoners, but*

Black September is adhering to initial demands and threatens to shoot all nine hostages if the noon deadline is not met. So far all previous deadlines have passed without incident. Olympic Committee Chief Avery Brundage has suspended the continuance of the games ... "

Jenny turns to her son's photograph. To her, he is very much there. Behind her is the father of this boy. Ahead of her, possible emptiness. It is not unlike the time they rushed the child to hospital with pneumonia. What did the doctor say? "We'll know in a few hours, if he's out of the woods." *There is no need to unravel time to remember how the threat of such a loss can drain one of wanting to live. Backward or forward, from the very beginning, to the very end, a mother's heart is a frail thing.*

There is a faint sound of helicopters. Those watching the screen and listening to the report of riot police inching silently toward the compound, pray that they remain unnoticed. But as they attempt to storm the building, the captors are alerted and the effort is aborted.

In her stricken state, Jenny feels catapulted onto the set of some evil movie. She must try to direct the lines and motions that will clarify and resolve the issue. But her part evades her. Weak with fright, her emotions tumble and lose direction.

She faces her adversary on the screen; the abomination commissioned from hell who scorns human life from under a white hat. Her chest constricts with images of her son caught in this barbarian's reign of terror. *What has Jaacov done to you?* she asks. *An age-old question... age old.*

Would you pretend to worship a just God... from whom you have taken control? If so, you defile that Deity with your mad interpretations of His laws!

Does that animal have a mother? Jenny agonizes. *What kind of mothers raise monsters? Or would that mother be experiencing waves of remorse for her failure to raise a decent human being in the eyes of God? Not likely.* Hadn't she just watched one interviewed on TV, with love in her eyes for her two little sons, make this statement, "I am going to raise them to kill Israelis." Just like that, expecting no retribution for the godless manipulation of her own flesh.

Have those full of vengeance not learned, all throughout history, that some Heavenly mandate has always commanded restitution for evil practiced on innocent people? Look you, with the white hat, at the history of a people who could never be conquered, though at times might have been divided. The source of that miracle, only the good Lord can devise and enforce.

But she, Jenny, would not wait for His permission. If she were there in that place, she would do what any mother would do, what that monster threatens to do. She would put an end to that evil mother's evil son—the child raised in hate—without a stab of conscience.

And for sure, she would not be alone. Imagining a team of Olympic mothers marching into the compound in Munich to take back their children, Jenny is certain that, with the heedless courage that marks such love, it would be quick work. If they lacked weapons, they would march in with kitchen tools.

In her mind she reverses these terror-filled hours as one would a home movie: to take Jack and his team back to Lod; to watch them change their minds and turn away…

Jenny blinks her eyes. ***"… are now leaving the Israeli compound in three helicopters, which are to airlift the terrorists and the nine hostages to the airport. The Germans have agreed to have a plane waiting to fly them all to Cairo."***

Jenny lifts an anguished face to Sam, "If they take him to Cairo, he's gone forever."

Across Queen Street, the bells from St. Michael's Cathedral toll the hour of four. A dooming sound in this valley of shadows, as memories of the little boy with his sweet dependency appear over and over, with his mother begging back time.

Maybe I could have been a better mother. Maybe I was sometimes impatient. I wanted to hug him again and again when he was little, but I didn't want to make him soft. Sometimes he was so cocky! So I would be purposely unsympathetic, to keep him tough… but always with my hand on his shoulder, if that's any good. I wanted to make him a good person… for his own sake. We made him a good person, Sam and I. So now, look what can happen.

He should have had more treats, more toy soldiers that he liked, the Davy Crockett hat he wished for with real raccoon skin instead of fake. But even with the cheap one, his smile was ear-to-ear, wasn't it? Was he disappointed? Maybe we should have given him more… more of our attention, more of our time. He should have had everything he wanted, that boy.

He landed in hospital with a broken leg once. A pretty nurse with red hair fed him porridge. He hated porridge, but he was smitten by her prettiness, so he ate it! Sam and I stood peeking by the door, giggling at the romantic attack on our three-year-old!

Jenny rubs her temples. She tries to breathe evenly. From her very soul, she never failed to love her son, no matter what… always wanting the best for him. *Did he know that? Does he know it now?*

I hate that cancer in the white hat. Enough to destroy him with my bare hands and to pay the ultimate penalty if need be. But hate doesn't help. I can't get to him, claw out his sight, cut off his gun hand, make him vanish. I can't reverse the danger, so that it will wash back over him. How can such evil expect glory in the next world by slicing this one to pieces? Not what anyone's God would want.

Jenny slumps once more into her vacant place. She is trapped in a desert, lost and confused, groping for a path to that merciful God who upholds her husband in his faith, but refuses to help Jaacov. Her heart crumbles. Her large eyes burn from sifting through hot, stinging sands in search of the fencer's sword, and finding that other mother sabotaging her courage, grinning her evil beside a life-size image of Jaacov planted in the sand… beyond Jenny's reach …

She can't locate the sword. She begins to shake.

Sam tries to maintain control, but his wife's suffering ends his restraint. Fear is visible in lines carved by love so deep and the violation of God's law piercing his world in such a way.

The light fades from the room unnoticed. *"This is CBS, bringing to you live coverage of the episodes in Munich as they unfold."*

Repetition, repetition. *Winners to be announced*, thinks Jenny, limp with fear. *The screen has lost its dimension. It is not possible to rescue anyone by holding onto a picture with eyes and heart. They've all gone, see? The screen is flat… like life from now on.*

She raises pained eyes to Sam's suffering. "I will make tea."

"Don't bother, Jenny."

"No bother."

Jenny stumbles around her own kitchen. She empties the water from the kettle, runs more into it, and places it on the stove. She takes a lemon from the refrigerator, slices it into wedges, one under each cup. She sets a bowl of cubed sugar on the table as the kettle begins to boil.

She turns to the man regarding Jaacov's portrait, this salt-of-the-earth father with a shawl draped over his head and shoulders and lips forming words of prayer. With shaking hands he opens the book he knows so well.

To Jenny, prayer at such a time is as sustaining as tallow in the heat of hell. But she wants to reach out to the man she has never praised enough, if only to tell him that if prayers are answered, his will surely be selected. At this moment, however, Sam walks solely with his God.

If you take this boy from us, Lord, let me follow, for I won't wish to live, she pleads. But what about the man so faithfully beside her? She has this partnership to maintain.

"Word has just been received from Feurstenfeldtbruik Airport that after a shootout between Arab guerillas and German sharpshooters, at least three Arabs have been killed. All nine Israeli hostages are believed safe and under the protetion of the Munich police."

Sam Rashman closes the Book but both parents remain unmoving. First they must take this in; then they have to believe it. Next they will be open to elation. Trembling, Jenny makes her way to her husband's side. "Sam," she whispers, "it's over? Jaacov... they say he is safe?"

Sam's eyes are veiled. He regards the woman beside him as one would a stranger, and directs his answer to The Almighty: "Our son lives. But will it ever be over?" Mindful of the presence beside him, in a strangled voice he declares, "If you're born a Jew, you need the courage to be one." With despair for a generation no more enlightened than those past, he buries his face in his hands and sobs with futility and relief.

"Come," Jenny coaxes as heartily as she can, "let's put together some sort of a meal." The telephone rings. The Consulate confirms the report.

It is two hours past midnight. Jenny fights sleep. Until she persuaded Sam to take himself up to bed, minutes had grown into hours, talking about times long forgotten. She turns off the television, unable to stand its rehashing of the event. She reaches for an afghan folded at her feet.

The wake of shock has left her numb, but slowly she dismisses what might have happened and comes to terms with what has happened. The substance of the last bulletin—"nine hostages believed to be safe"—flies repeatedly through her mind. The meaning is clear; but this mother is unable to dismiss a nagging fear. It shouldn't persist, but it does. *Who is doing the believing, and why can't they be sure?* One must have faith. But Jenny can't seem to draw on it. *It's dark out there, and vast.* And somewhere in that vast darkness, her son is 'believed' to be safe.

Relief doesn't follow; tonight finds her cautiously saving it… for when they can be sure. *One must trust… one must….* She pulls a pillow over her shoulder and tucks it under her face. With the intention of offering up a more elaborate prayer, she falls into a troubled sleep.

"Jenny?" Gently Sam shakes her awake. He is smiling. Full light comes through the window. She springs up, then lays back, dizzy, as events take shape.

"The morning paper." Sam waves it in front of her. "It's true. The news is good!"

Jenny smiles weakly. "Thanks be to God." But caution won't release its hold. *That newspaper, it was printed hours ago. This minute is not in it.* Brushing loose strands of hair from her face, she studies the phone on the wall, willing it once more to confirm. *If events change faster than the television can announce, what good is the morning paper?*

She pushes the thought into a collection of other thoughts she doesn't want to let in, but can't chase away. "You must be hungry Sam," she says. "I'll make us breakfast."

"I'll start it; take your time." While Jenny gets dressed, Sam switches on the radio, singing to himself as he cuts and juices some oranges. With lively gestures inspired by some blaring rock and roll, he swirls the golden nectar into two small glasses as one would a fine wine.

He switches off the radio and turns up the TV.

"We interrupt this program to confirm an earlier report from Munich. As a result of the shootout last evening between Arab terrorists and German sharpshooters, the final toll stands as follows: all nine hostages, five terrorists, and one policeman are believed dead."

Sam searches to find a place for the kettle he holds in one hand and a jar of tea in the other. He drops them on the counter with a thud and stares at the anchorman.

"What the... *hell*... are you... *doing in there* !" he hisses. *"Playing GAMES with me? While those VERMIN conspire with evil? WHERE... in that area of STINKING DECREPITUDE is MY SON!"* Last evening he pledged a debt to God. This morning... was he being called upon to pay it?

"We'll open the store Sam," Jenny declares. She stands in the doorway, her hand clutching the front of her blouse. She expresses no panic. Her face is like stone.

"Open the store?"

Jenny's eyes are bright. "Please Sam, go open the store. We must not let ourselves be battered, dying minute by minute in front of the TV. No matter how bad it looks, we must not weaken. We have to keep things straight.

"Any other way, we can be of no use to Jaacov. It would be like deserting our post, giving White Hat the upper hand. One must not reward evil." Jenny tastes bile as she recalls the less-than-human figure on the screen. "We must... we must carry on. That is how we show our faith." Her reasoning wants no argument.

If they were to accept the unacceptable, it would be like sitting shiva. They must not mourn. It is important to attend to their daily tasks as always. In Jenny's mind, that will shut the door on acceptance.

The rasp of a blind breaks the morning silence. The latch unlocks with a snap. Street sounds come from somewhere. A car door shuts, a tram swishes by, a tour bus chugs up from King Street, and a voice calls from across the way, all unaware of what is happening to Jaacov. The city sounds that Jenny always welcomed now seem harsh and unfeeling.

From the front of store comes a muffled sound of voices, ponderous and low. With her heart numb, Jenny puts on a face and straightens her back.

In the light of the shop window, the tall silhouette of a man stands with hands buried in the pockets of his blue denim jeans. His face is creased with concern; he looks to Jenny with eyes blue as cobalt, and whispers, "I came as soon as I heard..." In an attempt to insert hope into his words, the man hunts for the right ones. "All over the world good people are praying… whoever those thugs with their political mission are, they have to consider how they will be judged. This cowardly act… they won't get what they demand from it. They have to reconsider." He knows that the hope he is offering may be false.

He yearns to take on this terrorist muck, rendering them eunuchs, for they cannot be called men. Since the beginning of time, the world has produced its beasts—like these who take their orders from the mad and expect heavenly rewards for their treachery, which clearly expresses the simplemindedness of those so easily inflamed and manipulated by tyrants whose powers depend totally upon them. If there are such places as heaven and hell, he determines, such creatures will clearly go south.…

Kenneth Ryan tastes the truth of this prediction silently on his lips, as though the good Lord personally promised it. His way of balancing, but of little saving grace to the here and the now. He fixes his eyes on Jenny. She sees them: affection and strength in a pillar of support.

Kenneth Ryan is a renowned artist, still youthful at the age of forty-five. Their relationship is not merely professional. Ken has been coming to The Frame Shop since he began the struggle to make his name… a dozen years or so ago, with Jenny and Sam lending encouragement bordering on parental pride. Anytime Ken needs a renewal of some warm and tender attachment, or when he simply wants to check on his friends, he drops by to chat, always to be fortified by a warm welcome and Jenny's sensational cooking: "Just a snack; it's cooking itself in the kitchen… no bother, it's a pleasure!"

Today, she thinks, *there would have been apple strudel.*

They could be sure that Kenny would come from wherever he might be in this crisis. For this, he shortened a much needed holiday in the Bahamas, but good that he is here. Good to sense his nearness and devotion. She grasps his hand and holds it. "We must wait like the other parents are waiting," she says, her eyes unblinking, her features set. "We need to let the minutes tell us what to do." With her hand clasping his, Jenny leads him into the back room. "Right now talk to us, Kenneth. Tell us what it's like in the Bahamas… while we watch, and listen with the other ear," she says, pointing to the television screen.

With one fear and one hope, the three bond as one. For them, there are no precedents, no directions for dealing with this threat, for confronting it and smiting it, as one would a snake. Society is suffering a breakdown, Ken concludes. These people are approaching a dead end… and tomorrow may find them facing it.

Ken stares unseeing at a piece of lace draped over a kitchen chair, prompting Jenny's explanation, "It's from my brother… from Mexico. It came in the mail yesterday. It's a mantilla," she races on with a fixed smile, twisting a corner of the lace in an unconscious effort to wring out her distress. "He thinks I'm still his… pretty little sister," this time with no joy in her voice.

"Fascinating," Ryan remarks half-heartedly. But it wouldn't do justice to his little sister. If he were to put Jenny on canvas, the importance of the lace mantilla would be like a spoonful of snow in the warmth of her beautiful soul.

"That lady in your paintings," Jenny says in an attempt to be light, but with a catch in her throat at the thought of never seeing her son fall in love… never greeting his choice of a mate… never holding his babies in her arms. "Please take it for her. It would please me if you would paint her wearing this."

Jenny recognizes exquisite handiwork. In her anguish, she comments fully on that of the mantilla. "The patterns are not the same all over, which shows that it's all hand-knotted… hours and hours of delicate labor. The comb is real tortoise, see, and set with ivory and turquoise. They don't make them like that anymore. It's not like ordinary lace; it's like… some magic." Jenny parcels it in its wrapping and with all good intentions, hands it to Ken. "It's hers. No use to argue—"

A piercing ring from the phone halts conversation. Sam answers quickly while his wife stands transfixed. "Yes, this is Rashman. Hello? Hello? I can't hear, there's too much static!" he yells. He turns to his wife with anxiety and hope written on his face, "Jenny? Maybe you can hear better?"

Ken's hand squeezes her shoulder. She knows that this is the moment… when the last fragments of hope might be swept away. How can she make it to the telephone? *God, would you bless us with a son in our late years, only to take him away? Please don't… please reconsider… please… for just a little longer.*

Jenny takes a breath, shuts her eyes, and brings the receiver to her ear. "This is Jenny Rashman."

Copious static drowns out the echo of a voice. "Please, speak louder. Who is calling?" Weak with alarm, she recognizes the swishing sound in a long distance call. "*Oh my God!*" she gasps with a cry. "Yes! *Yes*, this is *Mama!* Jack, is that you? Dear God, my son Jaacov—he's *there!* That's *you*, son, it's *true*? Dearest, dearest God—my son is *safe!*"

At the sound of his voice, the mother sobs, emerging weak and trembling from some dark pit. "Where *are* you? Are you alright? Are you... *unhurt?*" Fearing a disconnection, she holds tightly to the phone, her knuckles white. "Speak *more*, Jack! I need to hear your voice telling me you're alright!" As she listens to the one she loves so dearly, tears finally flow, uncontrolled.

She and Sam share the receiver. Jaacov assures them in a somber voice of his well-being. As soon as trouble was suspected, their group came under heavy guard.

The fourteen survivors would be leaving for Israel immediately, along with the bodies of the nine victims to be buried the next day. His voice echoes with pain.

"I know a little something of how you must feel," says Jenny, not bothering to wipe away her tears. She places a hand over her heart, then reminds herself, "Here son, you must speak directly to Papa. He doesn't hear so good, but he needs to hear you say to him personally that you're okay."

Sam holds the phone with Jenny hugging his arm. "Of *course* we're okay!" he screams. "What would you *expect* from the parents of Jaacov! If *you* have to live with it, so will *we!*"

The mother's face is a map of gratitude. She falls wearily against Kenneth's waiting shoulder, sobbing with thanks for her son's safety, with sorrow for his lost teammates and their families so brutally robbed, and with futility for a world increasing with evil. *It will never be the same for any of us*, she thinks, *personally involved or not. Faith won't disappear, but neither will it be unconditionally embraced. If human life can be so trivialized, faith will always be tested and coated with caution.*

Ken lets his own thanks fall silently from his lips. Reports from Munich will be kinder to some than to others. But all of humanity will bear the scars.

Slowly, Sam puts the receiver back in place. His face glows with his answered prayer.

"Will he be coming home to us soon?" Jenny had forgotten to ask.

With a wide, determined grin, Sam answers, "Pack a bag, Mrs. Rashman! Close the store! We're going to Israel!"

———

Marjorie stores her carry-on under the seat ahead, fastens her seatbelt, and lifts the shade from the little window on her left. Vibrations rumble through the giant 747 as it positions for take-off, its huge jets whining and roaring. With a jerk, the brakes are released and the blurring runway releases its hold as the mighty aircraft heads for the clouds.

Lift-offs and landings always make this passenger nervous. She grips the armrests as if to help boost the plane upward. As it climbs and pillows, one level at a time, and the city recedes to toy-like proportions, the singing of the jets announces their undisputed control. Marjorie closes both eyes, sucks in her breath and wills the ship to remain airborne.

11:10, exactly on time. Tension begins to fade. The woman loosens her clutch on the armrests, her knuckles relax. She releases her seatbelt and lights up a Contessa Slim.

"Air Canada welcomes you aboard Flight 910 to Miami." It's a holiday voice: like jingle bells, trained for levity.

A twenty-four hour layover, caused by stormy weather, finds passengers in various moods. Babies cry, parents scold. Some grumble about the weather or the airline. Because people are exhausted, there is little holiday spirit left on this trip to America's vacationland. Marjorie looks to the man on her right whose mouth is already slack with sleep, so she turns to the patchwork scene below, its lakes and rivers golden in the sunlight.

Her reverie is interrupted. "Would you care for a beverage, miss?" Marjorie mouths her order to the flight attendant who flips down a tray from the back of the seat ahead. The frosty cocktail is good; it hits the spot where courage waffles.

She's done it. Safe that no one has missed her yet, she dismisses the pain left in her wake. She doesn't want to think about it.

She should have left a note.

Let's see: *Dear Phil: How are you? I am fine. I hope you are fine, too. I have some news: I didn't want to leave you... but sometimes it's necessary to choose, you know? So guess what?*

What words can explain abandonment ... of a husband and father who works so hard to support his family? What words will express his feelings when he finds her gone?

"She left me!" Or maybe, "Good riddance!" Or, "She went down in that plane." Most frightening of all, she can never go back... except to remember ...

—————

Marjorie regarded her husband as he lay on the sofa in exhausted sleep. She'd learned to be patient about these weekend afternoons, but lately she found herself invaded by a growing restlessness, difficult to control.

She closed the book she was reading , walked to a window overlooking the garden with its tiered decks, oversize swimming pool and cabana, and hugged herself with both arms in an attempt to squeeze out this recurring feeling. That cardinal in the apple tree. She wondered if the same one returned every year. She envied it its freedom. Life was closing in on her and she knew that it was partly her fault.

"It's a tribute to my toil!" Phil had cried when she rebelled against the purchase of their Georgian mansion. He had certainly earned it; she had to acknowledge that. So she had given in.

Phillip loved the rich setting of their antique-filled home, cherished the wine cellar with its select vintage labels, and continually stocked his walk-in closet which at present housed forty pair of shoes, dozens of suits and countless shirts, some never out of their wrappers.

Stuff. Something vital gets lost with every purchase, and life feels emptier. It will be worse in the fall when our youngest leaves for Queen's, she reckoned.

Everything was in place. So there was little to anticipate. No more goals to strive for, no exciting challenges. They simply did their separate things; he traveled, she stoked the home fires. It was senseless to look back. Yet… had they remained in their cozy bungalow, with the neighbors constantly popping in and out, she likely wouldn't be feeling so lonely. She missed the life they left.

But she wasn't being realistic: the past could never be recaptured, for many of the old neighbors had also "moved up." Nevertheless, Marjorie couldn't hold back an acute wave of nostalgia for the two babes in the woods struggling to get started, in support of each other and very in love. Now, with most struggles behind them, she ought to be relaxed and happy. So, what exactly was going wrong?

Phil was always somewhere else, that's what. Life was one adjustment after another. No sooner would their lives get back on track, he was off and away. Constant interruptions retarded maturing together, with the result that they were used to being "single."

A big part of that was the lack of connection with her husband's feelings, never shared. In a joke perhaps, or in an off-the-cuff remark, easily brushed over or tucked away in his insular place if she responded with too much caring. In all the years they'd been married, she'd never really got to know him. Too often, though they might be in the same room, Marjorie felt alone.

Was there any way to feel spiritually intimate with this man? From the beginning, I've been in his cheering section. Today, H. Phillip Campbell is successfully placing his medical machines into hospitals all over the world, saving thousands of lives every day, she estimated. Why isn't he attuned to mine?

Was she jealous of his freedom? Perhaps. Or worried about other women along the way? She didn't think so. Honest and independent in nature, she'd never questioned her husband's fidelity. Marjorie knew without a doubt that Phil loved her, that she would come first in any situation. She held him close as well, but not with a tight leash. In the twenty-three years they'd been married, she had seen so little of him.

Can't have it all, she lectured the possibly spoiled lady within. Phil wasn't used to a whining wife, and certainly wouldn't appreciate that sort of noose around his neck. Despite what one might achieve or possess, there will always be something to deal with, improve upon or repair, she reasoned. Simply put, that's life.

They had to attend a wedding at five. What a day for formal attire! A scorcher. Marjorie hated to hurry Phil out of his comfortable place. He seemed more exhausted than ever these days, and small wonder. To maintain their standard of living, he traveled more than forty weeks of the year. Watching him sleep, she summed it all up. With the acquisition of more and more wealth, the treadmill increased its toll.

At her touch, Phil stretched and rubbed the sleep from his eyes with clenched fists. "Hi kitten," he grinned sheepishly, the cleft in his chin and the corners of his mouth widening together. "Have I been out long?"

"Wakey wakey! Time to get ready."

"Hm? Oh yeah." He ran his fingers around a jaw sporting the second stubble of the day, and through silvery curls cut to a short Afro. He groaned, "What a day for a collar and tie."

"Be glad you don't have to wear a tight sari!" Marjorie laughed, as her husband bolted from the sofa and took the stairs two at a time. It would take him an hour to dress.

But in just a few moments he was back, calling to her from the top of the circular stairway. "How's this?" Her sari was draped over his torso. The back of one hand rested on his head; the other sat on his hip. From one nostril dangled the hoop of one gold earring. "Wanna trade?"

He looked like Chiquita Banana. Her laughter rippled. Funnier still was his expression, all agog in anticipation of her laughter. She wouldn't disappoint.

Lifting his skirt and with ungainly steps, the husband ran down the stairs, gathered the wife into his arms and murmured, "Do we have to go to that wedding?"

"Afraid so," she declared, her laughter on a slow fade. "Anyway, you hardly turn me on in that get-up, you know!"

"Okay." Phil gave her rump a slap and ran back up the stairs.

Marjorie shook her head in amazement. Phil was a tired old guy one moment and a funny kid the next. There was no in between. He seemed compelled to spend his waking moments entertaining her, to make up for the hours on end that he slept. No time was taken to address the things that mattered; so adept was he at avoiding them.

But he was witty, responsible and kind, and possessed many other attributes that she could go on listing. Of course she loved him. If she had her life to live over she would marry him again… wouldn't she?

Marjorie was adjusted to her life and was utterly unused to self-pity. But something was happening that couldn't be explained.

An hour to the minute, Phil was dressed, immaculate in a dark blue tuxedo, cut slim in the style of the day. White collar and cuffs showed just enough of themselves; a neatly tied cravat, gold cufflinks and soft calf shoes shone in harmony with the man's impeccable taste.

They met at the top of the stairs. "You're very handsome," declared Marjorie. "I'll try to do you justice." Up on her toes, she planted a kiss on the tip of her husband's nose. "Start the Jag, I'll be with you in a minute."

Marjorie scribbles around the maple leaf on her paper coaster. What exactly would she say was the matter with her marriage? Was it only "a matter" after all? Again she shifts her attention to the landscape below peeking through gauzy layers of clouds …

August had not been warm. Marjorie was wearing a bulky knit sweater as she strode through Edwards Gardens, viewing the various paintings displayed by The Group of One Hundred. With Phil gone, she often spent her Sundays this way. Beside a bold group of paintings she paused to light a cigarette.

"No smoking, please."

She looked around for the voice.

"Didn't you notice the 'No Smoking' sign?" His tone was severe. It drew her toward a display of paintings propped on a table, which made a perfect hiding-place for the red-haired man sitting in a deck chair. The artist, she supposed.

"No smoking," he repeated less severely. "These paintings are highly inflammable!"

"S-sorry," stammered Marjorie, dropping the offensive object on the ground and stubbing it out with her toe. She faced her accuser with large green eyes, which met impish blue ones. "Joke?" she ventured.

"The best I could think up at the moment. You seemed so serious." His grin was boyish, his manner gentle, and there was a quality in his tone that said he wasn't being fresh. However, she had come here to view art, not to joke. She lit another cigarette and studied the canvases. "Are these paintings yours?"

"As a matter of fact... they're not. I'm sitting in for a friend."

Marjorie cupped her chin with one hand, rested her elbow on the other, and closely examined each portrait. "The artist is a man," she stated.

"And how do you know that, young lady?"

Despite feeling patronized, she pointed to a canvas. "The strokes are bold. The artist catches his subject, but he doesn't capture the essence. For example, in this one, a woman's feelings on parting from a man in uniform, should express itself in her posture because it's only her back we see. There is little emotion as she watches him, knapsack over his shoulder, walk from her into the sunset. She could be modeling leisure clothes, for all it says."

To choke back his amusement, the man answered immediately. "You're correct about the sex of the artist, but I can't agree with your diagnosis. Why would lack of emotion rest solely with the artist being male? Have you ever seen a Schaeffer, a da Vinci... a Rubens?"

"Yesterday's man," Marjorie stated flatly. "This is today's."

The man's brow furrowed at her analysis. He began with his own, but the hurried steps of a short, husky man interrupted it. "Thanks, buddy," he waved, resuming ownership of his stall.

Ken walked the few steps to where Marjorie had wandered. "Did you want to discuss a painting with Bob?" At the shake of her head, he asked, "May I walk along with you, then?"

It's your park. "Of course," she answered, pleased with the company of one who could talk about art, even in disagreement.

"I'm Ken." He offered his hand.

She offered hers. "I'm Marjorie Campbell."

"So you think you're an expert, Marjorie Campbell."

Was he being supercilious? "No... but ..." Or was he teasing? Never mind, she found this chatter invigorating. "But I wasn't wrong, was I?"

The sun appeared, bringing with it a sudden humidity. She took off her sweater and swung it along behind her.

Ken's eyes twinkled. "Right. This time. Depends on whether or not you want a job as an art sexer."

"A what?" If she knew him better, she would hit him with her sweater. One more joker, she lamented. Her next comment had to be expected. "You can't be serious!" Of course he wasn't. "You funny men," she added with a sigh.

"You funny lady!" he mocked with a chuckle.

He was taller than she'd thought, and quite slim. His features looked chiseled, and faint lines wrinkled the corners of his eyes. His hair was wind-tossed, with streaks of salt and pepper running through the red. As he walked, he led with his shoulders. When he spoke, his voice was deep, but soft as down.

"Do you paint?" she asked, shading her eyes to examine a bronze. "Some."

"Are any of your paintings here?"

"Not today."

"Are you an only-when-you're-in-the-mood painter, or do you make your living at it?"

His smile deepened then sobered. "Both." An idea dawned. "Though in the mood, I'm in need of an inspiration. Would you mind if I sketched you?"

She flushed. "Now?"

He nodded, then grinned. "Now is always the best time."

"I'm... I'm not sure just how good an inspiration I would be."

"You'll be fine."

While Marjorie continued to wander, Ken went to his car for paints and brushes, an easel and a three-legged stool.

"Do you always cart that equipment with you?" she asked.

"Does a doctor carry his bag?"

Marjorie sat quietly on a grassy spot while the artist appraised her position, profile and figure. "Would you turn a little this way, Marjorie?" he requested.

Marjorie shifted, smoothing the sweater beneath her. She lifted a hand to brush a strand of hair from her face. "Better?"

"Much... now stay as you are." He became stern. "Keep looking this way. Think of someone important to you... or, if you don't mind, something of personal importance at this moment in time. I want to capture a look, any look, but it has to be real." Uh-huh. He'd pushed a button. Contoured by waves of gold stippled with sun and shade, two lips parted and a pair of emerald eyes turned wistful. "Excellent," he said in a low voice.

She was freshly showered and smelled of Estée's White Linen when she opened the door to Ken the following Sunday. She'd just had a swim and her hair was damp and curly. A full week of Indian summer sun added freckles to her tan. She looked youthful and not at all as sophisticated as she had the week before.

"Did you finish it?" she asked eagerly, as she ushered the artist into her home.

"I stopped working on it, if that answers your question. I never regard my work as finished, because I'm never totally satisfied with what I set out to paint. But that comes with the territory," Ken grinned.

Marjorie felt humble. "May I see it?"

With slender fingers Ken unwrapped the canvas for her inspection. After several moments he said, "Your eyes are getting deeper with your thoughts.... You don't like it."

"It's... incredible," she said, as the crossroads of her life looked back as though waiting for direction.

Ken wondered what the portrait conveyed to this woman. "Nevertheless, you seem puzzled."

"It's just that... you caught it so well." Marjorie paused, not without awe. "You couldn't have known, yet you've captured my thoughts... I swear it." Her eyes traveled down to his signature. "Hardly an objective painter, Mister Ryan. 'The' Kenneth Ryan, am I right?"

He looked apologetic.

"Forgive me for quizzing you last Sunday, burdening you with my opinions!" She couldn't have explained why, but instead of feeling embarrassed, Marjorie felt laughter. She bowed her head and shrugged her shoulders with feigned atonement, "To think I was helping a struggling artist with his idea of an inspiration!"

While Phil was still in Europe, Ken continued to paint Marjorie. In full sunlight on the deck of her pool and at twilight as she gazed at a darkening sky from his studio window. In blue jeans and sweatshirt, a flowing caftan, and regal in her silk sari. As he painted her, he couldn't help focusing on her eyes: large and questioning, smiling through sadness… exquisitely green. He couldn't know, just as Marjorie didn't know, that at these moments she was entirely at peace with her life.

"We are approaching Miami International Airport. Please remain in your seats, fasten your seatbelts and obey the No Smoking sign. We hope you enjoyed your flight. Thank you for flying Air Canada."

The landing is smooth.

From the lower concourse of the horseshoe-shaped terminal, Marjorie takes an elevator to the second level and the Foreign Exchange office. She trades some U.S. dollars for the equivalent in cordobas and stuffs the pile of bills into a zippered tote.

Accompanied by the strains of Christmas carols, which seem untimely in this climate, Marjorie wanders through the upper concourse where she buys a New Yorker, then backtracks to the elevator to push the up button to the International Hotel Restaurant. She occupies a small table overlooking Concourse B, and finds it lulling to watch B.O.A.C, Braniff and Caribair flights planing on and off the runway like a plait of hair being braided.

She orders a daiquiri. She's eaten nothing since breakfast, but pushes away thoughts of food. Halfway to her destination, as deceit stabs its painful thorns into her conscience, she begins to feel quite strange.

Ken was teaching her how to paint. He got her to mix different hues, to thin tacky oils, keeping them moist until they were no longer needed. "Decide what you want on your canvas, and stick with it. The great thing about oils, if you make a mistake or change your approach, you can paint over them."

Like most beginners, Marjorie was convinced that her attempts were trivial and stiff. But Ken insisted that she had a flair.

"Are you sure you've never painted with oils before?" he asked.

Convinced that he was being kind, she answered simply, "No, I never have." Then again, maybe he was actually seeing some quality in her work. Wouldn't that be something?

Marjorie worked with furious dedication, hands and face smudged with oils. During these sessions she and Ken got to know each other.

"What does your husband think of your paintings?" Ken asked one late September afternoon.

"He likes them. He thinks it's great that I've decided to do this."

"Mmm."

"He's an extremely ambitious person, so naturally he looks at everything with marketability in mind." There was a stall in her voice, like an unfinished thought. "Always reaching for the top, the best that he can be. Driven."

"In his field there's no room for imperfection," Ken concurred. "Where is he this week?"

"Switzerland. A large medical center is interested in the latest apparatus, a type of scanner for the entire body. If successful, it should eventually replace the x-ray machine. After that, he's scheduled to go on to West Germany for a conference."

"You must miss him."

"We've been married for twenty-three years, Ken. In all that time I've become used to long separations, though I'll never get to like them."

"I hear ya."

"Painting is good for me, my friend. When one is content, time speeds along on winged feet"

"You have talent," Ken repeated. "Your work bears witness to an artist hopefully not merely marking time," he said crisply.

Marjorie caught the bite in his voice. Her attention swung swiftly to the face that tried to be casual. Her rejoinder, "Of course I'm not. I wouldn't call doing what I enjoy simply 'marking time.'"

Ken slipped from the front of his easel, and bent over Marjorie's shoulder to examine the canvas she had propped on her knees, a position she seemed to favor. Fiercely he snapped, "What the devil are you painting?"

"Two people on a park bench." Her eyes were huge.

"Then paint them!" he barked. "Stop cluttering your canvas with birds and trees and pretty flowers! You're not in kindergarten! Paint your subject!" Regarding her half-hurt eyes, he pressed on in a gentler tone, "Look Marjorie, you're going along in an attempt to fill a canvas... but you're not showing a purpose. You've got to paint with the emotions that affect you. Remember the canvas you criticized at the art show? Feelings! In order to project them into a work of art, you've got to bare yourself—grasp them from your soul and bring them to your canvas! You've got to put yourself in there and live it, true to your inspiration and your reason for painting it.

"Everyone who sees your work has got to be moved by it. If you paint, as your husband expects, with 'success' as your goal, then you have to give a person who buys one of your paintings, an excuse to buy another!"

Spacing his words to give them emphasis, he continued, "Live... for your... art, and keep broadening... your horizons. There's a downside: you need to love what you do, but rarely are you a hundred percent happy with the result.

"Sometimes the subject captures your brush and paints itself, no matter how hard you work to turn it around. Sometimes the result resembles a collision between you and it.

"The way you are painting—like a contender in a Monet look-alike! The inspiration is okay, but... you've got to add your own strokes, insert your personality into the creation of your personal style... without an attempt to copy that of another artist, though your preference for his technique will show itself and might be pleasing. Trust me."

Ken gestured around his studio. "These paintings: some folks may not like them nor want them. Some may laugh; some may scoff or ridicule. Others may be puzzled or angered, receiving some message unknown to me. But hopefully they're going to be affected, Marjorie. They're going to think about them one way or another, because each was kick-started by intent and painted with emotion." Ken patted her shoulder. "Don't be afraid to put your heart into your work. Tackle your subject directly and honestly. It'll all fall into place, you'll see." He shivered as though a cold knife twisted inside him. He looked into her eyes. "You'll be happier, I promise you."

Marjorie's spirits soared with the meaning of his words, and she felt a new kind of ache. Ken was a compassionate man, yet he'd shot her down in flames. Which made her feel ecstatic! How come?

She answered her own question: because his role as teacher compelled him to honor it with professional honesty. She could definitely trust him. Her face on canvas wasn't all that mattered: he cared about her work, her desire to achieve, her self esteem. That part of her, so long on hold, she welcomed back.

She would do this. She picked up a brush, coated it generously with color, and applied it to her canvas with bold strokes and a point to make. "Move over, C.M.!" she joked. "Make way for M.C.!" Laughter rang, awkwardness faded. Marjorie dove into her work with zeal, and hope came tagging along.

———

"Pan American Flight 503 now boarding at Gate 4." Scooping up her hand luggage, Marjorie pays the bar tab and catches the elevator to the boarding gate.

In the half-empty 707, she clicks back the armrests, lifts her feet, and stretches her legs on the empty seats beside her. Placing a pillow under one shoulder, she turns her attention to the rivers and lakes below, scrolled in the first shrouds of night. They look touchable, those shadowed valleys between the sculptured hills, reminiscent of young David's fourth grade salt and flour mould of a native village, shaped together by mother and son. David... now halfway across the world.

In her thoughts: How many love affairs am I looking down upon? In this aircraft, where only I and the other passengers seem real, I wonder if unseen things exist. Do unseen people love? Hate? Silly thoughts. Still, over how many throw-away marriages do I now preside from my superior advantage of height?

———

It was late October. Ken and Marjorie drove up to Belfountain Park with their paints, easels and a picnic basket packed into Ken's Safari stationwagon. They settled on a wide flat rock surrounded by explosions of color.

Marjorie sat cross-legged, and whipped out her box of paints. Her challenge was nature's brilliant palette; her intent was to dazzle, and she painted with growing excitement while Ken illustrated how to add depth and action with the use of more than one color in a single brush-stroke. Caught up in the results, Marjorie wasn't aware that her instructor did no painting, that he sat and watched her instead.

With the beginnings of awareness, she lifted her eyes to his. Confusion tripped along with her heart. She could hear it! Their eyes locked. A blush crept into her as she tore her gaze away.

Ken placed his hand over hers and she read the question in his eyes. She felt happy; all emptiness had long disappeared. Such an unexplainable thing, this: a look, a stab of consciousness, a centering, and a woman knows. Clearly, here was where she belonged.

Lost in the commitment of the moment, two complete strangers who had met by chance in a city park, who shared a friendship with a smile, a touch, mutual interest... could hardly anticipate the pattern that fate was weaving for them both.

They drove in silence to Ken's apartment. It was twilight, and music gently filled the place. Stardust. A favorite. He would know. Because he knew her. Like they were kids running out of time, they had used theirs to get to know one another... and had taken note.

Was she in love with Ken? Or was she looking at him through the eyes of an adolescent? But for the gnawing guilt, Marjorie wanted to be nowhere else but here. You are right, Ken; each bold stroke... affects someone.

She could never leave Phil. Then what would her love be worth to this man? Left alone by a travel-happy husband, and facing an empty nest, she was likely on a dangerous curve. Had Ken been otherwise committed, this might be a harmless interlude, a sweet flirtation for them both, however irresponsible.

Her wisdom stated and her eyes implored, "No good can come of this for you."

It was another voice, in another place, in another world. "Love can't be anything but this." Ken stroked her brow. She let her head drop to his shoulder. He lifted her chin, kissed her eyelids, then kissed her lips.

His lips traced her earlobes, her throat, to circle her shoulders and tease their way to the valley between her breasts. She ran her fingers through his hair and slowly circled his chest. In mounting response, his kisses covered her; and she embraced the completeness of him. She didn't close her eyes. She had to see his face, share in his discovery of her, his pleasure, his passion and his release. And he had to share in hers. Touched by sweeping sensations, she gasped with the thrill of him, and breathed in the nearness of him that was like a series of tiny electric shocks in a warm bath.

They trembled and soared. They careened into the race to meet, leaving them spent, in some holy place, far, far above where they lay....

In the pale light of approaching dawn, Marjorie gazed at Ken's striking profile, half-turned to her in sleep. His arm still held her. All that was hidden was now theirs, with none of the guilt she feared may come with the morning. No regrets. With a sigh, she fell into the soft slumber that only comes before break of day.

———

Twilight doesn't linger at thirty-thousand feet. Without warning, darkness lays its cape over all, and it is suddenly night. Tiny lights flash off the wingtips, like children vying for attention: "Look at me!" Blink! Blink! "Look at me!"

Marjorie accepts coffee from the stewardess, lights up, and watches the smoky wisps from her cigarette rise lazily toward a nozzle that says *Oxygen*; to be whirled, lured, and swallowed. Dismissed. Just like that.

———

A ring of the telephone interrupted the reunion between husband and wife. Marjorie broke from Phil's embrace and turned to answer its insistent peal.

"Hi Marjorie. What're ya doin'?"

The voice was familiar. "Who is this?" she asked.

"Canchoo guess?"

"Afraid not," she snapped.

"It's Jerry Forrester!" sounding as though she'd just won a lottery.

Obviously he'd been drinking. But her voice warmed with relief. "Hi Jerry... how are things with you?"

"Not good a'tall. C'mon over. Wanchoo t' come over."

Marjorie was startled but remained polite. "Uh, Why don't you and Georgia come over here?"

"Can't. Georgia left me. All gone. Poof!"

Only a month ago, Jerry and Georgia had celebrated their twentieth anniversary. But Jerry's wife, a full-time crusader for whatever social or political issue prevailed—Marjorie forgot the current one—was never home. Turning away from each other would be their way of handling a problem, but this one right here would be nipped in the bud. "I'm very sorry about you and Georgia. Hold on a moment... I'll ask Phil if he's up to going out again. He's just arrived from Europe."

Marjorie handed Phil the phone, but his "Hi Jerry!" was answered by a dial tone. Phil looked to his wife. In the silence that followed, she said nothing.

To her dismay, Phil answered her stricken expression with a chuckle, "Well, you can't blame him for trying! The guy is always alone!"

How easily he understood. What about her? "Would you like me to make dates when you're away with anyone who happens to be available?" fumed Marjorie, with little expectation of a sensible answer.

She didn't get one. "Honey," he said, "you can do anything you want... as long as you come back to me!"

Trivialized. Or was this some kind of trade-off, wondered Marjorie. My freedom for yours, perhaps? Formula for the modern marriage: hold close, with one foot out the door. Such suggestions of entitlement represented a trend, but were nothing more than easy abdications of responsibility. She felt empty.

She wouldn't want an altercation with Phil over tonight's episode, but she was wise enough to know that in order to remain loving, partners had to review once in a while. At this point, Marjorie was questioning her husband's caring, his protection of her and their marriage, and the whereabouts of the warm feeling that comes with being cherished.

Phil might well be sending an essential message in an abstract way. Hadn't he always had trouble expressing his feelings up front? Perhaps this latest statement was meant to announce a new attitude furnishing a comfortable place for him, while loosening the strings for her. He trusted her implicitly; but there was a vast difference between trust and complacency, that of taking her for granted. She had never betrayed him.

Until now.

Now, in her mind, she'd lost the right to consider herself part architect of a happy marriage. Was this one hopeless, or worth a continuous effort to change it in the endless search for honest communication? How was it possible to enrich a relationship all by oneself?

"Marjorie," Phil announced two days later, "I've got to go abroad again."

Adjusting the thermostat on the chilly November morning, she simply asked, "When?"

"Friday." It was the Sunday before.

"Where to this time?" she said in a dull voice.

"London. But it'll be a short trip. Ten days, two weeks at the most."

Her response was sudden. "Take me with you?" she begged, like a frightened child.

He seemed annoyed, but said, "You know what business trips are like: same old, same old. Like the one in Paris two years ago. Can't be with you during the days. You'll be alone."

And what do you think I've done here all these years? was her silent rejoinder. Obviously, I'm not just a passenger in your vehicle, husband! My track record boasts a fair measure of independence. She'd had a fine time in Paris all on her own, which, she'd discovered wasn't always a terrible way to travel, especially in the City of Light, referred to as a woman's city.

"I think I can manage." Her voice was tired.

"If you really want to go...." he mumbled with a half smile. Back to his morning paper, he reached for a second piece of toast and buttered it without taking his eyes off what he was reading.

Marjorie poured herself some coffee, and repeated, "I do want to go." She waited for an indication that he'd actually heard her. When that didn't happen, she broke into his concentration. "It's important to me to get away with you for a while. Our marriage needs more time together." But the absence of his attention made her no longer sure of how it would help.

Ten minutes passed before Phil folded one section of the paper, put it aside and reached for another. "Our flight leaves at 8 PM. I'll call the airlines and book passage for you."

The following evening was cold, crisp, and starlit. Marjorie arrived at the studio unexpected. "It's beautiful out there, Ken. Let's bundle up for a walk?" Tramping through the frosty underbrush of Wilket Creek Park, she wanted to run from herself. After all their time together, with so many joyful memories, she had come to this hollow decision. As Ken had implied, "The only time is now." Tomorrow will be no good; she must get it done tonight.

Her words were planned to be kind, but came out sounding swift and harsh. "Ken... I'm going to London with Phil."

His breathing faltered. His silence made her shiver. "And then?"

"And then... I'll be traveling with him," she lied. Did she need to explain her decision?

Ken's eyes were dark blue in a face like a stricken mask. The shadows of two broken-hearted lovers trailed under the lantern lights, and there was little sound except for the crunch of their footsteps in the snow. Searching for logic, he broke the silence. "You love me, and you're staying with him."

Marjorie's mouth felt dry. She had to continue or not manage another word. "Forgive me for this, Ken. I love you, but I can't keep living this double life. It's disloyal to husband and children, and unfair to you. It can't go any further without added pain... for everyone. I love my family. I love you... more than I can express. But I don't have the freedom that you do."

They stopped walking and faced each other. "Then take it," Ken challenged, his voice gruff.

Marjorie stepped back and shook her head. He reached for her just as an errant breeze tossed her hair into wings of gold, as though ready to whisk her away. He pulled her into his arms, held her close for the minutes that were left, then kissed her under the swaying branches. He turned from her. She watched him go until she couldn't see him anymore.

———

"We will be landing briefly in Guatemala City to pick up passengers. Please remain in your seats, keep your seatbelts fastened, and obey the 'No Smoking' sign." Marjorie regards a full ashtray. Habit. We women are such creatures of habit!

Like a colony of busy ants, passengers file into the aircraft to fill the remaining seats. A woman in a flowered mumu guides a little boy by the seat of his pants, to station him next to Marjorie. Instructing her charge in a steady stream of Spanish, she fits her heavy frame into the aisle seat beside him, drops a picture book into his hands, and with hers placed stiffly on her lap, seems to concentrate on a spot straight ahead..

Marjorie replaces the armrest between her and the boy, and gestures toward the one on his right. Eager to imitate what the lady has done, he slips it down with a click, and a shy smile. She returns it with one of her own. "Okay?" The boy nods. Though silent, the exchange is easy. Marjorie wonders why communication is so difficult for some.

———

Phillip was right. But not for the reasons that he had foreseen. Marjorie spent her days doing all the things the tourists do: watching the Changing of the Guard, wandering through Kew Gardens, visiting galleries and museums, touring the Tower of London, or sifting through antiques and junk in the stalls of Portobello Road... all the while hoping that, with distance between them, her thoughts of Ken would fade.

But she saw his smile in the face of the Abbey clock, heard his voice in the rushing crowds, longed for his embrace as she wandered the city untouched and alone. Examining some paintings at the Tate, she felt him beside her, counseling, "Don't be afraid to live it!"

On the tenth day of the two week trip, Marjorie announced to Phil that she was going home. She hoped vainly for some leadership to harken her back to reality,... even an argument in response. "Told ya!" he chided.

She cabled Ken that she was coming home.

The last crescent of sunset flooded Ken's apartment, and the lace mantilla shimmered in its glow. "I want to paint you in that," he stated quietly. "But in the right setting. Come with me?"

"To where?"

"I arranged for some time away when I thought you weren't coming back. Remember Bob, the artist in the park? He'll be occupying this place for a few months."

Just as well, thought Marjorie. This had to end. "Ken, that's out of the question. I don't know what I'm thinking. I have my nerve coming back to you like this when I can't find it within me to leave my husband."

"Still? Why not this time?"

His impatience was deserved. "Because... he needs me," she faltered, disgusted with her own waffling. "We like each other, we really do."

"But you say you love me! Why would you want to stay married to him?"

Her promise on her wedding day. Her role as wife and mother. But it also involved loyalty and affection for her mate, not easily explained to one who had never been married. With Ken it could be all about passion... and the sharing of an interest.

With Phil it could be all about habit.

"I can't leave you," said Ken. "Not after finding you again."

She had no right to ask him to stay. Nor could she up and follow... an appendage of yet another man. Her eyes blazed, "Are you some kind of white knight, riding to sweep me away from the emptiness of my life?"

"I'm offering an escape!" he hissed.

"I don't want an escape!" she wailed.

Ken lifted Marjorie's chin and kissed the freckles on her nose. "I want to paint you before a Ponaloya sunset. We'll visit Peña del Tigre, a cave called Tiger Rock. According to legend, two lovers who hid there were joined by a tiger."

"What happened to them?" gulped Marjorie, her tears still wet on her cheeks

"The lovers or the tiger?"

"The lovers, you goof!"

"No problem. The woman charmed the stripes off him, ma'am."

When laughter faded, Marjorie repeated, "I can't come with you," momentarily destroying his dream. "But I'll try to come to you."

"When?"

"As quickly as I can."

Marjorie awakened the next morning, out of sorts. She had always enjoyed the ambience of her country French bedroom, but today it didn't look the same. It's affected, she decided, as she made the bed and placed the mantilla carefully in a drawer. Her choice of green and white toille on the walls now seemed to surge around the Monet above her bed. She hated it. She felt dizzy and couldn't remember having slept so poorly.

She ran a bath, lolled in its warmth, but couldn't relax. She dressed in beige pants matched by a cardigan over a white shirt, and sat in the den with her coffee and the morning mail. A wind whistled around the eaves. "I've decided to spend Christmas in the sun this year," Gail wrote from McGill University. "It was so unselfish of you to say that I could, Mom. Holidays run 'til a week after New Year's, so I'll detour by way of Toronto to see you and Daddy. Have a great holiday, you two!"

"That takes care of everyone," the mother fidgeted. Gail in St. Lucia with her friends, Midge skiing in the Laurentians with her friends, and David in Laos, translating mail for Foster Parents as a public service credit for his Social Science course.

The next letter was from Phil. "Back in a week." Marjorie examined the postmark and counted the days on her fingers. He could have called—or maybe he tried? Wildcat strikes were delaying mail deliveries. One day there'll be a method swifter than the post, she reckoned.

"This means he'll arrive on Christmas day. How about that? Too late to share in preparations... like the trimming of the tree—even the getting of the tree. Won't it be fun to drive up to Jake's farm in Maple all by myself? I'm sure they would load it for me into the station wagon, but then, it would be such fun lugging it into the house and putting a shoulder to it to get it upright. Like a real good sport.

"Or should I actually smarten up. This minute."

She read on: The scanner went over big at this exhibit. Key people want it shown in a few more European centres. Tomorrow Berlin, which will serve nicely as a jumping-off point to surrounding areas of importance. If Gail decides to go south, my trip back for the holidays may not be necessary. Think about spending the New Year in ..."

And if Gail had planned to come home, Mom would be humming a merry tune while baking cookies and stuffing the Christmas goose! And then, who knows? Something else might preempt time together, to bind husband to yet another "area of importance"!

Marjorie took stock of her daily existence: Monday, fitness; Tuesday, volunteer day at the hospital; Wednesday, the garden club and more fitness. Thursday's extension course... this year it was child psychology. Interesting, somewhat challenging. Fulfilling?

She wasn't making a difference in the world! Soon women would be entering the work force en masse. She could see it coming as the seventies rose to give women the push to educate themselves as extensively as men.

It's reported that these are the years of "liberation" for women. Exactly what does that mean? Marjorie wondered. *It wouldn't mean abandoning the home, because that's where women most want to be, creating and cherishing their families. As a first, liberation from being trivialized would be a major step.*

Aloud, she berated herself. "Take it, you fool!"

Marjorie looked angrily about her. At the French antique clock, the collection of pewter in the rosewood breakfront, the priceless Tsien-Tsien carpets, and all the tastefully selected Country French accoutrements. She wanted to toss the lot into that giant ice-covered swimming pool!

She glared at her hobby corner in which lay a half-finished shawl, a rug partly hooked and a stack of loose photos to be sorted. She was surrounded by things with which to fill the lonely hours. Surrounded to the point of suffocation!

No more. The desire to drag through Europe on her husband's coat tails one more time had simply disappeared, along with hope for their marriage. No more. She would spend Christmas in Ponaloya with Ken.

———

"Señora? Señora? We have reached our destination. We are now at the terminal." A gentle statement that seems to come from far away. "Are you alright, Señora?"

Marjorie is startled to see the aircraft almost empty of its passengers, the last one the mother in the muumuu, shoving forward the little son determined to look back with concern for the nice lady who went into a trance after showing him that fine manoeuvre. Patiently but in vain, he had waited with hope that, in her strange faraway place, she was conjuring yet another.

Marjorie waves a weak goodbye, then turns wearily to the stewardess. "Si, gracias... I'm fine... just tired, I suppose." But she isn't fine. A devil voice admonishes, "You're an irresponsible drifter!" She unhooks the safety belt that she doesn't remember fastening, and with trembling fingers reaches for her hand luggage under the seat ahead.

Tiger! Oh, he's out there alright... waiting for them both.

Marjorie asks, "Would you know when the next flight leaves for Miami?"

The face that responds remains bland. "You must check at the Flight desk, Señora. Next to the Departures Lounge."

How childish to expect an immediate turnabout, to carry her back to safety on lullaby wings! The world is real. The terminal is real. The people filing into it, real. And in there among them, the man waiting for her is so very real.

She is relieved to learn that to reach the Departures Lounge she need not pass through Arrivals. Forgive me my love.

The air is oppressively hot and still. Marjorie walks with effort the last few feet of the tarmac. Throwing away her heart, she turns toward Departures. "This is not part of a canvas," she censures herself, "to be painted over if not to one's liking!" She must return home, close the door to this love without end, and throw away the key.

But he's there, with his hands in the pockets of his white jeans. He knows her, alright. Better than she knows herself, checking both lounges to watch for her here as well. He is unsmiling. His marvelous eyes deeply beckon. Her heart leaps.

Fires. They don't belong to that other place. They belong in heaven, with Ken!

The metal fence between them acts like a magnet! Again she feels the ache that just the sight of him brings... coiled within, now stronger, more powerful for all its procrastination. Through the links, Ken laces her fingers with his, and with fingertips touching, they make their way to the gate.

"Your health card, please," an official demands. Marjorie extracts it from her ticket folder, but keeps her eyes on Ken.

"Your tourist card, please. Thank you Señora, enjoy your visit."

Marjorie walks directly to where Ken is standing. "Our journey... yours and mine," she whispers. He holds her tightly in the Arrivals Lounge, the way she needs him to....

Bienvenido

.....

AEROPUERTO DE LAS MERCEDES
MANAGUA, NICARAGUA

——————

For Luis Enrique, this morning is different. Mama is not singing over the charcoal stove, stirring the breakfast. The old bus with the horn like a frog has not come to carry Papa Jose to the coffee sierras. Even Raphaella, his little sister, is quiet. Her eyes that shine with mischief on other days, look timid and silly today.

Luis can sniff adventure. He peers closely at Raphaella. To be sure, she won't follow him this morning. She is hanging tightly to Mama, chewing on her thumb, a sure sign she won't.

With the curiosity of a six year old, Luis does not pause to heed the worried whispers of his parents and older siblings clustered together.

Forcing down the last of a banana, he slips away unnoticed, padding in bare feet through the stagnant water on which their colony of cane huts is built.

With all the speed he can muster, little Luis breaks into a lively run toward the Rama Road.

"Dios mío!" rasps an old woman, in an attempt to coax water out of a roadside pump. She regards instead its muddy regurgitation into her bucket.

In pursuit of excitement, the boy does not stop to help as he might on other days. Right now he must see for himself "the Devil's work" that the elders quiver about. For sure, the Devil knew how to shake his bed in the night with its rumbling bad temper—hard enough to make Mama smother him to her chest as she sobbed over and over, "Do not be afraid, Luis." Mama was afraid; but he, Luis, was not.

To remain unseen, the boy heads for the gutter, and scurrying like a centipede, darts through it toward his destination. With new respect he fixes his eyes on Mount Momotombo. Many tales have been told of her anger, but for Luis, she has always peacefully sat there, comfortably guarding their little municipio like a giant Mamacita. If he wanted to, he could actually make out her smile, just like he could the face he sometimes saw on the moon.

Why did she start shaking things up? And how did she do it from way over there at the bottom of the sky? What had made her angry enough to change into the Devil?

With speed important to his mission, Luis wends his way toward a giant boulder that marks a fork in the trail. Tall palms lean and teeter above a gaping cavern where the Rama Road should be, where a boy listens for the hum of automobiles, chooses the one he likes best, and dreams of steering it for miles and miles to wherever he wants to go.

But a smoking hole as big as a monster has eaten up the corner. Cautiously, he creeps toward the edge and hears muffled voices. "La tourista with the golden hair... esta muerta." She is dead.

"Él también." He also.

With his heart thumping far down in his belly, Luis peers over the lip of the cavern to face the mangled wreckage of what had been a shiny blue sports car. Beside it are two men in hard hats, a tall one with a handkerchief over the lower part of his face, the other with a mask to block the smell of smoldering rubber. The tall one nods grimly, "Sí, es horrible."

From where he is crouched, Luis strains to see. But fearing discovery as the voices grow louder, he coils his brown legs and leaps back behind the boulder. It is then that his hand catches a sweep of material slinking in the faint breeze, slinking like an iguana.

Beside him are other things that must belong to golden-hair. A brush with back so shiny that a boy can see his face in it. Tubes of toothpaste spurting glorious colors when the caps are loosened. A pink slipper, a black and gold cigarette case soft as goat's fur, and a capless bottle that smells of flowers when he examines it for its contents.

With his eyes glowing with puppy love, Luis studies the shimmering fabric, and considers how pretty it would look on tía Josie, his mother's youngest sister. The thought takes effect. Like the scoop of a pelican's beak, his hand sweeps the mantilla from the ground and stuffs it under his cotton shirt. He will return for the other things later, when the men with yellow hard hats take their siesta.

But Luis is grounded by his father who, in a rage fueled by anxiety, encounters his paint-smudged son on the trail. It is not until night that the child slips from his bed and looks hard at Raphaella to make sure she is asleep. Silently he runs a hand under his straw mattress in pursuit of a precious box containing such treasures as a little boy saves: stones, bottle caps, elastic bands; lots of stamps, crayons and postcards sent to him by tía Josie. From this collection he pulls out some brown paper with its wrinkles smoothed, and a bundle of knotted string.

With shining eyes, he thinks of the object of his love: "I do not forget you, my dearest Luis. Each time I perform, I will pretend that I am dancing with you, just like at Fiesta."

In the light of the moon that streams through the window, Luis wraps the mantilla as one would a firecracker, twists and ties the ends, then lovingly winds each of them with an extra supply of cord for this beautiful aunt, said by the family to be "too loose." For the address, he consults with a postcard just received, then poses his crayon....

To tía Josephina.... No. Maybe nobody will know who that is. Better her work name. In a childish hand, he scribbles:

tíA CaRmelitA VAsqez
HaciEnDA des AmistADes
MeXico, Df

Head
Over
Heart

I T'S IN THE FEEL of things, this freedom. In the polished pine floor
beneath feet that are bare. Along cedar deck rails, smooth and
grainy. In Muskoka chairs, warmed by the sun. It's in the wind,
in light caresses and cooling edges that kick up tiny waves along the
gray-green inlet, beating them into omelettes of foam, anointing the
rocks below in their frothy, mystic sway. I am bewitched... lulled...
cleansed.

It's like a purge, this place. I need this other world to break the
confines. To know the meaning of naked existence without the fetters
that bind... to sort out why we build them. If I can.

Cerebration. Belinda's definition. A good one. Her mom travels a
high wire of safety versus risk: what can be attained versus what might
go wrong. It's a mother thing.

I shouldn't have flicked that little bug. I hurt it. But people and
nature hurt each other all the time. People and people do the same,
often in good faith. All the same, they hurt each other.

Like Mattie and John. He claims he failed her, and wants to set her
free. Maybe he just wants to be free. He's hurt us, mostly because his
method of breaking free is so contrived, it can't be his alone. Of course
there's someone else. When anyone interferes in a marriage, I don't
wish that person well, and it's upsetting for me to feel such anger.

Belinda. She cares for the poor and downtrodden. I brought them
up to be the way they are, didn't I? Their goodness has hurt them—
and us for them. It's the parents' role to stand by, while hurting.

What frightened that crane not twenty feet away? "Graw! Graw!"
That's an answering call from the south island. Another crane or a
different bird? I can't be sure. But the crane knows. Its body is heavy; it
barely skims the water. Frenzy does not lend wings. I must remember
that.

Our cabin has a fireplace—a priority when renting this place.
It's chilly at dusk. We light some kindling and split branches, then
settle down with our drinks, snug in the protection of nature's bounty,
pleasured by her unspoiled beauty through a stretch of windows
overlooking the sound and surrounding woods ablaze in a fast-setting
sun. The kindling catches with a hiss, and a puff of smoke drifts to the
cathedral ceiling. On cue, split wood sears with its overture to the logs.
They crackle and laugh at us. *From the beginning of time, we've done*

this same dance, filling the air with the same woody perfume, offering the same contentment. And the waves lap on; not the same waves, not ever the same waves, but in the same way. Like Mama used to say, "Nothing ever changes. Though each generation might think itself different, the same laws of nature and human nature prevail."

So relax... which is what I came to do. To make some sense of life. I followed all the rules, Mom, the ones that were important in that day and age of raising me; I may have bent them some, but never enough to rip your heart.

As you pointed out, in raising my children I left out some of your rules. I wanted them to be free to reach out farther. I'd known too many limits, I thought. Love and support would fortify their journey. But the water ripples, the fire crackles and laughs at us. You were right, too, Dad. Rules work. For the kids' sake.

We should have tightened them more. Instead of being buddies, we should have made sure that our son-in-law was a little afraid of us. "John, you wish to marry our daughter? Then this is what we expect from you," might have saved the marriage. What was the reward for Mattie's loyalty? She is a beautiful, gentle woman who was a pleasure to raise. What now?

And Belinda. Here we are with Jim, making it a foursome. The fault lies with us, unable to be consistent. When we finally did meet Belinda at Pine Lodge Landing, after two tries, by which time we were pretty frantic ("We got our trees mixed up. We went to Elm Island Lodge, Mom, sorry"), there was Jim beside the van they'd rented for the gathering at Heaven's Rock. Thank goodness he hadn't just delivered her and gone. Not Jim, decent Jim; he's in love with our youngest daughter.

Spotting us, Belinda gathered her things, touched Jim's hand in goodbye, and boarded the water taxi, holding back the tears she's learned to hide so well. I read her thoughts: "He can't join us... because he's different. No matter how we try, you haven't been able to accept him, Mom and Dad." No bitterness. Just sadness.

"Where's he going to stay until we bring you back tomorrow?" I prayed she'd say that he'd arranged something.

"He doesn't know."

I knew it. And I knew I'd wave him back. "Tell him to come with us."

Well now, spoken like royalty, wasn't it? A supercilious offering.

I didn't like myself much as I waited for Belinda to deliver the message. Refuse, Jim, refuse. Slap us back. For rejection one minute, acceptance the next. Who do we think we are? He's going to shake his head and drive on. Do that, Jim. I would.

But not that strong young man. Slowly he backed the rusty van into a parking space beside the landing, grabbed a few things, and followed Belinda with a smile that must have cost him plenty, undeserved by us.

Once more, I hear my mother's echo, "I will not accept it. I cannot!" My daughter and her choice of husband not accepted? My daughter turned away because the boy she loves is not "one of us?" Mother knew racial persecution first-hand. It hardened her. In many cases, that's what happens: a generation threatened by memories, afraid of the unfamiliar, indifferent to dialogue, accepts no diversity.

What kind of memories are we making here and now? I am not in favor of marriage for these two, either. But my reasons are not the same. One can adjust to differences, but this doesn't seem like an adjustable situation. Jim is well-meaning, kind, good-looking, personable, and perceptive about many things… but it's not enough. He fails to reach out for the opportunities that are his to take. He is a sweet-natured dreamer, and a drifter.

"My sleeping bag is replaceable," he says, hoping the ferryboat captain will remember who left it at the dock. "But," with reference to our initial panic, he regards Belinda with stars in his eyes, "she isn't."

Not many young men would understand a mother's anxiety. Like many of his people, Jim is intuitive, almost reverent in his phrasing. For that, I love him. With human and spiritual priorities in order, he places values where they belong. I question myself: If you were "one of us," would I consider you a good husband for our daughter? Not so, I'm afraid. "If he were a doctor or a lawyer," someone once asked, "would you feel differently?" Most likely. He would have a goal.

When Belinda met you, Jim, you were just out of the American army, in Toronto on a rehabilitation program. You are an alcoholic. I can accept cultural differences, but this problem is difficult.

Belinda might have married you by now. But her choice is to have parental consent. Which places her future in our hands, to ensure her happiness. Oh, it's easy to be wise, but very hard to be right. This is our child!

You depend on Belinda, Jim, to keep you warm and fed. You don't hold a job for long. Through the G.I. Bill you are entitled to a free university or college education. You are not ambitious. And I'm afraid these parents predict your future through eyes programmed by their challenges and priorities.

Your first domestic quarrel, which you will have—will it be exacerbated by lack of education, inability to support a family because of an absence of skills, or answers not found (forgive me) in a bottle? Belinda is bright and ambitious. Right now, your quiet philosophy is precious to her. But lack of ambition creates a time limit. Reality sets in, often too late. Idealism can be an excuse department for continuous failure. If John and Mattie couldn't make it with all they have in common, what hope can there be for the two of you?

But it's not the same bridge to cross, you might say. One shouldn't compare. It's how one supports the other; it's the nourishment, the chemistry that counts. Maybe.

With Mattie and John, one always got the feeling that John was somewhere else. Possibly Mattie felt it too, why she over-praised any thoughtful gesture, cloaked him with protection from something she sensed was threatening. From us? Or from everyone? At times, the two of them looked stranded and unsure, like teenagers uncomfortable with adult values. They weren't much older than teens, come to think of it. Maybe they were just uncomfortable with each other. We liked John. Their relationship would mature.

But it didn't. "We don't want to be married anymore." Just like that. Someone took an axe to our hearts.

Maybe Jim was sent to us this weekend to teach us something. Yet, whenever I open my mind and heart beyond my structured world, I am punished. The worst punishment is through my children—their hurts, their broken dreams. I cannot experiment with them. It's one thing to preach acceptance, quite another to embrace it. Changes have to be weighed, studied… perhaps learned.

And what about our son, Grant? A long marriage to Lexie wasn't expected either. Rather than lend support, they spent their time outdoing one another. Too young. Since their breakup, Grant has been drifting from one girl to another. He cares not beyond the present. Clearly he has no intention of tying another knot.

And so they whiz along, a throw-away generation, not to be "trapped" more than once. In their differences, they are bound together with a sameness. And divorce, a well-worn highway, is now a universal shroud.

It's getting rough out there. The waves rise higher, break faster, stretch further, pummeling the rocks with crazy bubbles silvered by the metallic gray of an overcast sky.

After breakfast, Jim suggests a game of Trivial Pursuit. He shouldn't have, because he's not very good at it. But he knows that Belinda's father enjoys it. It's a damp, windy morning, unsafe for boating in everyone's opinion but Jim's. Belinda is still in deep slumber in the room she and I shared. They'll not be leaving for a few hours.

What peninsula do Spain and Portugal share? "The Sinai!" beams Jim. Well, we don't guess them all either. Belinda would likely regard the answer as sweet, open and honest, needful of her help. But oh, honey, over time, how such innocence loses its lustre! We correct gently with, "It could be the Iberian," as kindly as we can. Jim holds onto his smile; but it's set; and his eyes betray one more futility.

On the next round, I feign ignorance. Give him room. Make him comfortable. "We need to go back to school!" I declare, slyly working that into conversation. "Jim is considering going back." Where did I come up with that?

"Uh, I'm not too sure of that," he interjects, sagely stroking his chin.

"Oh? What makes you undecided?" I persist, with hope manipulating my mouth.

"Because our people will be lumped together, segregated in college as we are everywhere, and we want to be treated like everybody else."

"How might a decision not to attend remedy that?" At least we're into talking about it.

"Maybe if enough of us stand up to the system, it will be changed."

Where is the logic? "It probably will be, but it will take time," I continue relentlessly. "And to be in on it, you must be present. Right now, through the G.I. Bill, education is free, not just to your people, but to all who were in the service."

"Which is only valid for two years."

"Jim, no one knows for sure what changes will come in two years time. We must live for now. It's the only way. Consider this: lobby for what you want, while at the same time taking advantage of your free education."

His stubbornness remains fixed. I know, guy. One inherits so many ills. Your folks have been treated as inferiors, trampled upon, deprived of rights and choices. Now opportunities knock and you're suspicious of them. Think like one of us, Jim! Accept what is offered; regard them as your rights, and pyramid such rights into achievements that will work for you, your family, your people. The first Native American president of the United States will not have your defeatist attitude, my friend.

Whitecaps are disappearing. But the water is not yet smooth enough for four adults in a cedar strip boat. We four in the same boat? Or even just the two of you? You've got to question it, my dearest Belinda. Life is not flat. It is many-dimensional: it whirls constantly with new surprises and different challenges, like particles in a kaleidoscope. But unlike a plaything, if life's pattern becomes stuck, one cannot easily switch to another.

We lunch in the main diningroom. Our waiters are native people living in the area, who are pleasant to us, but shy about Jim, who might as well be invisible. They are obviously not comfortable about the four of us as a family. What exactly does that say?

It's time for Belinda and Jim to leave for the city. We wave them off at the dock as they board the water taxi back to the mainland. My heart breaks for a daughter so keenly alert to her parents' feelings, so troubled by them. Feelings still fraught with cultural fetters, despite the folksy songs preaching understanding and acceptance for all.

It's in the feel of things… in the weight that sits on my conscience, the shackles that tear at my heart, the rags that smother souls. The waves recede into a surface of tiny ripples. The fire begins to crackle. And to laugh….

Printed in the United States
141630LV00003B/13/P

9 780595 496860